THE
Promise
OF
Miss Spencer

SARAH L. McCONKIE

SWEETWATER
BOOKS

AN IMPRINT OF CEDAR FORT, INC.
SPRINGVILLE, UTAH

Praise for

The Promise of Miss Spencer

"Set against the backdrop of the smallpox epidemic, this sweet historical romance will give readers hope in a time of tragedy, with characters striving to do what's right and the promise of more than one happily ever after."

—ILIMA TODD, author of *A Song for the Stars*

"Intriguing premise, heartfelt emotion. This story tugged at all the right strings."

—JEN GEIGLE JOHNSON, author of *A Lady's Maid*

"I love it when a story can entertain and uncover a part of history that is new to me. *The Promise of Miss Spencer* does both extremely well. Like Miss Spencer's perfect baguette, McConkie's novel is warm and inviting with just the right amount of salt."

—ESTHER HATCH, author of *A Proper Scandal*

To Mark's children, in his honor,
and anyone who has lost a parent too early in life.

ISBN 13: 978-1-4621-3580-6

Published by Sweetwater Books, an imprint of Cedar Fort, Inc.
2373 W. 700 S., Springville, UT 84663
Distributed by Cedar Fort, Inc., www.cedarfort.com

Library of Congress Control Number: 2020931149

Cover design by Shawnda T. Craig
Cover design © 2020 Cedar Fort, Inc.

Printed in the United States of America

10 9 8 7 6 5 4 3 2 1

Printed on acid-free paper

December 1822

Jacob Grysham wrinkled his cravat in his hands and threw it to the ground like a discarded toy. "Coming to Berkeley was supposed to fix everything," his recently deepened voice muttered as he paced the hallway, sweat beading his brow. His mother's sobs from the other side of the door tore at his heart.

He pulled on the handle and opened the door. The scene looked the same as it had for the last two days: his perfect ten-year-old little sister lay motionless, stricken with fever. Red puss-filled sores dotted every part of her exposed skin, their poison ravaging her body. Her case of smallpox was worse than most. Jacob moved slowly to his mother and touched her hair, still beautiful and dark, as she clutched her daughter's hand.

Earlier that year, Jacob had been vaccinated—that was the word the doctor had used—against this awful disease by Dr. Jenner himself. Now Dr. Jenner sat next to Eleanor's bed, tears streaming down his own face. Jacob shifted his long, gangly frame toward them, wondering how his body had grown three inches in the last year while his sister had become so frail and deathly ill.

Jacob knelt next to his sister and whispered, "Isn't there anything we can do?"

The physician looked down and shook his head. "Not now. It is too late."

Jacob winced, clutching his open collar. His voice came out in a strained whisper. "Would your vaccination have prevented this?"

His mother's tears had become silent, and her eyes looked distant from across the room.

The doctor swallowed. "Since the time I was young and exposed to this devil, I knew I must do everything in my power to fight it. That is why I searched for a way to stop it. It doesn't save all, but it is far better than anything this country has ever had."

Jacob kicked the floor with his tall riding boot. Why had he not insisted his sister receive the same treatment as he did? Why did he not press his parents harder on the subject? He blamed himself for his sister's imminent death.

The doctor stood and placed his arm on Jacob. "I am so sorry."

"Thank you, Dr. Jenner," he said.

Heavy silence filled the room. Lady Haversley, Jacob's mother, went over to him and placed her hands on his. "I was sure coming to the country would improve her health. The air is so much better here."

Jacob shook his head. "Smallpox can destroy anywhere."

Lady Haversley's eyes closed as more tears slipped out. "My dear boy, promise me you will not be next."

Jacob took his mother's hand and kissed it. "I will always be here for you."

Chapter 1

OCTOBER 1839

L ord Jacob Haversley dismounted his sable horse and walked toward the shade of a large gazebo on the edge of the Chalestry estate. It had been more than fifteen years since his last visit, and his boyish mind of years ago had never noticed the expanse and wealth of the McCallisters.

But then he had only been Jacob Grysham, the younger son of Lord Haversley. That was before everything had changed. Perhaps he would have taken notice of the luxurious estate had he known then that he would become a lord. As an *unmarried* lord, it was high time he noticed which of his mother's friends had large holdings.

He hurriedly deposited himself on a marble bench to collect his wits before meeting Michael McCallister, Earl of Chalestry. No one expected him for a few hours, and Jacob would have gone straight on to Berkeley had his horse not slipped a shoe. He wished he could address the social part of the visit later, for Berkeley pressed on his mind, but now he needed to think.

It was his duty to make a perfect impression.

Jacob pulled a small leather-bound notebook from his vest and reread the hasty notes from Mrs. Tursley's ball two days previous:

Blanche Beecher—19, stunning, wide features, excellent singing voice. Seemed quite interested as I praised her song, excellent dancer. Quite flirtatious.

*Amelia Livingston—17, first ball, extremely wealthy, shy, but well-pro-
portioned and sweet temperament. Bright blonde hair, elaborate gown,
seemed quite taken by me (complimented my waistcoat).*

*Julia Tursley—21, eldest daughter of the Tursleys. Asked her to dance out of
obligation, as she sat alone. Quite tall and thin, overly giddy, a bit clumsy.*

He mulled over the other entries. There were twenty-nine in all, just
from the last six months alone. That was two fewer entries than the year
of his age.

*Surely there must be one female among these who could prove a suitable
wife,* he mused. He sighed, knowing the falsehood of his thought.

The problem did not lie in his effort but in his results. He had made
more than ample effort.

And so he came to Elmbridge, half-heartedly hoping that one of the
young ladies he met here might become more than just a small entry in
his journal. But how could Elmbridge have any more interesting ladies
than those from town?

Still, he tried to play the part—complete with his elaborate jacket.
The words of his friend Colonel Unsworth rang in his ears: "A well-
dressed man will obtain a lady with more ease." Jacob brushed a speck of
dirt from his lapel. He *did* always employ decorative cuffs and billowing
cravats, and none of it had helped him thus far.

Ever since his father's death, he felt bound to do his mother's bidding.
He would play the role of dapper, eligible bachelor, awkwardly on display,
to perfection. He knew his mother hoped to secure an engagement for her
son to her childhood friend's daughter. At most gatherings, eligible girls
flocked to him like seagulls to bread.

But with each girl, something was always missing. At times he told
himself it was the family they came from, other times their financial
status, or—although he tried not to be rude—sometimes the girl's
looks. But it was more than that. He had assumed for years that he
would know the right girl when he found her, that he would feel it to
be right.

Now he doubted such a notion. Who in their right mind went according to their feelings, anyway? That was a sign of a weak man.

Elmbridge would hold some answers. He could feel it. Something
tugged at him, prodded him forward, telling him he *needed* to be here. He
led Sylvester on, ambling his way to the gate of the McCallisters' estate.

He dismounted and adjusted his newly tailored coat and immaculate cravat and summoned his parliamentary charisma.

A robust butler dressed in dark maroon livery opened the door. Once inside, Jacob dusted himself off gingerly as he was let into a marble-columned entrance hall. He examined himself in the large mirror to his left and brushed his hand across his hair, hiding the few greys that had recently shown themselves among the mahogany strands. His ensemble, he had to admit, especially the deep plum vest, complemented his brown eyes and dark eyebrows rather well. He knew he looked the part.

Gazing around at the winding staircase and brightly hued floor-to-ceiling paintings, he admitted to himself that perhaps the country did hold some charm.

A dainty maid whisked through the hall as Jacob waited for Lord Chalestry. Then, hearing a slight sound of moving feet, he looked up and saw a young woman, barely visible behind a curtain on the second floor. She gave him one glance and then seemed to disappear as she stepped back for a moment. Her elaborate hair and gown must mean she was Lady Florence, the McCallisters' only daughter. Jacob watched her as she slowly descended the stairs. She lightly touched a blonde curl and wielded a demure smile. The staircase's curve gave this young woman the advantage of time as she slowly stepped down the stairs. She seemed to know better than to introduce herself before her father's formal introduction. When she finished her descent, she curtsied in silence. Jacob bowed back toward her, and then she exited toward the parlor.

Jacob smiled. Perhaps Elmbridge's females would impress more than he had anticipated.

A moment later, a round man with thinning hair and a silk paisley vest erupted through the door. His dark olive jacket fit snugly around his middle, and his smile extended across his entire face.

"Lord Haversley, it is good to see you again! Last time we were together, you were perhaps fourteen." Lord Chalestry quieted a minute and added, "I am so sorry for all that has befallen your family since our time together so many years ago. When you left Elmbridge, I thought your sister's death was enough grief for one family. And now . . . I am so terribly sorry."

"Thank you, Lord Chalestry. It has been a hard few years, but my mother and I bear it the best we can."

Lord Chalestry nodded. "Of course." He looked Jacob up and down, smiled, and said cheerily, "So again, welcome! My wife informs me that you, your mother, and niece plan to stay at least a month."

"Yes. Thank you for your hospitality," Lord Haversley said, his usual easy conversation now employing itself. "I arrived by horse, though the rest of the party should arrive this evening. I came early to attend to some business in Berkeley, but my horse threw a shoe not half a mile from here, so I decided to introduce myself here first."

"And welcome you are. My wife and your mother will have much to talk of, I am sure. We are all excited to meet your niece, Miss Grysham. I hear she has become quite the lady. Yes, yes." His hands bounded off his great belly in approval. "And of course you have pressing business. Please take one of my horses. I can tell you prefer to ride." Lord Chalestry clapped his hands and seemed filled with nothing but praise. "So we might expect you all at a late dinner, then?"

"Yes, sir." He had offered his horse without Jacob even having to ask. *How perfect*, Jacob thought.

"Splendid! I shall have my man show you your room." Lord Chalestry bowed and turned to leave. A servant entered as he exited. Jacob followed the servant up two flights of stairs and deposited his few personal effects in the striped forest green suite but had no intention of resting. He made his way to the stable to acquire his borrowed horse and pursue the real reason for coming to Elmbridge so early.

"Has Sylvester been fed and watered?" Jacob asked a towheaded stable hand who could not have been more than twenty.

"Yes, indeed sir, 'e has."

"Your master has said I can borrow one of his horses for the afternoon. Can you see that my horse gets another shoe? Sylvester is quite sturdy, and I need him back as soon as possible." Jacob thumped his large hand on the horse's left flank.

"Yes, of course, sir," the stable hand said, already placing the saddle on the back of a light brown mare. He handed the reins to Jacob, who mounted quickly.

Jacob knew he had only a few hours before everyone else arrived. He must make the most of his time. When his mother arrived, he would be almost entirely beholden to her wishes. Now, if only he could remember the exact way to go. He kicked his long leg over the side of the horse and looked down toward the stable hand once more.

"This way to Berkeley?"

"Oh, yes, sir." A thin hand pointed right. "About two hours or so down the east road there."

"Thank you," Jacob replied, determined to gallop all the way.

Miss Suzanna Spencer smoothed her slightly dirty work apron and checked the state of her unruly dark blonde bun. She reached for her basket and pressed deeper into her family's large vegetable garden. The fall sun shone with a warm hue as she smelled the rich, musky earth around her.

At the edge of the plot on a stone bench sat her sickly, coughing father, who dutifully inspected his radishes. She sat down a few yards from him and sunk her trowel near a carrot, unearthing a rock. Chocolate-colored soil flew all over the tidy linen cravat of Mr. Lacy, her father's studying vicar, who followed directly behind her, weeding the beds as she continued her story.

"You see," she said speaking quickly and with such animated hand motions that Mr. Lacy had no choice but to submit to the barrage of soil now covering his vest. "I could not believe it. That old man must have been nearly forty-five. What on *earth* did I do to give Colonel Newbold the idea that I would accept his hand in marriage?" Suzanna furrowed her brow toward Mr. Lacy, letting out a large breath. "Oh, Mr. Lacy! Your poor linen. I am ever so sorry. I just got carried away."

She shot a plaintive glance to her father, her light blue eyes reverting back to her schoolgirl pleadings. "Surely you do not blame me for my refusal, Papa?" She pushed her unmanageable hair out of her eyes and continued to drive the point with her look.

Mr. Spencer's dark hat shaded his white hair and conservative black suit. His modest clothing befitted his reserved personality, even though he stood as rector of the largest parish in Elmbridge, possessing one of the most robust livings in all of England. Coupled with his yearly sum as a younger son of an earl, he lived quite simply for one with so much influence and disposable income.

Mr. Spencer's curved back attempted to straighten a little.

"Colonel Newbold is a respectable man, Suzanna. And might I remind you, there are many 'old' men who are still very fine." He smiled warmly toward his daughter as he collected the last of his produce. "But I know that, from your infancy, you have never acted against your conscience. And your conscience, luckily for me, is quite well-mannered and amiable. So if he is not your choice, then so be it, I suppose. Although . . ." He coughed again and cleared his throat, and Suzanna noted it sounded worse than it had a few weeks before. "I would like it if you were married before God takes me from my mortal sojourn."

Suzanna nodded, for once not speaking. She feared her father might leave them much too soon. She lifted her basket again, this time analyzing the turnips, and glanced sideways at Mr. Lacy, who listened to the whole conversation silently. Thank goodness for him. His presence eased her father's mind and workload a great deal.

It was Lord Chalestry's duty as lord of the manor to fill the position. Consequently, he had asked Oxford for their brightest new vicar, knowing he would act as assistant for Mr. Spencer, whose health was deteriorating. The sad truth was that Mr. Lacy would then take over the rectory once it fell vacant. He had therefore arrived at the Spencers' home just a few months earlier.

Suzanna came out of her reflections. "You know I do *wish* to be married, Father. I have always wanted what you and Mother had. But not many men really interest me, and Colonel Newbold is no exception."

"All in good time." Her father smiled.

Then Mr. Lacy finally chimed in, only quiet enough for Suzanna to hear. "I did see a few of his false teeth fall into his glass during the last dinner party." He winked at her. "But you did not hear such a report from me."

Suzanna chuckled and smiled at Mr. Lacy as his strawberry-blond head dutifully returned to his produce. Mr. Lacy would do credit to her father. She could not have wished for a better friend and vicar, for he had proven an almost indispensable part of their family in their short acquaintance. His coming had been like rain on parched soil.

A few moments later, Mr. Spencer declared, "Mr. Lacy, I must return to my study, for I have had as much sunshine and breeze as my health allows. You and Suzanna finish collecting a few of the vegetables, and then deliver them to the cook before dinner."

"Yes, of course," Mr. Lacy said. "We shall finish in no time." He tried to brush the earth from his shirt.

Coming back to herself, Suzanna remembered she had not said everything as she ran her fingertips over the edge of the carrot stems.

"I am sure," she continued, becoming animated again, "the colonel is only fifteen years my father's junior. He could almost *be* my father. Surely I should at least *like* the man I marry. And he would expect me to entertain his old navy friends and their wives all day. I don't want to be some perfectly prim hostess who never thinks of anything but what carriage to order."

"Any sensible man could see that you care about far more than that. Your sense of duty always returns to your quest to help the less fortunate," Mr. Lacy said, his bright green eyes wrinkling. "The vivacity with which you proceed to buoy the world, one poor farmer's wife at a time, is incredible. I know no one with your kind of stamina toward good deeds."

Suzanna responded with a smile. He truly understood her. She rose from the garden, wielding a full basket of vegetables. "Everyone remembers my mother as the very best rector's wife—constantly serving those around her. At first, my desire to help others came only from a sense of obligation to her legacy. But now, I want to find a way to *really* make a difference. Not just helping here and there, but changing lives." She daintily brushed her apron, noticing how clean she seemed compared to Mr. Lacy. "Oh, I fear I have given you a sermon," she said. "Forgive me."

"On the contrary. I quite enjoyed it," he said. His smile lingered long enough Suzanna hurried to change the subject.

"Now if you could please take these inside," she said, briskly filling his arms with vegetables, "I will deliver some of them tomorrow morning to the Pincers, whose eldest three children have caught the croup. It will do them good."

Suzanna watched Mr. Lacy nod but did not notice he had shuffled the produce and extended his arm until he cleared his throat. She tilted her head and smiled, allowing him to escort her to the top of the root cellar, where she bid him farewell and continued with her usual bounding step down the stairs.

Less than an hour later, Lady Florence McCallister, daughter of Lord Chalestry, entered Suzanna's parlor.

"I feel it has been *ages* since I have seen you, my dearest friend," Lady Florence began, surveying the window treatments as though she almost approved of them.

"We have been quite busy these past few months," Suzanna answered. "I try to assist my father any time he needs me. His training of Mr. Lacy has been fulfilling, but it tires him."

"Ah, yes. Mr. Lacy," Lady Florence replied. Suzanna watched her friend's eyes twinkle toward her. "My father's choice for future rector is quite good, don't you think? I am sure *you* have spent much time with him then, as well?"

Suzanna *did* enjoy the presence of Mr. Lacy, but the way Lady Florence pried into her affairs caused Suzanna to stiffen.

"He has learned a great deal from my father," Suzanna said stoically, looking across the room.

"Just right!" Lady Florence continued with a dainty clap. She quickened the pace of her speech. "Then I shall extend *your* invitation to my ball to include him as well. Bring Mr. Lacy, to be sure! Tell me, dearest, that you will attend next Thursday. I promise it shall be the biggest event of the year, excepting our annual fox hunt! And my mother is quite set on showing off all the gems of Elmbridge, so you must be there. Of course she means to show me off, for we have invited Lord Haversley from town to attend. His mother and mine are dearest friends, you know. Quite old chums, in fact. He has not been to Elmbridge for several years. He's devilishly handsome, for I saw him after he arrived. He gallantly came by horseback. I assure you there is not a better specimen around."

Suzanna wondered for a moment if Florence meant the horse, but she rather doubted it. Lady Florence had paused for effect and air, and smiled toward Suzanna. "I daresay I drag on. Bring Mr. Lacy and your father, if he is able, next Thursday. We shall have a fabulous evening!" She stopped only long enough to begin again. "I must be going. I am to have a special dinner with Lord Haversley and his mother. Oh, and his niece who now lives with him. So good to talk with you, my dear."

Lady Florence gathered her ornately embroidered shawl around herself and gave a small wave. The carriage that brought her quickly bore her away almost before Suzanna had walked back to the parlor. She had not yet seated herself again when Mr. Lacy entered from the library into the sitting room.

"Oh," he said, lowering his book and quickly smiling. "Forgive me, Miss Spencer. I did not know you presently employed this parlor."

Suzanna gave a wry smile and folded her arms. "On the contrary, sir, I am sure you heard *every* high-pitched word of Lady Florence."

A guilty look crossed his face. "Quite thin walls here in Elmbridge," he said, gesturing with his book toward the doorway behind him. He looked down and scratched his head. "So she is to have a ball?"

"Yes, to secure her courtship to Lord Haversley of London, whoever he is. You are invited to attend, of course, she wishes me to add."

"I shall indeed! Sounds quite entertaining." He cocked his head to the side, a smile pulling up one side of his face. "And from what I hear"—he shifted his weight on to one leg—"Lord Haversley is one of the most eligible bachelors in all of England."

"And how do you come to know such information?" Suzanna asked, her eyes narrowing.

"All of the ladies sewing for the poor were talking of his arrival today. You know how they can be—times of service often turn into a bona fide gossip hour. According to the female report, he is thirty-some-odd, uncommonly handsome, well off, and has made it *quite* clear he desires a wife."

"Well, with such a list of attributes, we must assume him to be very picky or quite insufferable to have not yet obtained one," Suzanna declared.

Mr. Lacy nodded emphatically. "My thoughts exactly! Seems like the ball shall be quite the scene to behold." He stood proudly, like a pleased show dog.

"Definitely," Suzanna said. "We shall not miss it."

Chapter 2

Thursday afternoon the only daughter of Elmbridge's rector snuck down into the servants' quarters. Although brought up by the finest governess and given the finest clothing and training, it was not beneath Suzanna to steal away to the kitchen in pursuit of a masterpiece. She had a penchant for baking, and today she pulled a crusty loaf of bread out of the piping hot stove, slathered the top with a large pat of butter, wrapped it in linen, and then concealed the hot loaf in the folds of her apron. She had just untied it and had started up the stairs when she spied Mr. Lacy in the main sitting room. One hand checked her thick hair, which was coming undone as usual. Though it could have been worse. Today she only had to push two pins back into place. As she walked in, Mr. Lacy turned his head and stood.

"Thank goodness you have no visitor." She withdrew the wrapped loaf from her apron. "Here is my latest triumph!" She hastily broke the end off the bread and handed it to Mr. Lacy. He juggled the steaming morsel as though it were hot tar and then looked toward the tea tray and quickly located a saucer.

"Oh dear, I am sorry. I should have waited till it cooled." She sat down across from him, gingerly cradling the rest of the loaf in her apron, watching Mr. Lacy's face in anticipation. "Is it not the most delicious thing you have ever tasted? I have been trying for weeks to master a baguette, and behold, here it is!"

Mr. Lacy slowly chewed his piece, a grimace beginning to cloud his face.

Suzanna exhaled in exasperation. "Oh no. Oh no! It is *that* bad? I was sure I reduced the amount of salt this time."

Mr. Lacy swallowed forcefully and drank hastily from his cup. Then he looked Suzanna in the eye. A smile twitched at his lips. "I am just teasing you, Miss Spencer. It *is* much improved since last time. Still a bit too much salt, but the texture is to be admired."

"Oh posh!" She flung her hands at him. "How can you torment me so? Pretending it was completely awful!" She shook her head. "It will never be perfect for you, will it?"

"As my mother always said, practice makes perfect." Mr. Lacy smiled and inched closer to her. "It is very much improved. Your talents astound me, Miss Spencer." He paused a moment and then added, "Although I have to admit I am rather surprised that today you chose to practice more baking."

"Why is that?" Suzanna asked, confused.

"Because your carriage is scheduled to go to the McCallisters' in an hour or so, if we are to be on time for their ball."

Suzanna had begun the morning baking a single loaf. But when she recalled a few families who might benefit from the bread, she had slaved away the whole day and had just finished her eighth loaf. Having completely forgotten about the ball in the process, she had hoped to deliver the loaves that evening.

"Oh my!" Suzanna exclaimed. "It is Thursday!" She looked at her flour-dusted apron and hands and wiped the back of one across her brow, which only added to her general dustiness.

"I thought I ought to mention it," said Mr. Lacy. "With so many potential beaux there, you will surely wish to be presentable."

"Oh, I care nothing of the men. But I would hate to appear underdressed with Lady Florence and her mother watching like vultures. I must go."

Mr. Lacy nodded and stood once more. "I shall be ready. Perhaps in the meantime you could leave me with another morsel of your salty creation."

She nodded and smiled as she grabbed the bread from the table next to her and hastily ripped off a large section. She brandished it toward him like a knife and placed her other hand on her slender hip. "For your compassion, sir, although I am not sure you deserve it."

Mr. Lacy gave a gallant bow, and Miss Spencer wrapped the rest of the loaf in her apron and hurried upstairs, tugging at her unkempt bun as she went.

"Now let me remind you," said Lady Haversley to her son, taking swift jabs at his cravat. He cleared his throat and looked down at her. "We all expect you to dance with Lady Florence for the first dance and open the ball. But it is also wise to be cautious of your impressions, so you ought to dance every other dance with a different young lady."

"Mother, you need not direct me in ballroom strategy." He batted away her hand and turned toward the window. "Let me remind *you* I have served in Parliament these last two years using more tactics and negotiation than could ever befall a ballroom full of ladies." He repositioned the cravat she had skewed, inwardly admitting how over-the-top he looked. His appearance reminded him of one of those dogs with too many trimmed poofs on their tails and around their necks. But he would never admit to her or anyone else that he felt a little insecure at a dance. He hoped having the most lavish ensemble would bolster his confidence.

Lady Haversley's face and tone softened. "I know, love. I just hope to see you married and settled sometime soon, and Lady Florence would do the job wonderfully. I am sure you remember our purpose in coming here." He thought of his sister all those years ago. He remembered the pain on her face and the scabs and scars that covered it. His family had come then to try and cure her. Now they came to try to find him a wife. Perhaps that would be fruitless as well.

She rubbed her arm and then added, "None of us live forever, you know."

He thought of Lady Florence, who had descended the stairs his first time back in Elmbridge. She was indeed quite beautiful, with impeccable style. She seemed the verbose type at their first dinner together, but that could be tolerated.

He knew their purpose—his mother's purpose, really. Why did she have to mention that? Didn't she know the pressure he felt now that he was to inherit? His brother had died, leaving only a daughter. Now, with his father's death, Jacob felt all of the weight—taking his place in Parliament and running their family's affairs.

But he couldn't burden his mother with the ache of his heart, too. Jacob glanced at her in the oval looking glass and felt nothing but love. He came behind her and rested his hand on her shoulder. He stood a head and a half above her, his large frame taking her in as he said gently, "I am sure at times like these you miss Father a great deal."

"Yes, I do. And I know Lady Chalestry is a bit of a gab, and a little overwhelming sometimes, but I have not had this kind of excitement since your father's passing."

Jacob tilted his head and smiled, lips closed. It had been nearly two years. "Then let us both do our best to enjoy ourselves tonight."

She nodded gently and took her leave. Jacob straightened his midnight blue coat once more. His poor mother craved companionship—and the McCallisters' sociality was paramount. So, he would dance and flirt and flatter every girl in the room, just as he had all over London. He exhaled. Perhaps Lady Florence would be the one. She was quite beautiful, possessed high breeding and manners, and was reported to play the pianoforte like an angel. He would try his best to fall in love with her.

"Your lack of flour does you credit," said Mr. Lacy as he helped Suzanna into the carriage.

"I think that is a compliment," Suzanna said with a smile, settling herself next to her lady's maid, Kate.

"Why yes, Miss Spencer. All teasing aside, your dress and hair are quite lovely. I am sure you will be the belle of the ball."

Suzanna's cheeks colored as his eyes lingered again. Then he cleared his throat, and Suzanna noticed he looked out the window a great deal.

When they reached their destination and exited the carriage, Suzanna bit her lip and met her maid's eyes.

"Don't worry, Miss Spencer." Kate organized one of Suzanna's curls. "You are just as beautiful as everyone here and so much more real. *They are all show.*"

"Thank you," Suzanna whispered, sighing deeply as Kate walked toward the servants' entrance.

Mr. Lacy extended a gallant arm and led her through the entrance hall and past the great spiral staircase that glittered with lighted candles. They reached tall, open cherry wood doors that led into the McCallisters' expansive ballroom. The several cathedral-shaped windows, also cased in cherry wood, gave the cream paisley pattern on the walls the feeling that the ceiling went on forever. Suzanna expected as much, knowing the McCallisters prided themselves on a room twice as high as the average ballroom. Tonight a few tall tables topped with silver candelabras brought light high into the room, and a dripping chandelier added to the effect. It hung high above their heads, the ceiling rising even higher into the darkness. To Suzanna, it felt like a sparkling cave, the chamber surprisingly warm with the heat of the seventy or so people gathered together. Lady Chalestry must have invited every relative and acquaintance in all of Gloucester.

"Good evening, Miss Spencer," said Lord Chalestry, his belly dangerously close to bursting a button on his brown satin vest. "And Mr. Lacy. Welcome, as always." The men bowed toward one another.

"What a lovely way you have dressed the room," Suzanna said, curtsying toward Lady Chalestry, who, with such a compliment, beamed as brightly as one of the candelabras.

"It was nothing, I assure you," she said, waving her swan-feathered fan a few times. "We can hold nothing back for our dearest Florence, as you know. But dear me, allow me to introduce my illustrious friend, Lady Haversley, wife of the late Baron Lord Haversley."

"Delighted," Suzanna said, curtsying even lower. As she stood, she studied Lady Haversley's face, expecting the same pompous air of Lady Chalestry. Instead she saw a soft, unpretentious smile and genuine excitement for the evening.

"It seems, I am afraid," said Lady Haversley quite apologetically, "that my son has already entered the throng of guests."

"And I told Lady Florence she need not wait here any longer. There are far too many young people to mingle with, I say." Lady Chalestry did not possess equal remorse in her tone.

"Why, naturally!" Mr. Lacy said with a smile. "We shall join them." He held out his arm to Suzanna, which she took gratefully. He was her anchor here among a sea of over-important ships.

As soon as the two friends were out of earshot, Mr. Lacy turned to stand in front of Suzanna.

"Now, before I let you roam free, I wish to ask you for your first dance this evening."

"Of course," Suzanna replied.

"Why thank you," he said as Lady Florence approached Suzanna and linked her arm through her friend's.

"My dear friend!" Lady Florence exclaimed. "Oh, and Mr. Lacy. A pleasure." Her tone fell flat. Lady Florence offered the briefest of curtsies, dismissing him before she pulled Suzanna toward the back of a very tall gentleman. "I must introduce you to Lord Haversley at once. And his dear niece, though she is *incredibly* shy. She has said hardly a word to me at all! But it is no matter. I am sure we will become great friends. Here we are now." She led them around the side of Lord Haversley, and Suzanna saw him for the first time and analyzed him while he was deep in conversation.

She was close enough to notice the silk sheen of his dark blue coat. His cravat boasted a scalloped gold pin to keep it in place, and voluminous ruffled cuffs cascading out of his coat sleeve added to the effect. Not one hair of his head seemed awry, and even his stockings met his pants with quite a fair amount of gold trim. It was too perfect, with too much gold. All of this overcame her before she even looked at his face, which was not unhandsome but paled in comparison to his peacock-like outfit.

"Dear me," Lord Haversley said as soon as he turned. "Who do we have here, Lady Florence?" His voice drawled on as he brushed nonexistent lint from his sleeve. Suzanna had to bite her lip to suppress a chuckle.

"This is Miss Suzanna Spencer, daughter of our rector, Mr. Spencer, the youngest son of the Earl of Salisbury."

"Ah, I see," he said as one leg jutted forward and he rolled his hand too many times as he bowed. "What a pleasure to meet you. I have heard much about your father, but I daresay people should have warned me about his daughter!"

Lady Florence sidled close to Lord Haversley. "Miss Spencer, this is Lord Haversley, son of the late Baron Lord Haversley." She paused as Suzanna gave a guarded nod. "Oh, do not look so alarmed, Miss Spencer. Lord Haversley has a tendency to flirt with every female under the age of fifty. He means well, I assure you." Lady Florence gave a simpering smile in his direction. He looked as though to speak when Lady Florence cut him off, grabbing his arm in an instant.

"Now do not be shy, Lord Haversley," said Lady Florence. "Ask her for a dance straight away! She *is* one of my dearest friends, you know, and when you ask my friends it makes me ever so happy!"

Suzanna looked around, wishing she could escape. Lady Florence could be very overpowering at times, and at this moment she ruled her realm. Lord Haversley's eyes remained quite distant and somewhat unimpressed, as though he would not be told what to do. Panicking, Suzanna stuttered, "Oh, no, I assure you, you need not feel obligated . . . I . . ." She spoke in a rush, trying to make up for the awkward predicament her friend had thrown Lord Haversley into.

"No need to apologize, Miss Spencer," Lord Haversley said, seeming to find command of himself again. Before she knew it, he had her gloved hand in his and kissed it. His momentary pointed look toward Lady Florence had melted away, and he was again all pleasantness. He was nothing but bravado as he asked, "Have you a partner for the quadrille?"

"I do not," Suzanna almost whispered, not sure she wanted to accept a dance from this man. How could she entertain such a dandy? His only impressive trait thus far was his ability to recover quickly from Lady Florence's tiring antics.

"Then may I have that dance?" Lord Haversley said, his charm thick as he leaned forward, his dark eyes never wavering.

"Of course," said Suzanna with a low curtsy. Suzanna noticed Lady Florence and the few other men around them smiling pleasantly. No one else seemed to notice Lord Haversley's momentary frustration. He continued to lock eyes with her as she measured him until a tall, slender girl came to Lord Haversley's side. He swiveled on his freshly shined boot and said, with much less affectation, "This, Miss Spencer, is my niece. May I introduce you to Miss Anneliese Grysham, my older brother's daughter."

"Pleased to meet you," said a soft, sing-song voice.

"The pleasure is mine," said Suzanna as she smiled and curtsied, noticing the stark difference between Anneliese and her uncle. Anneliese wore a beautiful baby-blue gown with a white overdress. Her hair was mostly pulled tight, accented with only a few blonde curls, but her overall appearance was tasteful and quite modest, unlike her uncle's outrageous outfit.

Lady Florence had launched into another animated conversation, warning everyone of who in Gloucester had been taken ill, most likely with smallpox. She practically pulled Lord Haversley by the arm toward a few other acquaintances in the circle. Anneliese seemed a bit uncomfortable, and Suzanna wished to rescue her. "Is it your first time in Elmbridge, Miss Grysham?"

"Oh!" Anneliese smiled toward her, alarmed to be addressed directly. "Why yes, it is."

"And how are you liking your stay?"

"It has been quite enjoyable. It was very kind of my grandmother and uncle to allow me to come with them." She nodded a few times.

Suzanna turned so that she and Anneliese formed their own little party. "And this is your first time traveling outside of London?"

Anneliese looked down quickly. "Yes." Her eyes shot up toward Suzanna. "Is it so very obvious?"

Suzanna threaded her arm through Anneliese's. "Oh no, a lucky guess." Suzanna found this girl's naiveté and humility quite endearing. She started to walk with Anneliese. "I once traveled to a friend's ball in another town. I was so scared, I had to leave before the third set had even begun!"

Anneliese's shoulders relaxed a little as she giggled. "Dear me, I *am* a bit frightened of the dancing, although I have had the best teaching in all of London, my uncle assures me. He prides himself on *his* ability and says I am even better than him."

"Is that right?" Suzanna asked, shooting a look toward Anneliese's gaudy uncle. "Well, if you are nervous, perhaps I can suggest someone who will do you no harm." Suzanna scanned the room, locating a strawberry-blond gentleman standing with a few other men near the punch. "Come right this way."

Suzanna watched as Anneliese's eyes brightened and a shy smile crossed her lips.

"Mr. Lacy," Suzanna said as they reached his side. "Allow me to introduce Miss Anneliese Grysham, with whom I have just become acquainted. As Lady Florence is otherwise engaged to make such introductions, I thought she ought to come meet you. She does not know many people at the party yet, but I assured her you would be worth knowing."

Mr. Lacy bowed as he chuckled. "Miss Spencer does me too much credit. Miss Grysham, it is a pleasure to meet you." As he spoke it, Suzanna gave a purposeful glance toward Anneliese and half lifted her arms into a dance position.

Catching Suzanna's meaning, he looked back at Anneliese and said, "If you are not otherwise engaged, may I ask for a dance this evening?"

Anneliese gathered herself and looked courageous as she said, "Yes, I would be delighted."

Suzanna stepped behind Anneliese and bestowed a grateful smile toward Mr. Lacy. He had done exactly as she wished.

"Tell me, how do you find Elmbridge, Miss Grysham?" Mr. Lacy continued.

"It is beautiful. Such a change from London," Anneliese answered, barely above a whisper.

The three continued a short conversation. Mr. Lacy mentioned the smallpox in the neighboring village. Tomorrow Suzanna would have to see if anyone close to them had fallen prey to the sickness yet and needed her help.

Suzanna came back to the conversation as Anneliese spoke. "It was a pleasure meeting you," Anneliese said, looking at Suzanna. "I think it best I return to my uncle."

"Of course," Suzanna said. She stayed close to Anneliese and started walking in that direction. "You know, Miss Grysham, I think you and I might become great friends. And, although this might seem selfish on my part, I always love someone to go on visits with me to the poor and sick of Elmbridge. You seem just the type that might enjoy such work."

Anneliese's face brightened like a flower beginning to bloom. "How right you are, Miss Spencer. I visited the poorhouses back in London with my grandmother. I have a sturdy constitution for people who are ill, too."

"Then perhaps you could come to my home, day after tomorrow, and we shall have our first outing." Suzanna smiled at her new friend.

Within a half hour, Suzanna had filled her dance card. As the music started for the opening set, Mr. Lacy came around again. His confident smile met her with a teasing look in his eye.

"You know," he began as he bowed, "I do believe this is only the second time we have ever danced together, excepting the small assembly at the beginning of summer."

"You are quite right, Mr. Lacy. How kind of you to condescend to my clumsy feet once again."

The dance called for a spin, and Suzanna noticed Mr. Lacy's eyes almost never left hers.

"On the contrary, Miss Spencer, I find you one of the most graceful dancers of my acquaintance."

She turned, grateful the set led her blushing cheeks away from his face for a moment. Was she discovering the enigma of Mr. Lacy? He was kind but not overly complimentary, exactly as she imagined a brother. Yet every so often he came remarkably close to flirtation and interest, which made Suzanna rather uneasy.

She did like him, as a person. But she did not fancy him—not yet. If she had to choose someone to marry at that very moment, she supposed it would be him, but she did not think what she felt was . . . well, she shouldn't be thinking in such a way.

What had led her to such thoughts? She had time to fall in love, with someone, someday. In the meantime, she ought to help the vicarage. Find some way to make sure the smallpox everyone kept whispering about stayed away from Elmbridge. She remembered the surge of illness that had torn through their parrish years ago. She had been vaccinated, she had been safe. But too many around her had died.

A few more dances followed. Suzanna always had a partner. She found the evening quite pleasant, and the food was some of the finest she had had in months. Lady Chalestry really did hold nothing back. As it came time for the quadrille, Suzanna steeled herself for the dance with Lord Haversley.

He sauntered her way, tugging on his ample cuffs as he walked. A low, drawn out bow met her as he said, "Our dance, Miss Spencer?"

Suzanna reminded herself to be courteous. She nodded and held his hand as they took the floor. Lord Haversley escorted her to the head of the set. Of course he would place himself there.

"I believe Lady Chalestry could not be more pleased to have your family staying with them," Suzanna said as they lined up.

"Yes, they are longtime friends. And if our host continues to feed us and entertain us as they have done, I shall have no complaint about their hospitality." With a slight affectation in his voice, he continued. "And I am so very grateful we have met many other pleasant people, your beautiful self among them."

This attempt at flirtation did not impress Suzanna. "Oh, I assure you, Lord Haversley, there are many more interesting and prominent ladies among us who you would do well to connect yourself with."

Lord Haversley's jaw clenched. Suzanna noticed he seemed a bit taken aback by her lack of awe. She liked the effect of her disinterest. She did not know exactly what she held against him, other than his outrageous outfit and desire to banter with every girl, but she continued. "Lady Florence, for instance, seems to appreciate your London flair. The rest of us are just simple country folk."

She drove the point home with a little shrug and thought she saw his lips purse as he turned away from her. Lord Haversley stayed silent for the next few minutes. Suzanna's conscience pricked her as they continued, thinking herself too harsh for a first meeting. Endeavoring to make amends, she stated, "Your niece seems quite lovely."

His face, which had hardened by degrees as they danced, seemed to lighten one shade. "She is a most wonderful girl. I only hope when we return to London, society and balls full of people who presume to know others they just met will not ruin all of the goodness in her."

Suzanna was the one who now bristled. He was commenting on *her* behavior? She saw clearly what a coxcomb he was. He ought not be so put out even though she was different from girls who threw their flirtatious selves at every eligible male.

The quadrille could not end soon enough.

The final chords of the music rang. Lord Haversley's charm returned like a wave.

"Thank you for the dance, Miss Spencer," he said as he bowed low and smiled large, his eyes already hunting for the next interaction.

Suzanna gave a shallow curtsy, glad the evening had almost drawn to a close.

An hour later, she entered the carriage, sleepy and eager to return home. Mr. Lacy sat back against the cushion and smiled toward Suzanna and Kate.

"And how did you enjoy your evening, Miss Spencer? You did not lack for a partner."

"I found the ball quite pleasant, I must admit. Except for the quadrille, it was all very lovely."

Mr. Lacy's eyes widened for a moment. "You did not enjoy your dance with Lord Haversley?"

"Oh, yes, he was my partner for the quadrille," said Suzanna, feigning a yawn, surprised Mr. Lacy would know such a detail. "And why should it shock you that it was not enjoyable? Did you see him? Or speak to him?"

A bit of moonlight shone across Mr. Lacy's face as he looked out the window. He kept a steady gaze. "I did have the chance of being introduced to him by Lady Chalestry. And I was glad for it, as he is the most sought after man in the ballroom, with the most power, if not the most money."

"Oh, definitely not the most money," Suzanna responded, waving her hand. "Besides the McCallisters, Haversley's friend Colonel Unsworth has the *most* money. Apparently an uncle left him quite a fortune. He did not tell me himself as we danced the allemande, but Lady Florence made it quite clear over dinner. I have to say I learned a great deal about all the guests while sitting next to her. She is always so informed." She smiled. "No, people like Haversley for his status in Parliament, that is all."

"And is that *not* impressive? Many young ladies seem charmed by his manners and looks."

Suzanna could tell he was measuring her reaction. "His manners and dress are insufferable. He is as fine looking as several of the men there tonight. Not ugly, but nothing extraordinary."

"My goodness, Miss Spencer. Sometimes, for all of your piety and charitable ways, you are quite the critic."

"I mean no ill-will, I assure you. It is just that it is all equal in my eyes. A gentleman is a gentleman, regardless of the number of frills on his cuff. I did not expect Lord Haversley to be such a dandy. It makes him quite unlikable." She shot a look at Kate, who nodded sleepily, trying to show support.

"Well, you are entitled to your opinion," Mr. Lacy answered as he looked down. Suzanna thought she noticed a thin smile creep across his lips, although her weary eyes may have played a trick on her.

Jacob pulled out his brown notebook. There were too many ladies to record every dance. But he did remember his first. How could he forget?

Lady Florence McCallister—20, perfectly elegant dress and hair, handsome face. Excellent dancer. A bit sure of herself, and quite talkative.

He paused a moment, before adding:

Mother's favorite.

He could go through and list the other women who filled his evening. But what was the use? His mother expressly wished him to court Lady Florence. She had been quite lovely, except when she felt threatened by other young ladies. Then she had become slightly altered, putting on airs. And although he thought that a bit obnoxious, had he not done the same?

Miss Suzanna Spencer had been an excellent dancer, though she seemed very put off by him—a sentiment, he had to admit, that was terribly unlike all of the other women he danced with.

He dipped his pen again.

Suzanna Spencer—21, beautiful features, unassuming style, confusing. Rather blunt and unimpressed.

He recalled Lady Florence.

He would give her a second chance. Perhaps she had more to her than met the eye.

Chapter 3

The day after the ball, Mr. Spencer seemed unusually healthy. Because the weather did not threaten rain, Mr. Matthew Lacy suggested that the two of them take the carriage to Berkeley. Mr. Spencer owned a small house, Norling Place, and had mentioned for weeks that he must show it to Matthew.

The two men exited their equipage and began to slowly circle the grounds. Mr. Spencer leaned heavily on his walking stick. Matthew listened carefully as Mr. Spencer began.

"You see, I would not say this near my dear Suzanna, but I think I shall not live through another autumn. She despises hearing such things, but deep in my bones I know it to be true. And when I do die, I wish her to live here, until an eligible man finally suits her fancy."

Matthew stopped moving and furrowed his brow. "Mr. Spencer, you will live past this autumn." He looked straight at his mentor for a moment.

Mr. Spencer coughed. "I think not, Lacy. Let us speak as men should. I am lucky my father left this house to me." He shot a glance to his right, and Matthew said nothing more. "It has been a wonderful source of income. However, my last tenants have nearly ruined this place. I was hoping you could help me improve it, for I am glad they have finally quit it."

"Of course," said Matthew.

Mr. Spencer gestured to a stone-covered gate to his right. "The garden is atrocious. And Norling needs more furnishings. The exterior of the house calls for a few updates, some attention here and there, but the bones of the place are good." He pointed to the front door surrounded by climbing ivy, which seemed to hold the house together with finger-like tendrils. Matthew noticed a few small cracks in the mortar between the stones.

Mr. Spencer held a kerchief to his mouth. "After a few months of working the garden and having the house painted, it will be quite nice. And if by some miracle I am still alive when you find a young lady to take as your bride, you may live here." Mr. Spencer smiled ruefully at Matthew.

Alone with Mr. Spencer, Matthew knew this was the right moment. He buoyed up his courage. Better now than never.

He cleared his throat, his hands shaking with nerves. "About that, sir, about matrimony. I have been meaning to talk to you. I do wish to bring a wife here and start my family. It would add greatly to my happiness, for a clergyman ought to enjoy the joys of marriage." He squared his shoulders toward Mr. Spencer. "I wish to ask for Miss Spencer's hand."

Mr. Spencer stopped walking and placed both hands on his cane like an old stooping crow. He looked toward Mr. Lacy and said, "I have been wondering when you might ask."

Unsure of Mr. Spencer's sentiment, Matthew remained motionless. Mr. Spencer took a deep breath and continued. "Of all the young gentlemen I know, you would be my choice for her. I know your character. I know your heart. And so, I most readily give my consent."

Matthew's shoulders relaxed and he stood a bit taller, looking over the leaves that had just begun to fade on the trellis. The first bit of autumn breeze began to blow. The color of the leaves reminded him of Suzanna's wispy hair. He had liked her from the first, but now, after their dance at the ball . . .

He realized he had not replied. "Why thank you, sir," he said. "If she'll have me, I promise I will watch over her and see that she is always safe and well taken care of."

Mr. Spencer nodded. "Yes, of course. You are like a son to me." Mr. Spencer's mouth drew into a crooked smile as he wagged a finger at him. "Now let me give you this bit of counsel. She must like the idea of marrying you before you ask her. She is, I am afraid, even more strong-willed than her mother, and I can tell you from personal experience it is better that she think falling in love and marrying you is her own idea rather than yours. I know she does want to marry, but only to a man she loves, who treats her as an equal."

Matthew looked thoughtful and nodded, thinking back on what Suzanna had said over the past few weeks. "What an adept observation, Mr. Spencer. Right you are." He nodded a few times. "I will do what I can to make sure our love grows." They walked a few more paces, and Matthew folded his arms. "Right you are," he said under his breath again.

The next afternoon, Anneliese Grysham stood in Suzanna's parlor, wearing a simple cream and brown dress, overlaid with an apron, and sturdy, though elegant, leather boots.

"Welcome!" said Suzanna. The butler bowed to them as they walked toward the kitchen. "The people I wish to visit are close enough to walk."

"Oh, I do enjoy a good walk, especially since the weather is so fine."

"Splendid," said Suzanna. "If you will just wait here, I will retrieve a few things."

Suzanna made her way to the back of the house and spied herself in the glass before entering the kitchen. After she smoothed two stray bits of hair, she brushed off a smudge of flour still on her cheek, hoping Anneliese had not noticed. She then scurried into the kitchen and wrapped the loaves she had left to cool. She smiled proudly at her homemade goods but would never tell Anneliese that she actually baked them herself.

"I was just told this morning," Suzanna said, her face flushed with exertion as she hurriedly walked back up the stairs with more supplies in her arms. "Mrs. Smith's daughter has fallen ill, and some think it's smallpox. They could greatly use our help, if you think it agreeable. Thus far none of the smallpox sickness from over the river has crossed into Elmbridge, so I pray this isn't the case."

Anneliese took a step backward. "Are you not afraid of infection, Miss Spencer?"

"I most surely am not," Suzanna said, placing a hand on her hip. "I have been protected against it. I guess I assumed you had the vaccine given to you."

"For smallpox? Yes, though I am still a bit hesitant that it works. But my uncle insisted I receive the treatment a few years ago. I was quite scared when the doctor gave it to me. Who would not be? I fell dreadfully ill for two weeks, but I have never contracted smallpox."

Suzanna nodded. "It was right he insisted on it." It was the first time she had thought of Lord Haversley as possessing some kind of sense. "The smallpox shall not harm either of us. It is a great tragedy to me that many of our poorer families are still too destitute or too ignorant to fight against the horrid disease. I am sure it is the application that scares most of them. After the last outbreak, my father made sure the parish understood the need for the vaccine."

"Yes, of course," said Anneliese. "My uncle says many people are too scared of the fever that sometimes comes, or afraid the treatment of it is unnatural."

"If they only knew the benefit," began Suzanna. They were still standing in the parlor when the door swung open, nearly hitting Anneliese.

"Oh, forgive me, ladies," said Mr. Lacy with a bow that, to Suzanna, seemed a bit contrived. He eyed their parcels. "I seem to be interrupting your charity work."

Suzanna raised her eyebrows and pursed her lips, wondering if he had heard their whole conversation and trying to silently scold him for eavesdropping.

"It is nice to see you again, Miss Grysham," said Mr. Lacy, avoiding Suzanna's chastising eyes.

"Yes, Mr. Lacy, a pleasure." Anneliese curtsied, missing Suzanna's look.

"I have actually just received a note from your uncle," said Mr. Lacy with a triumphant, upturned chin. He shifted his weight with importance, waving the letter in his hand.

"Lord Haversley has invited me to shoot with him this afternoon."

"Hmm," said Suzanna, "and shall you go?"

"Undoubtedly." He turned toward Anneliese. "How good of your uncle. I trust he is a good shot."

"They say his aim is impeccable," said Anneliese.

"Naturally," said Mr. Lacy as he pocketed the letter and turned out of the room, having stopped only to share his triumph.

Suzanna picked up her wicker basket from the table, loaded with four loaves of bread and some carrots, and turned to Anneliese. "Shall we be off?"

"Yes, only let me tighten my bonnet," said Anneliese. "Grandmama is always warning me against more freckles from the sun."

Suzanna noticed her pale, blonde friend did have a few freckles sprinkled across her nose, but she found it added to, rather than detracted from, her beauty.

"Now tell me, how did you come to live with your grandmother?"

They had started down the lane when Suzanna noticed Anneliese's face fall.

"My father was to be Lord Haversley, but he and my mother died within the same year, when I was nine. Since then, I have lived with my grandmother and until just over two years ago, my grandfather."

Suzanna took a deep breath. So many of Anneliese's family members had died. She wanted to know what happened to Anneliese's parents but thought perhaps that would be too painful. She knew what it was like to lose a mother. "I am so sorry for your loss."

"Thank you. Unfortunately, my family has quite the history of bad constitution. Not me, but several others. Before I was born, they used to keep a house here in Berkeley. They even moved here because of the air several years ago to try and improve my aunt Eleanor, the youngest daughter. But it did not help. She should have been vaccinated, but Grandmama was too scared it would make her worse. My uncle has since sold that house. It is amazing he will even come to Gloucester. The memory of her death still haunts him."

How awful. Perhaps he employed a pompous air in part to hide his sorrow.

Anneliese fiddled with her small purse. "And my poor grandfather. He had always been rather sickly, since I knew him. Something from when he was young weakened him, just like his daughter, and eventually he passed away. Lucky for him he had two sons, instead of just one heir."

Suzanna swallowed. How could Anneliese endure so much grief? Suzanna had only lost her mother, but it had changed her forever.

Suzanna finally spoke. "So your uncle comes to lordship only upon the loss of his brother and father?"

"Yes, unfortunately. My grandmother had three children, the youngest dying first, when she was ten. So my uncle is her only living child."

"I am so sorry," said Suzanna. They were almost to the Smiths, for which she was grateful. She knew the pain she felt in her own heart, and she did not wish Anneliese to have to dwell on the subject any longer.

"Miss Spencer and Miss Grysham, please don't tell anyone," Mr. Smith pleaded as he put his arm around his wife.

The Smiths' daughter Elsie did indeed have all the awful signs of smallpox, though they had tried to keep that fact hidden from everyone. The parents had been vaccinated, they said, but it was years ago, and the man who did it seemed to not know what he was doing. Therefore they had not taken such a precaution with their daughter.

"I only wish to help," said Suzanna, stooping down to the bedside of the sick little girl. "When did she start to fever?"

"More than ten days ago, miss. As soon as she did we put her in the barn and stayed clear, except to bring her food once a day."

Suzanna looked down. Poor Elsie wasn't more than seven. Left all alone, in the chill—if only Suzanna would have known. How could a parent allow such a thing?

"Now that her pox are starting to crust and fall off, we thought her safe to bring inside. We never should have let her visit those awful cousins in Cheltenham."

Suzanna shook her head. If only he had vaccinated his daughter. She did not know how to teach these people to have more compassion and more faith in vaccination. How many people remained ignorant of what good it could do?

"She needs nourishment. Feed her this gruel and bread, and often. Keep her linens and clothes away from others. Burn them if you can provide new ones. And don't leave her outside anymore, I beg you."

"And I beg *you* not to tell anyone. I did not ask you to come barging in here. I still wonder how you knew," the father fumed at Suzanna.

She heaved a sigh. "We won't mention it. Good day."

As soon as they were out of earshot, Anneliese began, "What a proud, insensitive man. Did you see the scabs all over his daughter's face? The large red craters all over her arms, on her cheeks—how could he speak of all of this like that?"

"I think anger and resentment is how some people cope. His daughter will never be the same, if she lives," said Suzanna. "Still, it is inexcusable."

Jacob knew that one of Lord Chalestry's first orders of business in securing him was to give him full access to all of the excellent hunting on his land. But when Lord Haversley invited Mr. Lacy, he had a different reason besides decreasing the number of birds at Chalestry Manor. He could not have cared less about the fowl. For one, he needed a diversion from Lady Florence, whose clutches proved overwhelming in word and action. For the last day she had insisted on being at his side, even turning up in the hallways around the house a few times.

He could like her, he admitted, but she came on quite strong. He wished to give his feelings some time to develop. He had not made up his mind yet, and *she* ought not act as though he had.

His second reason for inviting Mr. Lacy to go hunting was that he seemed to be one of the most sensible men he met at the ball, and he would know information about Elmbridge, maybe even Berkeley or Gloucester.

Mr. Lacy arrived on horse in his tall leather boots and thick black jacket at a quarter past two. Lord Haversley and his friend, Colonel Unsworth, bowed and exited Chalestry Manor quickly. The groom brought Sylvester and two other horses, along with a pair of grey hunting dogs. The three men were off quickly, Lord Chalestry having declared earlier that he was quite fatigued and too out of sorts to join their party. Jacob wondered if Lord Chalestry remained at home in order to recover from his wife's most recent lavish expenditure of money and refigure his accounts. Jacob dusted off his grey paisley hunting jacket, tucked a few folds of his cuffs into his sleeve, and smoothed his hair before setting his horse in motion.

"Thank you for accepting my invitation," Jacob said to Mr. Lacy as soon as the men rode up the hill. "It is no easy task to remove Unsworth and me from those ladies, and your presence has saved us."

Colonel Unsworth laughed at his friend and added, "Not that I wished to be removed. I actually find their company rather easy, but it is only because they do not have a particular interest in me. Your familial connection is winning you all the glory, I am afraid."

Jacob knew Unsworth might find every lady's company easy. His friend had never found a woman he did not like.

"I trust you have met all of the promising ladies in the area," Colonel Unsworth said, wiggling his eyebrows toward Mr. Lacy, who looked over a ravine next to them and shook his head.

"A clergyman is not the source to learn about eligible young women, I am afraid."

"Come on, Mr. Lacy. Surely you have noticed some young women you can tell us about, for you have been here a few months at least. Lord Haversley here might have found him a desirable match, but I am *always* looking to increase my connections, as it were. I saw some rather fine ladies in the ballroom, but there was not time for me to meet all of them, you see."

Mr. Lacy cleared his throat. "I assure you, sir, I am quite new here."

"What about that Miss Spencer, the rector's daughter? You seemed acquainted with her."

Jacob watched Mr. Lacy's shoulders bristle like an agitated animal. "I am *acquainted* with her father."

It had been many months since Jacob had spent time with Colonel Unsworth, and he had forgotten exactly how pointedly brash his friend could be.

Mr. Lacy swallowed and smiled toward Colonel Unsworth. "I am sorry that you have not found a lady as quickly as Lord Haversley. Perhaps, as a *clergyman*, I might direct you to the story of Rachel from the Bible. It might just be your lot to wait seven years—or longer—for your wife."

Jacob smiled, hiding a laugh with a cough and avoiding the colonel's furious glare. Unsworth steeled his gaze and raised his chin in disgust as he rode forward a few yards.

Jacob shook his head and turned toward Mr. Lacy, adding in a whisper, "Right you are. Do not let Unsworth haggle you. His delivery and motive are sometimes found lacking." He cleared his throat. "Now, tell me about your background."

Mr. Lacy pursed his lips and sat taller in his seat.

"I have lately come from Oxford, this summer, in fact, as vicar under Mr. Spencer. His health is failing him, and I believe it to be Lord Chalestry's wish that I take the position of rector when it unfortunately becomes vacant."

"What good fortune for you to have a living to take so early in your career," Jacob said.

"I actually find it rather sad, for I have come to respect Mr. Spencer and do not wish his passing any time soon."

"I have heard only good things about him and would love to meet him," said Jacob. "Perhaps you could introduce us at the next gathering."

"I would be delighted, but I fear he does not go to many social outings due to his frail health. It would have to be in his home, I daresay."

"Oh, is that right?" Jacob said slowly, hoping an invitation would follow but trying to mask his interest. Mr. Lacy seemed quite focused on his shotgun and said nothing.

Jacob wondered exactly what excuse he could make to visit Mr. Spencer. They rode on for a moment. He *would* like to make the man's acquaintance, and the intriguing disposition of his daughter contributed to his desire to visit. Miss Spencer had seemed thoroughly vexed by him, and somehow that made him want to see her again.

Colonel Unsworth, who had been listening to the last half of the conversation, circled his horse back around. "Perhaps you and I should call there during our stay," he offered, fidgeting with his reins.

Jacob straightened his broad shoulders, staring at his friend in warning, surprised Unsworth would again drive his point. He had also danced with Miss Spencer at the ball. Jacob wondered if she was slightly rude to Unsworth as well. Surely Unsworth must have deserved it more than he did.

He then watched Mr. Lacy's eyes tighten in the colonel's direction. Jacob feared he found them a bit presumptuous. Jacob cleared his throat and said, "Oh I am not sure, Unsworth. I would not want to impose on the man, especially considering his health. No, it would be too much."

Jacob watched Mr. Lacy's shoulders relax as he answered. "I do not think Mr. Spencer would mind if you called, especially if it were a brief visit." He pulled his horse to a stop and again examined his shotgun. He then raised his eyebrows and shrugged. "I must warn you, however, his daughter is often away serving those throughout her father's parish who need assistance, so it would be best to seek his company, not hers. She is almost never at home."

The men dismounted from their horses and began to ascend a small hill that faced a larger ridge.

"Naturally," said Jacob. It was clear by Mr. Lacy's stiff posture as they walked that he wished Jacob to change the subject. "We would not overstay our welcome in any way." He gave a purposeful nod toward Colonel Unsworth. Mr. Lacy seemed appeased, relaxing his shoulders and uncrossing his arms as he prepared his gun. Perhaps the man had feelings for Miss Spencer. It did make sense, as she was the rector's daughter.

"Also, as you are familiar with Elmbridge, you have not heard of anyone contracting smallpox, have you?"

Mr. Lacy's eyes turned grave and dark. "No, not yet. I know that Cheltanham has had several cases, God bless their souls."

"So the whisperings are confirmed," said Jacob. "You have been vaccinated, I trust?"

"No. But as a boy my mother exposed me directly to the smallpox. I nearly died, and the pain I endured those weeks, outcasted in a barn while I suffered, still haunts me at night."

"Then you are protected, too. But that is far too savage a method, Mr. Lacy. Let us hope more people want to apply the vaccine."

Jacob paused again and then motioned to the McCallisters' hounds, who began flushing the birds.

"And now," said Jacob as he lifted his gun to his shoulder, "should we see who is the best shot?" They crested the hill. Their horses stood silently as a few birds flew from a bush. His eyes tracked a large pheasant before he pulled the trigger, sending it directly to the ground. One of the grey hunting dogs set off running, retrieving it within minutes. Mr. Lacy shot next, easily landing another bird.

"Good shot, Mr. Lacy," Jacob rang out.

"It must be luck, Lord Haversley, for I am quite out of practice," Mr. Lacy replied, bringing the gun horizontal against his shoulder.

"Have you ever hunted for reds, Mr. Lacy?"

"Indeed I have not," he replied as another shot sounded. "I have been away from the country for many years."

"Lord Chalestry holds a spring fox hunt every year. Surely you must come. I've been told it is quite the singular experience."

"I would be honored," Mr. Lacy said. His smile widened, ease filling his countenance.

A few moments passed, and Jacob was reminded of the beauty of autumn in the country. Leaves began to be afire, their warm hues decorating the landscape like the embroidery on women's gowns. On the hem of Miss Spencer's ball gown, he remembered.

After landing another bird, Jacob came over to Mr. Lacy. "The more I am here, the more I remember how much I like the country. Wouldn't you agree?"

Mr. Lacy nodded. "Indeed, sir."

"Well, then," Jacob said, "tell me what you believe these people need addressed in Parliament. Based on your good sense, I am sure you have several pertinent insights that should be brought to town."

"Indeed, I think I do," began Mr. Lacy. He spoke of including more of the poor in worship services, which Jacob thought quite amiable and reflected his good character. Jacob decided then that he liked Mr. Lacy. He seemed sensible, well-mannered, and direct—and had a fine shot to boot. The more reasons to rendezvous with others besides Lady Florence the better, and Mr. Lacy had now been added to the list of friends with which to distract himself.

Suzanna sat in the parlor in her customary place on the maroon settee. She had taken dinner with her father and now sat ensconced by the glow of the fire, embroidering a handkerchief. The sun had just set and her father sat near her, an open book in his hand, already dozing. Mr. Lacy shut the door almost imperceptibly, but Suzanna immediately noticed his shuffling boots.

"A full evening, was it, Mr. Lacy?" she called out.

Mr. Lacy divested himself of his outer clothes into the butler's arms. He turned the corner and walked into the parlor, his hands resting on the back of the one available chair.

"Who all went hunting?" Suzanna continued with curiosity. She gestured for him to sit down, and he did readily, thrusting out his feet and crossing his ankles, looking quite comfortable.

"It was just Lord Haversley, Colonel Unsworth, and myself."

"And tell me, does he wear voluminous cuffs even when riding?"

"I assume," said Mr. Lacy running his hand through his hair, "that you are referring to Lord Haversley, and I did not notice his cuffs." He sighed. "He did not seem at all the dandy you found him to be. Quite level-headed and a good shot. He even asked me my opinion on a few matters. He invited me to the fox hunt in the spring. Lord Chalestry is holding the biggest in the county." He shot a proud glance toward Suzanna and then furrowed his brow, adding, "Oh and he definitely possesses better manners than his friend."

"Hmm," Suzanna said. "More civil than Colonel Unsworth? Unsworth seemed the better of the pair, to be sure!"

"No, I think you are mistaken. I was not as impressed with him." Suzanna thought she saw his lip twitch. "He mentioned you specifically."

Suzanna raised her chin as she waved her hand at him, a chortle escaping her throat. "No doubt he remembered me due to my clumsy allemande. I have to admit my dancing was uncharacteristically poor at Lady Chalestry's ball. But never mind that. That famous fox hunt happens every year. It *is* truly grand. You, of course, would have been invited, even if Lord Haversley had not extended such an invitation." She would not give that fop of a man any credit.

Employing a more cheery tone, she continued. "Miss Grysham and I had a productive afternoon. She wasn't quiet at all! We had quite a meaningful talk on our walk to the Smiths. Their daughter is improving." She wished for a moment to speak of the smallpox but did not want to scare her father, if he stirred.

She looked up momentarily as Mr. Lacy sat with his hands folded across his lap with a cocked ear. She liked how well he listened.

She thought to tell him more, but he began to speak again. "At the risk of offending you, I do not think you understand exactly what I meant earlier about Colonel Unsworth and Lord Haversley."

Suzanna cleared her throat and cursed herself for thinking he actually listened to her. "Excuse me, Mr. Lacy, but I believe I was talking about Miss Grysham and the Smiths."

He quickly waved his hand. "Yes, but the point I was trying to make is that one day you will have to give up constantly serving and perhaps consider marrying someone." His voice grew more serious. "I must point out that you *glanced* over Colonel Unsworth. I believe he will try to court you. I saw the look in the man's eye. He shouldn't be trusted, not with pursuing you. And if *he* doesn't, perhaps Lord Haversley will try. It behooves me, Miss Spencer," he said, trying for a lighter tone, "to warn you that whilst you seem to ignore the men in your life, *they* are noticing you."

Suzanna's shoulders dropped into the upholstered backing of her seat as she lifted her head. What nerve!

She had met Colonel Unsworth and Lord Haversley but one time. Colonel Unsworth did have a fine face and seemed pleasant, but all of that did not tempt her in any way, even considering the large sum he possessed. Now that she thought of it, he did seem to snake over to her at the dance and act too familiar. Mr. Lacy could not think she would ever consent to the colonel's overtures. She would end up as a pretty-faced accessory on his arm, not as an equal who could help others together.

And she would never, never consider Lord Haversley. If there was one man who wished for a trophy piece of a wife—a beauty without a brain or ability—it was Lord Haversley.

Did Mr. Lacy, and Unsworth and Haversley for that matter, not understand she wished to be more than a title? To actually feel she were the man's companion, helping alongside him?

Suzanna ran her hands over her face and then clasped them together on her lap, forcing a smile. "Mr. Lacy." She let out a long, purposeful sigh. "You are *so* kind to warn me of those gentlemen, but I have only met them once, and they hold no harm for me. I think it would take a great deal for me to consent to marrying someone. To even be tempted toward marriage I would need to know they thought of me as an equal, not some fox to be hunted."

A smile spread across Mr. Lacy's face. Suzanna tilted her head, perplexed by his reaction. She tied a knot in her embroidery, feeling their conversation ought to be finished. Such discussion had gone on long enough.

"So if you did know someone better—who treated you as an equal— are you saying you might consent to marrying him?"

Suzanna looked from side to side, processing his words. Could it be possible that this conversation spurred from the fact that Mr. Lacy cared about *her*? That his intention was to try and *marry* her? Goodness, things had turned rather quickly. She must escape this talk. Now.

"Perhaps. At present, I do not feel most men understand what I want in a marriage," she said, rising and curtsying. "Please excuse me. I am suddenly feeling quite fatigued. I ought to turn in."

Chapter 4

"Thank you, Kate," said Suzanna to her lady's maid as she placed a braiser in her bed. The night was cold, but even with the warm toes, the recent conversation with Mr. Lacy made her shiver.

Suzanna felt she must have just fallen asleep when she heard a rap at the door. The braiser had lost its heat, and she looked askance toward the small opening.

"Beggin' your pardon, miss, but Mr. Spencer needs you immediately."

Kate's voice quivered, and Suzanna sat up directly in bed. She threw on her dressing gown over her nightgown and went to the door immediately. Kate met her with a candle, her eyes looking deep and empty, and the two of them hurried down the hall.

The butler held on to Mr. Spencer's shoulder and assisted him to a seated position. The dim candlelight revealed quite a large amount of blood on the bedsheets. Suzanna rushed immediately to her father's side. His face was pale and looked fatigued.

"I heard much coughing," the butler explained quickly, "and checked on Mr. Spencer. I have called for the doctor. When I found him, he lay on his side, with blood coming from his mouth."

"Thank you. Kate, fetch us some clean water and rags." Suzanna brushed her father's hair out of his eyes, noting his dazed expression. She clutched his hand tightly and prayed for the doctor's arrival.

Minutes later Kate returned with a basin of water and linens, and Suzanna began wiping her father's face. She heard quick footsteps coming down the hall. She was amazed the doctor had come so quickly. When she looked up, however, she saw the face of Mr. Lacy in his nightshirt sans cravat, barefoot and in brown knickers.

"What can I do?" he asked urgently. His light green eyes opened so wide Suzanna could see white around them even in the dim light.

"We have already called for the doctor," Suzanna answered quietly. "But of course you can always pray."

Mr. Lacy bowed his head so solemnly that Suzanna knew he was silently pouring out his heart to God.

Time dragged on until the doctor slipped into the room and took off his hat. "I came as quickly as I could. How does Mr. Spencer fare?"

Suzanna stood and allowed the doctor to take her place. He took Mr. Spencer's hand and felt for a pulse, putting his ear near her father's chest as he coughed again.

Suzanna drew back into the edge of the room, and Mr. Lacy came closer to her. He took her hand for a brief moment and pressed it, his touch calming her like a cool drink of water.

"It is going to be all right."

She smiled at him, surprised how natural her hand felt in his. He *was* one of her truest friends.

The doctor stood and gestured for Suzanna to come over toward the corner. Reducing his voice to a whisper, he began, "I am afraid your father's condition is quite severe. Symptoms such as these indicate a very deep infection of the lungs."

"Perhaps there is some treatment available?" Suzanna asked, stepping closer. She felt a heavy weight wedge its way into her stomach.

"I have done all I know how to do. This is just the next step. I fear he does not have much time to live. Especially with the weather turning."

The doctor pulled out a few bottles and placed them on the nightstand, giving instructions to the butler. Suzanna walked in a daze, like a ghost, over to the corner. She fell into Mr. Spencer's reading chair and cradled her hands in her face, trying to shut out the words she had just heard. She silently uttered a longer, more fervent prayer.

Mr. Lacy exited with the doctor. Suzanna could hear only a muffled conversation through the door. She stayed by her father's side for the rest of the evening, wiping his brow every so often and constantly clutching his hand.

In the morning Suzanna opened her groggy eyes when her father stroked her face.

"My dearest Suzanna. You must get some sleep."

"I am fine. How do you feel?" She willed herself to keep back her tears.

"I have been better," he said with a soft smile. He looked around the room and then back at Suzanna.

His eyes rested on her face, and he tried to clear his throat.

"There is something I must say." A barking cough interrupted his speech. "I should have spoken to you before now. I must explain myself before it is too late."

"Go on, Papa," Suzanna whispered back, gazing into his steady eyes. What could he wish? His urgency made the situation seem all too final.

"I feel the need as a father to set my affairs in order. And as Mr. Lacy has come to take over here, my clerical duties are secured. But you"—he lifted his weak hand to touch her chin for a moment—"have not been taken care of."

Suzanna looked at her hands, wishing this conversation was not so necessary. She felt her tears form into a small river down her cheek.

"I shall be just fine, Father," Suzanna said quickly. "You have left me with a few hundred pounds per year and Norling Place."

"It is not simply the money, Suzanna," he said, attempting to shake his head and coughing up more blood. Suzanna's tears flowed as she handed him a clean cloth. Though his voice was raspy, he continued. "I want to know you will be taken *care* of. As my daughter you have prestige, rank, opportunity, and status." He looked into her eyes, searching them. "When I am gone you may be looked over or, heaven forbid, someone undeserving might prey upon you."

"Papa—" she began, but he persisted.

"It is my greatest wish to see you married." He swallowed and looked at her again. "Therefore I have one request. Someone we both know desires to ask for your hand. He is a good man, Suzanna. He will treat you well, and you will have this house. You will become a great mistress of this living. When he asks, promise me you will say yes."

The speech had taken much effort, and Mr. Spencer closed his eyes and took a deep, wheezy breath, almost settling into a fitful sleep. Suzanna watched his closed eyes through her wet ones as she tried to still her breathing. She wanted nothing more than to set her father at ease. She loved him so. He had given her everything. Indeed she owed every happiness in life to him. How could she refuse him his one wish— one that was so completely and utterly in her favor and for her benefit?

Was it Mr. Lacy of whom her father spoke? She searched her heart for a moment. She did not love Mr. Lacy, that she knew, but he was the best sort of man. They would have a very amiable life together, and at least they were friends and not strangers. She bit her lip and closed her eyes, gathering courage.

Her will fought against her aching heart. Mr. Lacy would treat her as an equal, and she could serve by his side. That was better than most men. But there was a part of her that wished for love—romantic, deep, exciting, and enduring love.

But how could she answer no to her dying father? It was out of the question.

When she opened her eyes, her father's eyes were watching hers.

She caressed his hand.

"If it is Mr. Lacy you speak of, he is a wonderful man. I did not know of his intentions, but if he asks me, I promise I shall do as you wish."

Mr. Spencer sighed, and Suzanna thought she saw his shoulders raise two inches.

"Thank you, my love. I can now return to my God in peace."

"Oh, Father, you must continue to try and live as long as possible. You may recover yet! And be here for the wedding!" Suzanna patted his hand emphatically.

"How I pray that to be the case," he said, his eyes clouding with sadness. "You really ought to get some sleep."

She knew she could not rest but did want a moment to think about what had just transpired. As she stood, Mr. Spencer said, "Would you mind sending Mr. Lacy to me?"

Mr. Lacy. Her future husband. At that moment Suzanna realized the weight of her agreement. A wash of grief for her father had already encased her that night, and now another layer of dread fell over her as she realized her fate. She did not know how, but she nodded her assent and slowly approached the door.

As she exited the room, she saw Mr. Lacy pacing the corridor down from Mr. Spencer's room.

"Trying to listen through thin walls again?" Suzanna said, her voice tight and her eyebrows drawing together in pain.

"No," Mr. Lacy replied, a small, sad smile crossing his face. "I have been praying. For Mr. Spencer, of course, and quite honestly, for you."

His eyes looked at her so gently, with deep love and tenderness. He loved her. The future would not be unkind in his hands.

"My father wishes to speak with you," she said quietly.

He nodded and left her in silence.

If only she could love him back.

Chapter 5

Suzanna returned in the afternoon and often gazed out the window. The leaves had not fully changed, for it was only October, and no one had expected the sudden snowstorm. The chill echoed her heart at that moment. How had so much of life drained away overnight?

Her father looked at her, taking her hands in his.

"It came early!" he said with a faint smile. "I know how much you love it when it first falls. Go outside. It will do you good. I am feeling much stronger."

Suzanna shook her head. "No, not his time." Snowflakes seemed less magical with so much coldness inside of her. Winter should hold off. Her soul already felt too frozen.

"Suzanna. It will boost your spirits." Mr. Spencer gave a soft smile.

She sighed, holding back tears. She did not want her father to see her crying and decided that leaving briefly would be for the better. Donning a coat, she headed outside, making her way to the small stone bench in their garden. Her back faced the house—trying to block out all she knew. She breathed deeply as large tears came, streaming down her cheeks.

Why did her father have to get sick?

Why did the doctor say there was no hope?

He was all she had left in the world.

Except, she reminded herself, if Mr. Lacy did ask for her hand.

It would not be so bad, would it? Many women had married in worse situations. He was kind, she thought he loved her, and they would have means and social standing. What else could she hope for? She was really making quite a lucky match, she told herself, except for the fact that she did not love him. She did not know exactly what being in love felt like but had always imagined excitement, all consuming joy, romance.

Instead she felt duty bound. Not elated; instead, trepidatious.

A few more snowflakes danced across her lap as the sun began to fall behind the hills. She sat on her hands, thinking how silly it was that she left her gloves inside. She really ought to go back, as the temperature had fallen significantly since she came to the garden. If the frost persisted, they would need to collect all of the vegetables soon. She brought her legs to the edge of the bench and placed her hands in her lap, preparing to rise when she saw Mr. Lacy standing behind her against a tree. He smiled gently, one side of his face drawing up.

"I was trying to give you some moments alone before I interrupted," he said, walking toward her.

Suzanna nodded and kept her place on the bench. "Thank you."

He sat but left a good amount of space between them. For several moments neither person broke the thick band of silence that hung between them.

Finally Mr. Lacy heaved a great sigh. "Miss Spencer," he said as he continued looking forward. "I know your father has spoken to you, and I am too simple a man to pretend to be what I am not. Since the moment we met this summer, I must admit I was taken by your beauty."

He paused his speech, and Suzanna stole a glance at him as he scanned the landscape. He had noticed her beauty? He did not seem one to notice any particulars about anyone. And now he was proclaiming it?

He continued. "Do you remember that time in this garden when you spoke of refusing Colonel Newbold? I knew then I wished you to be mine. Your love of life, your service to others, and your desire to do right have not been lost on me. Although, you have too many amiable qualities to enumerate here. And then, when you shared your secret penchant for baking . . ."

He thought this a display of affection? She wanted to say something—what she did not know—but he continued quickly. "I know you are opposed to most men, fearing they will see you only as a lovely prize. But I do not. I wish you to be my equal, to continue to love and serve those who need you." He looked down and shook his head. "I am getting ahead of myself. This may all seem quite abrupt, but I wish to honor your father before he gets any worse."

He turned toward her and took her hand in his. It was warm, comforting. But it sent no thrill through her.

Finally she met his gaze. "Miss Spencer—lovely Suzanna. Will you honor me and be my wife?"

Suzanna looked down. She *had* agreed already. She had made a promise to her father and would not change her mind now. She closed her eyes, shutting out the world for a moment. It would be best to start on a pleasant foot, trying to show this brought her as much joy as it brought him, so she made sure to smile as she looked at him.

"Mr. Lacy, I have spoken to my father, and he cannot say enough good about you. As the future rector, you should take a wife. So you ought to know that I do say yes."

She tried to look pleasant, like a blooming flower, but inside she felt like nothing more than a dormant seedling.

"The walls in Elmbridge are quite thin," he said, his eyes twinkling at her. "I am glad to know now I have his approval *and* yours."

He scooted closer to her, and she let his arm encircle her shoulder. Again there was no rush of joy at his touch. At least she did not feel disdain. These feelings could grow, she promised herself.

"You are quite chilled," said Mr. Lacy after a few moments. He lent her a hand. "I think it best if we return inside."

Just before she stood, Suzanna heard Kate yelling across the snow, almost running toward them. "Miss Spencer, come quickly! Mr. Lacy!"

Suzanna gave one look to Mr. Lacy and lifted her skirts, taking off in a run. Within moments she was inside, bounding up the stairs as Kate exclaimed, "He has turned for the worse."

Suzanna hurried to his room and threw open the door in time to see her father's bed and shirt soaked in blood. He coughed again, more spittle and coagulated bits of mucus spewing from his mouth. Mr. Lacy rounded the hallway, taking one look into the room and exclaiming, "I shall go for the doctor!"

Mr. Spencer closed his eyes upon seeing Suzanna and took her hands in his. He blinked again after a few moments, visibly calmed. "I think the worst of it is over," he said, breathing slowly. "I am being called home, Suzanna. Mother wants me near her side. My soul cannot take its mortal frame any longer." Suzanna clasped his hands tighter and kissed his cheek. "But I did have Kate draw the curtain for me when you left so I could see your beautiful snow. And"—he stifled a cough—"I saw Mr.

Lacy with you outside." He looked deep into her eyes, asking a question without any words.

"Yes, Father," Suzanna said quietly. "I shall always be taken care of. You need not worry about me."

Mr. Spencer gave a soft smile, blinking up at her. "I love you so, Suzanna," he choked out.

Then he closed his eyes, gave a labored exhale, and his head drooped to one side. Suzanna laid her head on his shoulder as the tears fell uncontrolled. The cold from the outside seemed to envelop the room. She still held his hand as she sat in the silent space, which seemed to darken all around her.

He was gone.

Chapter 6

Suzanna could not relinquish her father's cold hand. Thoughts and memories swirled around her, like the dark leaves on an autumn day. Why did he have to go now? Why did he have to become sick? She cried and cried, sunken low in the armchair next to his bed. She recalled their life together—her younger years with her mother still healthy, then her mother's death when she was only twelve and how much that affected them both, and the years between then and now. Every dinner, every trip, listening to every sermon. Those days would be no longer.

Why?

How could she be so lost? So alone?

How could she endure it?

She had Mr. Lacy. Although the prospect of their marriage still made her uneasy, Suzanna took a small comfort that this wholesome man would always be there for her.

Mr. Lacy gave her space for the evening, retiring to the servants' quarters.

It wasn't until the next morning he spoke to her. "I am so very sorry, Miss Spencer. I did not think he would pass so soon."

She looked up at him with a soft, sad smile.

"Nor did I," she said, tears again welling in her eyes.

"I do not wish to cause any more grief, but we must think of the funeral now," he said, putting an arm around her. She slightly recoiled, not used to his touch. He perceived her movement and immediately moved away.

She tried to look pleasant. "Perhaps tomorrow we ought to bury him. Thank goodness the snow did not linger. And you shall perform the rites?"

"Yes, if you wish," he said and then stood. "I will go directly to Lord Chalestry to make my position official."

Matthew Lacy paced slowly as he waited in Chalestry Estate's drawing room. His ride over had been filled with several emotions that he tried to understand. With Mr. Spencer's passing, he was the new rector, as soon as Lord Chalestry declared it as such. It was an illustrious position for one so young, and he felt a bit of excitement at the prospect. But to lose the wisdom, friendship, and guidance of Mr. Spencer seemed unbearable. How could the good Lord take that man so early? There was so much Matthew wished to ask Mr. Spencer, to glean from him yet.

And then there was the engagement. He would not speak of it; it was too soon. Surely Suzanna would mourn for a six-month period, and then they would address it. He would take over the rectory, and she would have to move to Norling Place until they were married. How he wished her father's death did not displace her from her own home. If only they could have been wed before Mr. Spencer died.

Matthew looked around at the elaborate furnishings of the Chalestry drawing room. Each chair was upholstered with gold accents, each piece of wood masterfully carved with twirls and twists. It was too busy, much like his swirling mind. He then heard a rustling behind the door, a swishing skirt, and the muffled tones of an argument.

"Please, dearest, it will be fine," said Lord Chalestry in a hushed whisper.

The shrill voice of Lady Chalestry, who seemed to care nothing for a lowered tone, responded, "It is all very sad, to be sure, but you ought to make it clear that Miss Spencer leaves quickly, or better yet marries our new rector. She has always been a pretty girl, but now with the death of her father, she will undoubtedly wish to catch the first man who comes along so she can guarantee a more secure future. I am sure as soon as her mourning is over she will be flirting with every man in all of our circles."

"Dearest, Mr. Lacy is one of the most sensible young men I have ever met. Of course he has thought of these things. It would insult him to suggest it, man to man, and she *is* in mourning."

"Then perhaps I should say something."

"I think not," said Lord Chalestry. Matthew recognized the sound of a sliding boot, as though Lord Chalestry was hedging his wife's entrance. That man did possess more sense than his spouse. Matthew heard a few more deliberate loud strides as the door swung open.

Matthew stopped pacing and removed his hat.

"I am sure you have heard," said Matthew, knowing very well by the conversation he had just listened to, "but our venerable Mr. Spencer has just passed out of this life."

Lord Chalestry nodded gravely. "One of God's best men and one of the best I ever knew."

"Yes. I am quite sorrowful. I will feel his loss greatly," said Matthew as he twisted his hat.

"Indeed. Thank you for informing me." Lord Chalestry ran his hands over his large belly. "Now, I know it is soon to speak of it, but I give you all authority to move forward as the Rector of Elmbridge—including conducting his funeral and all future meetings. I trust you will take care of the logistics. Miss Spencer will need a new home. She is welcome here, of course."

Mr. Lacy cleared his throat. "Her father has a small home in Berkeley, which I think she will take as soon as he is buried. She wishes to have the funeral tomorrow."

"Very well. Thank you for all you have done."

Matthew bowed and exited the room. Lord Chalestry had enough sense to not discuss Miss Spencer any further.

As Matthew entered the carriage once again, the prospect of his future came before him. He was now the rector, and the weight of such a duty staggered him. He watched the crimson trees out his window, wondering how his life had changed faster than autumn had come and gone this season. Despite it all, he felt honored, and he pledged that he would give his whole heart to God, to the people of Elmbridge, and of course, to Suzanna.

Thank goodness Lord Chalestry had said nothing about Miss Spencer's future marriage. Matthew had already taken care of that in his own way. He did not wish to discuss something so personal and so new with Lord Chalestry—or anyone yet. He would marry Suzanna! Oh, to allow himself, at least in mind, to use her Christian name. Her beautiful face came before his eyes. Her teasing smile. Her hand on her hip. Her basket filled ready to help.

He was indeed a lucky man.

As he rode away, Lady Chalestry's words gnawed at him. He did not wish to marry Suzanna only because a rector ought to have a wife. How awful a sentiment. He truly cared for her. Perhaps Lord and Lady Chalestry had forgotten how wonderful true companionship could be.

Matthew and Suzanna Lacy. He could not contain his grin. They would make a splendid pair, as soon as they could announce it.

Lady Chalestry might just have to fret until that time.

Chapter 7

Suzanna's pride for her father's life swelled during Mr. Lacy's extremely eloquent and touching speech. If any soul was to be well received in heaven, it surely was her father. How she wished to emulate his legacy.

The day after the funeral, Kate packed every article of clothing and every possession for Suzanna. A letter and necklace from her mother, her father's Bible, and his hat and cloak were among her most prized. A servant had gone ahead to Norling Place, and Suzanna could not have been more grateful to Mr. Lacy for recently ordering a few new pieces of furniture.

"Is that everything, Kate?" said Suzanna, a slow tear falling from her cheek. She had not been able to stop crying, despite her efforts, and everything Kate tucked away reminded her of some memory from her father.

"I believe so, miss. Shall we make our way downstairs?"

Suzanna looked around her, as though she could take the very walls of the place with her if she stared at them long enough. She wiped another tear. "I suppose so."

As they came to the parlor, Mr. Lacy stood.

"I think we have the last of it," said Suzanna, trying to be brave.

Mr. Lacy nodded slowly, his eyes a deep cavern. "Kate, can you go check on Miss Spencer's bags with the footman?"

"Yes, sir," said Kate as she curtsied.

As soon as they were alone, Mr. Lacy stepped closer. He did not touch Suzanna, but she could feel his breath on her face.

"I wish you did not have to leave."

"Me too," she said. "It makes my father's passing all too final."

He placed a hand on her shoulder. "I figure you will be in mourning for quite some time."

"Yes," she said. "I plan on the traditional six months. And after that we shall announce the engagement?"

Mr. Lacy offered a soft smile. "Yes, when you are ready. Please write and tell me when you are settled in Berkeley. And if you have any questions about the house or furnishings, I would be happy to help."

"Thank you," said Suzanna. "I am much obliged for your kindnesses."

He stared at her for a moment, stepping even closer, lifting her chin gently.

Kate's quick steps caused Suzanna to step back, and Mr. Lacy dropped his hand. His eyes did not leave her.

"The coach is all prepared, miss."

Suzanna stood frozen, unsure of what Mr. Lacy had intended. But she nodded toward Kate and returned to the present.

Mr. Lacy accompanied Suzanna to the threshold, walking behind with his hand on the small of her back.

"Well, we must be off," said Suzanna, swallowing as she tried to hold back another wayward tear. "Until we meet again, Mr. Lacy."

He took her hand and held it a long moment, then brought it to his lips. "Safest of travels, Miss Spencer."

She watched him wait at the gate until they turned out of sight.

Besides her father, there never was a better rector.

Chapter 8

Three weeks later, Jacob stood in the Berkeley cemetery directly in front of the entrance, grey headstones greeting him from slightly askew angles on every side. At his left stood a man and his wife. Mr. Phipps was a thin man, but the work of the fields as a laborer had earned him taut muscles and a strong constitution.

Jacob turned toward them. "I realize this cemetery might seem a strange place to meet, but I must know more of your childhood and wish to tell you more of mine." He surveyed the grey stones, knowing each possessed a story unknown to the common bystander.

"Do go on, sir," said Mr. Phipps almost reverently.

"You see, we are drawn together through this place. I have not always lived in London, and my family used to own a home on the outskirts of Berkeley. Over seventeen years ago, my family moved here in hopes that the better air would improve my sister's health. She did become a little better but was never vaccinated against smallpox because my mother thought her too weak. For a time she seemed perfectly healed, but the next winter, she contracted smallpox from a servant who had visited a family member in another village. People thought surely she would recover because she was then almost eleven, but nothing could have been done."

Mr. Phipps looked up with pained eyes. "She is buried here?" He spoke reverently.

"Yes," replied Jacob with a nod, gesturing to one of the nearest headstones. His mind went back to his sister's illness all those years ago. Her body in pain. Her pock-covered face, only finding peace in death.

Dr. Jenner had suggested that his sister be vaccinated. If only she had been. Jacob rubbed his arms and turned back to Mr. Phipps. "I understand your benefactor and great friend, Dr. Jenner, is also buried here."

Mr. Phipps nodded, and his wife wrapped her arm around her husband.

Jacob continued. "Though I only met him twice, I recall him a great man. Mr. Phipps, I want to know everything you know. I want to understand what you went through, what Dr. Jenner learned, and how to promote this knowledge. I know he gave you a land and home to live on because of your bravery and friendship, but I wish to spread your sacrifice and his knowledge further."

"My sacrifice was nothing, really," said Mr. Phipps with a humble shake of his head.

"Dr. Jenner didn't think so. He knew the risk." Jacob looked directly at the man. "If he hadn't first tested the vaccine on you . . . if *you* hadn't been the first patient all those years ago, how would we know it works now?"

"I have always been grateful Dr. Jenner took a chance with me," said Mr. Phipps. He furrowed his brow. "What do you propose, sir, to stop smallpox?"

"I want everyone vaccinated. I want to rid England of this disease. I want to build up an immunity even among the poor classes."

The afternoon sun had not extinguished all signs of a beginning frost, but the cold did not affect Jacob's speech. He sighed and uncrossed his arms. Over the last few years since his father's death, he could not stop thinking about how to save more people. He remembered far too often the day his sister died, and the knowledge that her death could have been avoided had haunted him all these years. Had their servants been vaccinated, had he insisted on it, had more people had access to the vaccination, the sickness would not have prevailed.

Mr. Phipps cleared his throat, and Jacob could not help but notice the skeptical look on his new acquaintance's face.

"This is an ambitious goal. How do you propose such a thing to be done?"

"We must broadcast everything Dr. Jenner learned. We need scientists and doctors to collaborate." Jacob stood a little taller. "And we must pass a law in Parliament."

Mr. Phipps paced a moment in the cold November breeze. He shook his head slightly.

"It sounds mighty difficult, sir. I think many people of your circle and mine will resist such actions. Many people will even fight against your cause, for the procedure is feared by many. Passing a law sounds impossible."

Jacob paced toward another grave and brushed some snow off the headstone. He rotated slowly, hands clasped behind his back, and looked again at Mr. Phipps.

"It must be *our* cause." He lowered his chin and studied Mr. Phipps. "I need your help. I promise you I will not stop until we are successful."

Mr. Phipps looked down at his wife and back at Jacob with a face almost as steady as the stones around him.

Jacob pressed him. "When shall we meet again?"

Mr. Phipps' gaze did not leave Jacob's. More cold moments passed until Mr. Phipps finally said, "I can see you are quite determined. I do not think my wife would mind if we went back to my home so I can show you the documents."

Jacob smiled and clasped his shoulder. "This is the beginning of something great, I promise."

Suzanna felt she had settled into Berkeley nicely, although it was rather lonely. She almost never received visitors—and she knew why. She was new, virtually unknown, and in mourning. She did not attend any social functions besides church.

She had felt so lost since coming here. She missed her father daily. His absence had left a large hole in her heart. She wished to fill it but didn't know how. The prospect of Mr. Lacy should lighten her spirit, but she still felt dark. How could she honor her father's legacy? What would he wish her to do? Perhaps if she could figure out what that was, she might feel closer to her father again, less lost and alone.

Amid these reflections, Suzanna's maid entered the quiet drawing room, informing her that Miss Anneliese Grysham had come to call. Suzanna filled with surprise and delight.

"How unexpected! And does she come alone?"

"Yes, miss."

Suzanna sighed in relief. The last person she wanted was Lady Florence to criticize her reduced circumstances. The door opened, and

Anneliese entered, walking so unassumingly she reminded Suzanna of a dormouse who had just found a morsel. Suzanna's love for this girl came rushing back—her sweet face, her calm demeanor, and her genuine smile. She bore a basket of cheeses and jams and set it down on the side table before coming to grasp Suzanna's hand.

"I hope I have not come too soon. My uncle had business near here, and I asked him if I could come along with him. I know you must be grieving and lonely, and sometimes a bit of company eases that weight," said Anneliese as a tear pooled in her eye. "I was young when I lost my parents, and I still remember the pain—the loneliness—I felt. I still feel it, really. Death affects us all, I suppose."

Suzanna nodded slowly. "Oh, I am so grateful you have come. It *has* been a bit lonesome." Suzanna gestured to the spot next to her and thoughtfully considered what she was about to say.

Anneliese seemed aware of the silence and cleared her throat as if she had prepared a speech. "I know it is hard to speak of your loss. But I find that sometimes speaking of these things acts as a balm." The clear countenance of Anneliese smiled softly. "Shall I go first?"

A wave of emotion washed over Suzanna. She placed her hand on Anneliese's and nodded, afraid any answer would lead to an inability to control her emotions.

Anneliese inhaled and a thoughtful look took place of her smile. "I was only nine years old. They say it was really a miracle I was born, for in the next eight years my mother miscarried three times. On her fourth pregnancy my father decided more drastic measures must be taken, so my mother was on bedrest and high supervision by the best doctors in London. She carried the baby full term, but the poor little boy was born a stillbirth." She took a deep breath and said in almost a whisper, "And my mother died from excessive blood loss." She paused, letting out a slow breath. "My father was at her side then, and I think he never quite recovered from the loss of his sweetheart. He was different after that. My grandma convinced him to take a trip to France six months later to try and ease his mind, but then . . . he was killed in a violent storm." Anneliese looked up and gave a weak smile. "I comfort myself that at least they are together now."

"As are mine," said Suzanna, nodding thoughtfully.

Suzanna came closer on the couch and took both of Anneliese's hands in hers. "There are not many people who understand me as you have."

Anneliese gave a half smile, and Suzanna thought she saw another tear in her eye. "Now tell me your fondest memories of your father," she said.

Suzanna smiled, adjusting her skirt and moving closer to Miss Grysham. "There was the time I found a mouse in my bed, and he spent the whole evening looking everywhere for it." Suzanna smiled. "Or the time he tripped over his own words in his sermon, teaching about Cain and Mabel."

The rest of the afternoon Suzanna told memory after memory of her father. As the sun fell lower in the sky, Suzanna finally changed the subject. "So you will quit Chalestry?"

"For the time being. My uncle declares we must go to London to prepare for Parliament." She gazed out the window at the sky. "He shall be here soon to collect me."

"I see. Lady Florence must be devastated."

"Perhaps, but she bears it well," said Anneliese kindly. Suzanna wondered if indeed she had more thoughts that she did not voice. "She always has some new social event to look forward to."

Suzanna laughed. "I am sure you loved having such a robust schedule. You must have received visitors daily."

"Constantly! I am actually quite tired of it. I am glad we shall be back for the start of the Season and especially Christmas, though I expect my social calendar to be rather quiet. I am not the type to draw attention."

Her dormouse shyness returned once again.

"Surely not!" said Suzanna, clasping her hands together. "Your first London Season? You will be quite in demand, I suspect!"

Anneliese shook her head and blushed. "Can I ask you what your plans are now in Berkeley? I must admit this was part of the reason I came to call today. I was hoping—if it is not too bold—to invite you to London. I would like some company there and thought you might enjoy some time away from everything here during the holidays. Perhaps you could spend Christmas with us." Her lightly freckled face stared eagerly toward Suzanna. "Of course . . . you may think about it before you decide."

Suzanna looked out the window toward the icy, frosted garden. Her heart felt the weight of her solitary existence. Going to London and being in the easy company of Miss Grysham sounded delightful.

"I would enjoy that." Suzanna smiled. "Thank you for thinking of me. Christmas alone sounded miserable."

"Really, you will come? We will plan on it! Grandmama and I shall still be at Chalestry for three more weeks, even though my uncle leaves in ten days. We shall send our coach to you and shall meet up in Elmbridge and go on together to London."

Apparently, with such a plan, Anneliese had been sure she would accept.

A few minutes later, an elaborate equipage rumbled to a stop outside, and Lord Haversley rapped the door.

"Good to see you again, Miss Spencer," he said with a lingering bow, customary of his overly dramatic manners.

"Likewise," said Suzanna with a much more brief curtsy. "Thank you for letting Miss Grysham spend the day with me. It was delightful."

"Of course. I hope to visit Berkeley again."

"Oh, indeed?" She tried to remain cordial. "You and Miss Grysham are always welcome."

"Thank you," he said as he extended an arm to Anneliese.

She turned and embraced Suzanna.

"Until Christmas!" she whispered in Suzanna's ear.

Suzanna watched the tall man escort his petite niece to the carriage. Then Suzanna thought she saw a lady part the curtain and peer out. Who could she be? She certainly was not Lady Florence. Could Lord Haversley be courting more than one woman? Was he the kind of gentleman who played with ladies' hearts? Many women were interested in him. Surely most would fall at his parliamentary feet. Maybe this explained why he always sought occasion to travel to Berkeley.

Suzanna waved toward them, masking her curiosity. She would never understand that foppish, self-centered man. What right did he have to toy with female feelings like that? Even if that female was the overly self-important Florence.

She sighed. He really did have a wonderful niece, and at least she would miss her.

Chapter 9

With the illustrious position of rector, it was now time for Matthew Lacy to visit his home, even if his father's family did live quite a distance from Elmbridge. He would take the texts of his best sermons and visit, for it had been two years. He made arrangements for another clergyman to give the sermons over the few weeks surrounding Christmas, took his leave of the McCallisters, and set out.

By next Christmas he would be married. Perhaps his family would come to Elmbridge for the wedding, if his parents' health allowed. They would love Suzanna—not as much as he did, but no one could. He remembered her in every part of the garden, every walk to the church, every moment in the parlor. And every time he broke a piece of bread, he wished it came from her hand.

He had received a few letters from her, one upon her arrival and two more in the past month. She remained proper and easy in her correspondence, never giving a sentiment that was overly flirtatious or inappropriate. Her letters had been amusing, heartwarming. She would be the perfect wife.

He packed the letters too, which he had stacked and tied with a blue bow, so he might show them to his mother when he told her of his engagement. His secret would be safe with her.

Bundle in hand, he saddled up his horse, deciding to ride and take lodging at inns on his four-day journey. There would come a time when he could not so easily move about the country as a married man, and for now he wished to return to his home on horseback and ride through his father's rolling hills like he did as a boy.

Jacob arrived in London before his niece and mother. But once there, he realized he did not have enough compelling evidence and details to really drive his point at Parliament. His argument for the smallpox vaccine law must be undeniably convincing. He had found it necessary, therefore, to make a quick trip to Berkeley to gather more evidence from Mr. Phipps and to confirm the smallpox outbreak had not made it to Berkeley.

With a stack of papers tucked neatly into his leather riding sack, Jacob thanked Mr. Phipps again and mounted Sylvester, prepared for the long ride home. The morning air pricked his cheeks, although not a cloud hung in the sky. He wrapped his thick jacket tighter around him and adjusted his scarf to almost cover his face.

He would ride two long days before he would reach his estate outside of London. His mother had asked him countless times why he insisted on riding a horse during the winter months. But she would never under-stand—not many people did, let alone a sensible older woman. He did his best thinking on his horse, and the temperature did not matter when there was much thinking to be done.

Today he had to decide exactly how to convince the richest, most powerful men in England that what he believed in was worth believing in too. If only he could take a few of the poorest people in Clemsford and Cheltenham and show their scarred faces to the men of Parliament. Smallpox had to be stopped.

The next morning he was a bit sore. Although his horse was built for long rides, his muscles were not.

His ride yesterday had provided no solid conclusions. His plan was still quite expensive, and many did not think as he did. The pres-ervation of rank was too ingrained in many. Shouldn't everyone have at least some of the privileges he enjoyed? If he could not give them all enough money to live better, at least he could give them health. Couldn't everyone be free from smallpox? If they accepted vaccina-tion, nearly all could be saved.

He had also promised himself he would at least think about Lady Florence. She was beautiful, quite accomplished, and as far as rank and family were concerned, perfect. But did she have a mind for serious things? Jacob appeared the part of the perfect eligible bachelor, but he wondered if as a new benedict he would wish for a woman next to his side who would fight for right. One who would approve of time spent with people below his class such as Mr. Phipps. What would Florence think if she knew he enjoyed spending time with people far below his station? That he wished to do something bigger than just attend social functions?

Suddenly he realized for the first time what he longed for—someone who cared more about doing good than her trousseau. Someone who might care less about the next ball and care more about changing the world. He sighed as he slowed on his horse. Lady Florence was not that woman.

But the likelihood of finding that kind of young lady, preferably coupled with wit, refinement, and a pretty face . . . who was he kidding? No wonder he was over thirty and unmarried. He dug his heels harder into Sylvester and galloped on. He would reach his estate before nightfall—perhaps before the late afternoon—if he kept up this pace.

He took the post road and passed through one of the small hamlets two hours outside of his estate. The thickness of the trees shielded the sun. The road was riddled with scattered divots of wet soil. Large patches of snow clumped in far greater density than anywhere else on his ride. He had reined Sylvester in to carefully navigate a few large mud puddles when suddenly his eyes were drawn to a cluster of snow to his right. It reflected a deep crimson, and the surrounding area had large streaks of blood seeping into the ground.

Jacob pulled Sylvester into a walk. Whatever animal had found its dinner—or had become someone else's—must have been large to create so much sanguine liquid bespeckling the ground.

The hair on Jacob's arms prickled as he slowed to investigate. He saw the back of a man, crumpled in a heap. Matted hair crusted with blood covered the man's face. Jacob leapt from his horse and crouched, carefully turning the man onto his back. He lay unconscious, his face completely overspread with blood and soil.

The attack was recent. By the look of the man's coat, he was most likely a gentleman. His face was lacerated and had started to swell and discolor. He was covered on all sides in dirt, probably kicked down the hill.

He had been attacked on the road by thieves. It was the only plausible explanation. They must have stolen his horse and his money and left him there to die. Jacob struggled to pull the limp man up toward the road. A low groan escaped the man's lips. Jacob watched the man try to squint through his one good eye, the other completely swollen, unsure of who was touching him. Blood ran from his forehead.

"I shall need you to help me, if you are able," said Jacob. "I promise I am taking you to safety."

"The papers," the man let out with pain. "We must not lose the papers."

Jacob turned his head over his shoulder. About a pace away from the road he saw what might have been the draw to the scoundrels. A large leather bag lay open, the contents spilling out to the side. It looked full of only documents, bound together in small stacks, but a thief would surely have assumed such a bag contained large amounts of money hidden somewhere inside.

The injured man attempted to pull his feet up and raise himself.

"Are they there?" he asked, straining.

"Yes, I see the papers," Jacob reassured him. "But we must get you on my horse and to a doctor. Can you put your weight on me? I will lift you."

"I cannot leave without them," the battered gentlemen groaned.

"I will collect *them* once I have collected you," said Jacob firmly. The man attempted to stand, but his right leg gave out. Jacob braced against him, pushing him up the hill as though he was directing a stubborn farm animal. The man groaned and grabbed his head, which was bleeding profusely. Jacob laid him down, ripped off his cravat, and created a bandage around the man's open wound. The man winced as Jacob hefted him onto the back of his horse, and he clutched his severely mangled hand.

Once the man was settled, Jacob turned, collected every paper he could see, and put them back in the satchel. The man raised his head and squinted again. "Do not forget that bunch." The man attempted to point with his left elbow.

Jacob lifted a half-covered stack of letters bound by a blue ribbon. For being almost mortally wounded, the man was quite concerned about a few pages.

"I think I have got them all," Jacob said loudly. "May I proceed with saving your life?"

Jacob watched as the man's straight white teeth cracked through a dirt-smeared smile. "Yes, Guv'nor," he said, either loopy or sarcastic, "let us be on our way."

Jacob resolved at that moment that whomever he carried must have hit his head quite hard or possessed a very agreeable sense of humor.

It took them nearly four hours to reach Lysetter Hall. Sylvester had kept a slow, steady pace, and at first the man seemed to start at every uneven bounce. After a half hour, though, he fell asleep, slumping against Jacob.

When they arrived, the butler and groom were the first to notice them. "Fetch Dr. Willows quickly," Jacob called as he dismounted and carried the man inside and up the stairs to his own suite, laying him on the bed. The man kept even his good eye clamped shut most of the time, his face drawn in a permanent grimace. Jacob wrapped some fresh linen around the large gash on his temple, gathered a rag, and began washing his face and arms.

When the doctor arrived, he cut the man's shirt off and ascertained two broken ribs. The doctor then moved down to his right hand. The man smarted as the doctor reset some of the bones and wound it tightly. His good eye shot open and looked from the doctor to Jacob before clamping it shut again. Jacob continued to remove dirt from the man's skin, until finally he beheld a clean face. Jacob cocked his head to the side and peered deeper into the gentleman's countenance.

"Mr. . . . Lacy?"

The man's eyebrows raised as high as they could considering his bruised forehead, and he let out a cough.

"At your service," he attempted, a bit slurred.

"My goodness," said Jacob as he reached absently to his missing cravat.

He watched Mr. Lacy try to pry his eye open long enough to get a good look at him.

"It is I, Lord Haversley," said Jacob.

"Hav—Haversley." Lacy seemed to search his slogged memory. "Yes, of course, the man interested in Lady Florence? With the large cuffs?"

Jacob inspected his shirt sleeve, which had small cuffs on account of seeing Mr. Phipps that day. He only dressed in his elaborate shirts when meeting with well-bred ladies. Still, to be known by his cuffs was rather appalling.

Jacob nodded as Mr. Lacy's eye tried to focus on him.

"I am much indebted to you, sir." Mr. Lacy grimaced again as the doctor lashed some sort of stabilizer around his leg. Then, with as jovial a tone as he could muster, he said, "Doctor, what all is the damage?"

Dr. Willows dressed another cut and replied evenly, "Your hand is fractured and your leg is broken. Your forehead will require stitches."

Mr. Lacy winced through a small nod. "A minor scrape, I say. "

Jacob remembered why he approved of this man in the first place—his good sense of humor ranked high among his amiable qualities.

"Now I must attend to your head," said the doctor. He reached into his bag to prepare the needle.

"Keep him as good looking as you can, doctor," said Jacob, watching Mr. Lacy become more lucid by the minute. "He has not as yet secured a wife, and he must look handsome enough to win one someday."

Lacy shot a glance toward Jacob and then seemed to register the joke and cracked a smile. "I am not sure his stitching can fix the face I was given, *Guv'nor.*" Jacob's chuckle was stifled as he watched Mr. Lacy grimace as the doctor sewed up his head.

"Such humor at a time like this," said the stoic doctor. "He could have easily lost his life back there. Bleeding or freezing to death."

"I do not give up that easily, doctor," said Mr. Lacy.

"And I do not leave old friends on the side of the road," said Jacob with a smile.

The doctor continued on in silence. "Lucky, I daresay," he muttered under his breath. "Exceedingly lucky." Then he administered the last stitch.

Chapter 10

Three days later, Jacob listened as Mr. Lacy tried to coherently describe his attack. "I know there were two men," Mr. Lacy said. "The first one ambushed me from behind, and the second must have been waiting in the trees. They seemed sorely disappointed when they found only papers in my satchel. But I did have a good horse that they quickly made off with. He was my favorite."

"I am truly sorry for your loss," said Jacob. "Taking a man's horse is a low blow. But we have many here you can ride."

Jacob watched as Mr. Lacy looked down and tried to move his hand into the motion of gripping an imaginary set of reins.

Mr. Lacy chuckled. "I will not be riding anytime soon."

"May I ask what your papers were?"

Mr. Lacy's eyes shot to the side. "Personal documents. A few important letters, manuscripts of my best sermons, and my official certificate from Oxford."

"I see. I am impressed you thought of it at the time," said Jacob, thinking of his documents and paperwork from Mr. Phipps, as well as his leather notebook, where he wrote more personal details.

After a few moments, Mr. Lacy spoke again. "I do not plan on trespassing here any longer than is necessary."

"I assure you, you are welcome as long as you need. If there is anything I can do or arrange through my servants, please let me know."

Mr. Lacy shifted his weight. "There is one thing I was hoping I could ask of you . . . if it is not too much of an inconvenience."

"Anything, Mr. Lacy."

"I ought to send a letter to my parents and to Berkeley, and Elmbridge, for that matter."

"Naturally! I am sorry I did not suggest it earlier." Jacob looked at Mr. Lacy. "Let me gather a paper and my quill, and you can dictate whatever you wish." He made his way to the desk and sat down.

"To whom should I address it?"

Mr. Lacy cleared his throat and looked out the window. "I must inform my friend who is taking over during my absence that I will not be back for a few weeks. That letter must go to Elmbridge."

A few minutes passed as Jacob neatly dispatched a note.

Mr. Lacy then gave Jacob his parents' address. Jacob wrote it down and then transcribed Mr. Lacy's letter. When Mr. Lacy approved it, Jacob waited for more instruction.

"And the one to Berkeley?" Jacob asked finally, unable to contain his curiosity. Who did he know there?

"That one needs to go to . . . to Miss Spencer, the rector's daughter."

Jacob looked down, trying to hide the amusement in his eyes. "I see. Is she expecting a letter from you?"

Miss Spencer *was* beautiful, and Mr. Lacy would have been smart to choose such a girl to write letters to, but Jacob had not heard that there was an understanding between them that would necessitate correspondence.

"Oh, well no. We are not in the habit of writing letters. It is just that I have recently obtained my official documents from Oxford, and I promised to let her know when that happened, for the sake of the parrish. I know she cares about her father's legacy, so I feel some responsibility to her."

"Naturally," said Jacob, swallowing and looking down. "Of course you must set your affairs in order. Should I mention your injuries?"

"Perhaps only briefly."

Jacob cast a quick glance toward Mr. Lacy, who nodded dutifully. Five minutes later Jacob had a concise letter written to Miss Spencer.

Jacob stood and bowed. "I shall send these for you straight away."

"Thank you," said Mr. Lacy.

As he shut the door behind him, Jacob's hand still felt warm. He had never actually written a letter to a female other than a familial relation. Somehow writing to Miss Spencer had caused a flood of emotions to course through his body. What would it be like if he actually cared enough about someone to write to them? Why did he feel so nervous about exactly how and what he said? Perhaps he ought to practice more and start with writing a letter to Lady Florence. He sighed and looked across the room for a moment.

He shook his head. Lady Florence did not deserve one yet.

At the sound of a loud knock on the door, Suzanna scurried up from the kitchen downstairs. Dust from her latest loaf of bread was still scattered across her apron.

She walked as fast as she could, hoping to pass through the entryway before Kate let the visitor in.

She was too slow. The front door opened as she attempted to slide past. Suzanna caught herself and turned sheepishly, hoping to seem at least presentable.

"Anneliese? Good heavens! What are you doing here?"

Suzanna noticed a timid lady's maid just within the doorframe as Anneliese continued. "I know through our correspondence we agreed a hired coach would take you in two days, but I thought it ever so much more fun if I collected you a little early."

"And your grandmother approved?"

"Only just. I told her I am old enough to do things on my own, and if Miss Spencer can live alone, surely I can travel in a coach a few hours with my maid."

"Goodness," said Suzanna, brushing her hands together. "I fear I am a bad influence on you."

"Not in the slightest," said Anneliese as she walked up to her friend. "And what have you been doing?" Anneliese looked her up and down, gesturing a small swipe across her cheek toward Suzanna in suggestion. Suzanna's hand shot up to her face, briskly wiping away a large streak of flour. If the apron had not needed an explanation, surely her face warranted one.

"Well, since you are here, would you like to come upstairs with me while I change?" Suzanna motioned to Anneliese with an outstretched hand. "I know I look dreadful. It is just that I love to sneak downstairs and try my hand at baking bread." The girls were halfway up the stairs by now, and Anneliese said nothing. Suzanna hoped she did not find her *too* eccentric. "I assumed at your estate," Suzanna continued, "I might not be able to steal off to the kitchen, so I had to make one loaf today."

They entered Suzanna's room, both lady's maids following them. Kate quickly untied Suzanna's apron, and then Suzanna went to her wash basin to freshen up.

"You don't think I'm crazy, do you?"

"Only a little," said Anneliese. "Crazy because you thought I would not approve. I want to learn to make bread, too. It sounds rather challenging."

Suzanna smiled at her friend. "I assure you it is. The consistency is hard to master. But never mind, we have more important matters. I have debated whether to bring this second trunk or not. It contains my more ornate dresses." Suzanna rubbed her hand over the large luggage next to her.

Anneliese looked over the large traveling trunk on the bed. "I would say yes. There is a chance my grandmother or uncle will host a few formal parties, and although you are in mourning, you still ought to have formal black dresses so you could at least attend one or two with me."

"I will bring it then. But surely your uncle will be much too busy to plan any social functions. When he arrives, will he not have just started attending Parliament's new session?"

"Yes, but of course he attends any social function he can! He is always at the most prominent parties. And Grandmama says I am getting to the age where I might also receive an invitation. My uncle actually does not know you are joining us, for I have not told him. He will be ever so surprised to see I have brought you! And think of the people we could meet! I am sure you would love to snatch up some London beau."

Suzanna shook her head and smiled. "You sound rather excited. I thought it was to be a *quiet* holiday. You forget that I am in mourning. Perhaps I will come to some events, but I shall not dance. I have never cared much about men anyway." She recalled the engagement to Mr. Lacy. Even without trying, she had already caught herself a man.

"Oh, of course," said Anneliese with a frown. "I should not mention gentlemen when you are in mourning."

She was in a state of mourning and in a state of denial, if she were to be truthful. But no one knew that. "It is no matter! I am just grateful to have company this Christmas."

Anneliese reached over and pressed Suzanna's arm. She smiled back and then called to have her trunks brought downstairs. It was fortunate she had packed most of her things so early.

"It takes two days to reach Lysetter Hall?"

"Once we collect Grandmama from Elbridge, it might take even longer. She prefers short days in the carriage. Our home is in Ealing, not quite inside London proper. Far enough removed to have beautiful grounds but close enough to attend to business in town."

Suzanna smiled. For the first time in over a month, Suzanna actually felt excited about something.

Three days later, Jacob sat alone in his sitting room as Mr. Lacy rested upstairs in the master bedroom. Jacob had just begun reviewing a few notes from Mr. Phipps when he heard a carriage pull up through the back gardens. Who would call at such an odd hour?

He spied his own carriage through the large side windows and strode to throw open the door.

"Please, allow me," he said quickly to the footman as he reached the carriage. Jacob extended his hand and said, "Mother! I did not expect you so soon. How was your trip?"

"Splendid, my dear son! Though I would have stayed a few days more had Anneliese not been so anxious to return home."

Jacob watched the dark green taffeta of his mother's gown swoosh past him. He turned back to retrieve Anneliese, whispering to her, "I don't blame you. Was Lady Chalestry getting a bit verbose?"

Anneliese had confided in him that she found the McCallisters too ostentatious at times. Today, however, she seemed rather shy as she replied, "Oh no, Miss Spencer and I were just eager to start our winter holiday!"

Miss Spencer? What did she have to do with his niece returning home?

Anneliese cast a long glance deeper over her shoulder into the carriage as Jacob let her down.

"I invited Miss Spencer to spend Christmas at Lysetter Hall with all of us! Is it not the best surprise?" She placed her arm on his as he walked her to the door. She quietly added, "You remember she is in mourning over her father. I could not bear for her to be alone at Christmas."

Jacob nodded and patted his niece's hand. He turned back and in a few paces extended his arm toward the carriage for a third time.

"Welcome, Miss Spencer. It is a pleasure. Please come in."

Miss Spencer gathered her charcoal traveling dress around her and descended from the carriage. He gave her his hand, and as soon as she took it he felt a strange feeling run the length of his spine. He had not forgotten that she was beautiful—and he had taken the gloved hand of many a fine woman before. But with her . . . what *was* it?

She nodded a thank you toward him, looking down at his hand for a moment. Another thrill shot through him, and he willed himself to stop staring.

Miss Spencer let go and walked ahead toward Anneliese. He suddenly wished to accompany them inside but thought better of it. Instead he discussed the journey with the footman and groom. He had no idea his niece felt this close to Miss Spencer, but something told him their company would be good for each other.

Suzanna Spencer noticed immediately Lord Haversley's lack of lacy cuffs. It seemed odd, uncharacteristic—almost as strange as the look he had given her as he helped her out of the carriage. Her coming was a surprise, and apparently it had thrown him off. Hopefully he would not be upset with Anneliese.

As Suzanna caught up to Anneliese, she tried to take in the whole of Lysetter Hall. The grounds rambled on and on, not to mention the several wings that jutted out from the house like jetties on a beach. The hills sloped down behind it all, an expansive garden flanking the back of the building.

Suddenly Lord Haversley's normal ostentatious clothing choices made sense. It was all so . . . much.

"The grounds are so expansive!" said Suzanna as she placed her arm inside of her friend's. "I was hoping you could show me around the gardens and the house, but I fear that may take a few days!"

"And I fear that every Haversley man has felt the need to add on some wing or garden or something. It is over the top, if you ask me."

"I am sure each addition was the pride of its master."

"Perhaps," said Anneliese, "though my uncle has had the good sense to not add anything. At least not yet."

Suzanna wanted to look over her shoulder and analyze Anneliese's uncle for herself. Every time his niece spoke of him, he seemed the sum of most amiable parts. But every time Suzanna had watched him, he appeared to be nothing but a coxcomb.

The two girls entered the main entry, which boasted two curving staircases off to either side of the grand foyer. Through a large arch underneath, there were two marble statues and beyond them Suzanna spied a sparkling silver ballroom. Off to the left through a doorway she assumed were the drawing and dining rooms.

"Now, Miss Spencer, I see your eyes," said Lady Haversley. "I know this front entrance is too large and far too drafty, if you ask me. Mrs. Hatch here will take you to your room. Upstairs you will find fewer rooms than one would surmise."

Before they started up the stairs, Lord Haversley finally came through the front door behind them.

"Mother," he said, coming quickly, "I forgot to mention. I have given my suite up."

Lady Haversley cocked her head to the side, wanting an explanation. Lord Haversley clasped both hands behind his back and said slowly, turning to look at Miss Spencer, "Mr. Lacy of Elmbridge is here staying with me. I gave him my suite. It is much easier to access from the stairs, and the view is best. I thought it would help him recover more quickly. Mrs. Hatch, perhaps you could send some of the maids right away to change the linens in the first guest room. I shall be up shortly to remove my things."

"I am happy wherever is easiest," said Suzanna quickly. She looked down, feeling a warmth spread across her cheeks. "I do not want to be an inconvenience to anyone." She suddenly wished they had told Lord Haversley of her coming.

"I assure you it is no problem," said Lord Haversley with a wide smile.

Suzanna continued to study the marble floor tiles. Had she heard him correctly? Mr. Lacy was in this house? Why on earth was he here? Mr. Lacy was only loosely acquainted with Lord Haversley and did not know that she was coming for Christmas, and the people of Elmbridge needed him. Of all the places he could be at this very moment! Could she never escape him?

Suzanna's eyes met Lord Haversley's, which seemed to be watching her.

He continued with a much more serious face. "I came upon Mr. Lacy during my ride here. He was attacked coming to London, ambushed on the post road. I sent a letter, but it must not have arrived before you left."

Suzanna's hand flew to her mouth, and she looked at Anneliese, who already employed the same reaction. She looked back to Lord Haversley and said, "Oh my goodness—how terrible!" Suzanna immediately wished she had not been put out by Mr. Lacy's presence. How could she be so unfeeling toward the man who had always cared for her, who loved her?

"Is he . . . all right?" she asked slowly.

"He will be, in time. He has a broken leg and a fractured hand, so it will be a slow recovery. He was cut up quite badly when I found him."

Suzanna closed her eyes and took a slow breath. "He is quite lucky then, to have you come upon him."

"I am so grateful I did," said Lord Haversley, and Suzanna noticed he lacked his customary bravado in his voice. She wanted to thank him more, but it was not her place.

Lord Haversley continued with astonishment in his voice. "He was in such a state, I did not recognize him at first. Imagine my surprise when he was lain here at my house and I finally made out his features!"

Anneliese walked over to Suzanna's side. "Well, this is quite a story, Uncle. And you seem the hero. But perhaps we ought to get settled, and then we can discuss it all further."

"Oh, yes, of course!" said Lord Haversley, and Suzanna noticed he seemed rather sheepish for going on. "How right you are, Anneliese. Forgive me for my long explanation. We shall have ample time to discuss things over the holiday."

Suzanna wished he *had* shared more details. Mr. Lacy's recovery would surely take the whole of her stay. Suddenly her visit became much more complicated.

She tried to remain calm as Mrs. Hatch led them down the corridor.

"I shall be just next to you, which shall be great fun!" said Anneliese. Suzanna smiled back at her friend but could not stop thinking about Mr. Lacy. Would he make a full recovery? How did he feel? She also admitted that she had hoped coming to London would provide diversion from him and her imminent future.

But now with him here in the same house, how would she fare? Hopefully he would not try to announce anything before the mourning period was over. She still needed time to adjust to the idea of marriage. And if he tried to show any romantic overtures, like what had almost happened as she left Elmbridge . . .

No. He wouldn't try. She was sure of it.

Yet despite her uneasiness, a part of her longed to see him, to care for him as a friend, and make sure he would heal properly. If only they could just be friends again, instead of so much more.

Jacob tried to stay out of the girls' way as he turned the corner and strode down the next hallway, depositing his stack of paperwork in an extra room.

The master suite's door was ajar. Mr. Lacy was sitting up in his bed, staring across the room in a daze. It had been only four days since his arrival, but his face already looked much improved.

"I did not expect you to be awake," said Jacob.

Mr. Lacy looked at him with groggy eyes. "The sound of ladies' voices woke me. I fear I had a most unexpected dream."

"It is no dream, my friend. We have indeed been invaded by several women."

Jacob watched Mr. Lacy wrinkle his eyes in question.

"My mother and my niece, who brought her new friend, Miss Spencer of Elmbridge."

Jacob noticed Mr. Lacy's eyes open wide. "Miss Spencer, the rector's daughter?"

"The very one," said Jacob. He continued with an easy tone. "Perhaps the ladies could come visit you this evening."

Surely Mr. Lacy felt beyond bored being confined in that room for so long. Jacob knew he himself would have nearly gone mad. He watched Mr. Lacy's eyes cloud, and Jacob was not sure if his friend felt overly tired or was thinking quite intently about something.

"That would be . . ." Mr. Lacy paused a moment. His countenance seemed to restrain his words, or perhaps it was that his wounds made expressing himself hard. "That would be nice. Those two ladies do enjoy visiting the sick and infirm, so I suppose I now qualify."

Jacob chuckled but wondered if Mr. Lacy had more feelings toward Miss Spencer than he let on. Something about Mr. Lacy's tone carried more weight than usual. Jacob felt like he had come across a stone with only a bit of edge above ground and much more buried beneath the surface.

Why did he care? Mr. Lacy and Miss Spencer would be well suited. Their ranks and temperaments were more than compatible, and she seemed respectable in every right, as did he. Plus those eyes, that face. Jacob felt his hand warm suddenly, remembering her touch. Any man would be lucky to have her.

As he walked down the stairs, the less noble part of him felt lucky that he had no injury to keep him from dinner that evening with his niece and her new guest.

"Good evening," Lord Haversley said when Suzanna and Anneliese had been seated. He had changed into a nice jacket and had smoothed his hair. "I am afraid Mr. Lacy cannot manage the stairs as of yet, but I told him perhaps the ladies of the house could pay him a visit after dinner, if you are willing."

At the end of his speech, he eyed Suzanna and waited for an answer.

"Why yes, if Anneliese finds it agreeable, we can surely visit him."

"It *was* our visits to the sick around us that brought our friendship together!" Anneliese smiled.

Suzanna tilted her head in agreement.

Lady Haversley changed the subject. "Now I do hope, Jacob, that you plan on attending all of the engagements we have this next week, just as you did before Elmbridge. I know you may miss a certain young lady, but that does not mean we should attend any fewer social gatherings. Several people have invited us to dine and dance, and they expect to see you."

Jacob? Suzanna realized that until that moment she had not known Lord Haversley's Christian name. He was in the middle of a bite and seemed to chew his meat like a pensive cow in order to avoid answering his mother.

Suzanna analyzed him as she buttered her bread. His dinner jacket was outrageously orange, with a gold paisley vest. His cuffs, though visible, were a bit more tame than the ones he wore at the last dinner at the McCallisters, but the ruffles were still too big for someone named Jacob. The name seemed all together much too conservative for him. He warranted something more avant-garde such as Nathaniel or Bartholomew, although Suzanna admitted one does not choose one's own name.

"Of course, Mother. I would not miss any party." He had finally swallowed, his tone full of politeness. "I never do! And, Anneliese, you will be attending with Miss Spencer?"

Anneliese gave a nervous glance toward Suzanna. "I think I shall have the courage to attend if Suzanna comes."

They all looked at her. Suzanna nodded quickly, wishing the attention were somewhere else. She supposed she could still wear black and go with Anneliese only for support.

The dowager seemed to approve and continued, "Perfect. Tomorrow night is the Yule Ball at the Tursleys'. We shall leave here at five in the evening so we can make it into London proper."

Anneliese leaned over and whispered to Suzanna, "The Tursleys always throw the most lavish parties. I am sure there shall be several men there wishing to dance with you."

"You must remember," Suzanna whispered, turning toward Anneliese, "that I am still in mourning and therefore do not plan on dancing at all. I will only come so you are not alone."

"Miss Spencer and Miss Grysham," said a very happy Mr. Lacy, "you are a wonderful sight for a man who has been pent up in this room for days."

They curtsied, and Suzanna looked at Mr. Lacy. He was badly bruised, with a large scab on his forehead, but he seemed in good spirits. Thankful he wasn't worse, she glanced a moment around the large suite. It was remarkably stark for a master bedroom, especially for someone who dressed as Lord Haversley did. Only a few pictures hung on the walls: a large painting of two boys and a girl, a single picture of a girl not more than eleven, and a large oval rendering of an older gentleman.

There was a complete sitting area and what seemed another room entirely adjoining it. Mr. Lacy motioned to the couches as Suzanna came out of her inspection. "We are so glad you are well."

"A true blessing," he said, his eyes lingering on her for a moment. Suzanna cleared her throat as he continued, and he shifted his eyes toward Anneliese. "If it had not been for your uncle, I might not be here at all."

Anneliese nodded. "Yes, he is the best sort of fellow. However, he was not injured. I cannot imagine what you have been through!"

Mr. Lacy looked as though he would reply when down the hall Lady Haversley's voice rang, "Anneliese dear, can you come here? I must know what you have to wear for tomorrow."

She gave a labored sigh. "Excuse me. Grandmama is always so particular about gowns." She rose and headed for the doorway.

Suzanna stood to leave as well when Mr. Lacy extended his hand.

"Miss Spencer," he whispered, "don't go."

His hand held hers, and she sat back down. "I have worried about you. I am glad you have so many friends who wish to take care of you just as I do."

Suzanna stopped and faced him, recognizing the good in his sincere countenance.

"Yes . . . I am rather lucky. Before now I thought you my only friend left in Elmbridge, but it seems I have a few others. How curious to have ended up in the same place." A grin crossed her lips. She withdrew her hand from him and clasped her palms.

"I wish for your father daily," he said even quieter.

"As do I," Suzanna answered.

"How . . . how do you fare without him?" he asked tenderly.

She looked across the room for a moment, thinking of how much she missed her father. She was then captivated by the picture of the young girl. The painting must have been the younger sister Lord Haversley had lost. *Too many early deaths in their family*, she thought. *Too many in my own.*

As she studied the girl in the painting, she felt drawn to her. She had the same eyes as Anneliese and Lord Haversley. The artist had captured a glimmer of light in her eyes and just the right pink hue to flush her cheeks with joy. What had Lord Haversley's relationship been with this sister? Were they the best of friends, playmates, confidants? Perhaps inseparable. As she looked at it again, she caught a breath of sadness in the portrait. One small brushstroke in the young girl's slight smile was given by the artist, not by the subject, and Suzanna felt the pain of it almost acutely as her own. She had lost her best friend, too.

She came back to Mr. Lacy's question. "My aching heart cannot convey the right words. I miss his sermons, his presence, the way his mouth twitched when he ate soup . . ." She trailed off.

"We all feel his loss." He fiddled with the couch cushion and moved closer to her. He grabbed a stray tendril of her hair and followed it with his finger. "And of course I shall say nothing of our engagement until you deem it long enough, my dear." He added the last two words in a whisper and Suzanna nodded, offering a small smile.

She looked toward the door and stood. "I am so glad you are well. I . . . had better go. I hope you plan to join us downstairs as soon as you are able."

She could feel his eyes lingering in her direction all the way down the hall.

Chapter 11

The Yule Ball at the Tursleys' was overcrowded, just as it was every year. Jacob knew they tried to showcase their importance with an inflated guest list. The ballroom felt stifling hot. The sweat of too many people dancing close together wriggled his nose. Jacob was unsure if it was the large fire or the ever-searching eyes of Miss Julia Tursley that caused him to feel even warmer at the moment. She had followed him around most of the evening with either her actual presence or her gaze, and he stood in dire need of an excuse for why he would not ask her for the before-dinner dance. It was his only dance left open, and he did not wish to be with her throughout the meal.

He turned the corner, noticing his niece unemployed at the moment and made his way to her side.

"How are you enjoying the ball, Anneliese?"

"It is much more pleasant than I expected." Her lightly freckled countenance looked aglow with exercise.

She had no sooner declared it than a tall, thin man came up to her and extended his hand. "Miss Grysham," he said with a smile, "the quadrille?" He bowed. "Good to see you, Lord Haversley."

It was Lord Rytting, whom he had met a few times in Parliament.

Jacob nodded and found himself suddenly alone again, with Julia across the room tracking him like a hound.

Then suddenly Miss Spencer walked in his direction, her soft blue eyes scanning the ballroom. She hung to the edge of the wall, far away from any dancers.

He immediately strode toward her. "If you are searching for Anneliese, she is quite busy." He nodded his head to the left, toward the center of the room.

Miss Spencer peered at him with a look of surprise. He had snuck up on her, just a bit. "Hello, Lord Haversley." She curtsied but did not look him fully in the eye. "Thank you. I fear she has become quite the dancer for the wallflower she proclaimed to be."

"Indeed," he said as he saw Miss Tursley edge closer. He must act now. "Would you do me the honor of the quadrille?"

"I have not danced at all this evening, Lord Haversley. You know I am still in mourning over my father." Jacob watched her hands spread over her dark black taffeta gown. It seemed like quite a few months since Mr. Spencer had died. How long had it been?

She wore black because she still mourned her father? He was sure the dress was navy blue, and he simply thought she found the dark shade rather complementary to her complexion, for indeed it was. How daft he was! How insensitive. But as he shifted his eyes, embarrassed, Julia Tursley approached even closer. He must do something.

"*Please,* Miss Spencer?" He took her arm and placed it in his and led her into the throng of dancers. "I shall explain it all, and I remember you being quite adept at the quadrille."

This was the dinner dance. Sitting next to Miss Spencer seemed a lovely prospect.

The music started, and Miss Spencer stared at him with a quizzical expression. What exactly did her knit brows and bright blue eyes convey? Disdain? Agitation? Something like worry, but with more fire behind it.

"I am sorry," he said, trying to improve the silence. "I realize I am acting in my best interest and not considering your feelings."

"I am sure you are seldom told no and seldom consider others' feelings," she said, a tight smile stealing across her face. She spun gracefully, and he remembered their dance back in Elmbridge, where she had just as much skill, just as much beauty, and just as much pointed language.

"You are right. I am hardly ever told no. But besides that, you have saved me just now." He lifted his arm as she passed under it. "A certain lady has been hunting me the whole of this evening, and I do not wish to lead her on, so I thank you for this dance."

"What a predicament," she said with mock gravity. "I am glad I was conveniently close enough to spell you."

He inhaled sharply at such a comment. Now he had done it. Her face steeled a little, her eyes narrowing in a challenge. In truth he thought her quite pretty and did want to get to know her, really understand her. But she thought he was just using her. This, coupled with the fact that she was clearly still in mourning, surely must have made her think him an imbecile.

"It is not that at all, Miss Spencer. I . . . I . . ." He should not be stuttering. He was a member of Parliament, and she was simply his niece's friend.

"I understand. I am sure this happens at almost every ball." Her slender back faced his for a minute, a soft curl lightly bouncing, and he wished to touch it.

He swallowed hard and determined to right himself. "I assure you this does not always occur. But it happened today, and I am very grateful you helped me."

Her eyes wrinkled a little as she watched his face.

"I would have asked you to dance even if I had not been fleeing across the floor," he told her.

"Naturally, as I come with Anneliese."

"Well, yes, but it is not just because of that." He paused for a minute, wondering if he should elaborate but only added, "At any rate, I am sorry for your mourning."

Her face changed instantly. The brash smile she had just worn vanished. Perhaps inside, she was not as light as she seemed.

"I know how you feel," he offered.

"You do?" She was curtsying. The music was sounding the last chord, but their conversation was not finished.

Just then Anneliese returned with Lord Rytting at her side. She lowered her voice. "You asked her to dance, Uncle? She is clearly in mourning."

"Yes, I know." He rolled his eyes, shifting his weight. "I have violated custom, and I apologized. But your friend is quite skilled at the quadrille."

Anneliese smiled and shook her head toward him. She looped her arm through Miss Spencer's. She dropped her voice to a whisper. "Well, after dinner we can leave him to his next conquest. I must say that my partner was an excellent dancer." Lord Rytting stood on the other side, making sure to stay close to Anneliese as they walked toward the dining room.

It took Jacob a moment before he realized how stupid he looked in the center of the ballroom, mouth slightly agape, wondering how his niece and a rector's daughter from Elmbridge could cause him—the Lord of the manor and a Member of Parliament—to feel like a little boy left out of their childhood game.

Chapter 12

———— ❧ ————

Suzanna looked down at her gloved hands for the fifth time since entering the carriage. She promised to come to this dance only to act as a companion to Anneliese, to support her, whom she *thought* shy in these social situations. But Anneliese proved a whole new creature during the ball and continued now eagerly, recounting each dance. Suzanna nodded and responded with an "of course" or "naturally" when her friend paused but was not actually listening too closely.

How she had ended up dancing with Lord Haversley still amazed her. He had practically dragged her onto the dance floor. She glanced toward him as he sat stoically in the corner of the carriage, mostly looking out the window into the dark trees. For being such a tall, broad man, he seemed to pull away from them, especially her, with a palpable disdain.

The reason she even gave him a second thought must have been that he was the only person she had danced with in so many months, or had any real male contact with, excepting Mr. Lacy's occasional dialogue. Suzanna still felt the press of Lord Haversley's hands on her gloves and the look of his eyes meeting hers. She recounted their conversation. It was nothing out of the ordinary, but somehow it felt different from every other discussion she had ever had with him. It was as though she found a chink in his over-decorated, pompous armor. He was surprisingly genuine and kind. And what did he say at the end of their dance? That he knew what it was like to lose someone. He had spoken it with so much genuine feeling, such true concern. She wished then, and again now, that their conversation had not ended there.

But, by the look of his scowl, he seemed to have forgotten she ever existed.

The next morning, Matthew Lacy limped as fast as he could to catch Suzanna alone on the patio. Shimmering crystal flakes sifted through the trees, landing perfectly on her hair.

"I had hoped it would snow for Christmas Eve," he said as she looked over her shoulder.

"It is so good to see you walking around."

"Yes, Dr. Willows came again yesterday and says he does not think my leg broken but badly sprained. He says if I use a crutch, I can walk. " He scanned his surroundings, wondering when Anneliese would join them. "Something about you in the snow drew me out. I suppose it reminds me of . . . the day I asked for your hand."

Matthew came to her other side, further from the doors that led inside, and brushed his fingertips against her hand.

"How long do you plan to stay here?" Suzanna asked. She swiftly clutched the railing.

"I suppose until I am healed." He swallowed, wanting to put his arm around her but unsure of her quick movements. "A few more weeks, at least. And you?"

"Until Twelfth Night. But I am anxious for our return, for I just received a letter from the cook saying the poor Nobbs family have taken ill with the smallpox."

"Oh no." He reached out and put his hand on hers, which still clung to the railing. "Perhaps you ought to stay here longer. Berkeley is unsafe."

She shook her head. "I should not have mentioned it, for now you will worry. I have had the vaccine and am immune. I just wish to return so I can help those who can't help themselves."

"Suzanna—" he caught himself. "Miss Spencer. How can you be sure you will be spared? It is too dangerous!"

"No harm will come to me, I promise."

Matthew shook his head. This was pure foolishness. Why did he have to fall in love with a girl so unaware of self-preservation, so willing to throw herself into harm's way?

He looked at her, wishing she would stare back at him, but a few of her curls clouded her face. She was so good, so kind. And so beautiful.

"Well . . . please protect yourself."

She nodded.

He waited a moment, debating if he should say what was on his mind. He came to face her directly and lowered his voice. "Do you still find our engagement agreeable?"

He watched her gaze shoot to the ground. After a pause, she looked up with a smile. "Of course, Mr. Lacy."

He studied her eyes, which finally looked at him. She was smiling, but it almost seemed forced.

He hurried on, not wanting any uncomfortable pause. "Six months takes us to March, which is the Chalestrys' fox hunt and annual ball. I would so like to dance with you there."

She glanced to the side, as if she were recollecting something. Was she thinking about their dance together so many months ago? Perhaps she missed dancing.

"Although," he continued, trying for their old easiness, "if we announce it there, Lady Florence will be a bit vexed she does not have all of the attention."

A small chuckle escaped Suzanna, and she looked as light as she used to. But then her face suddenly became serious. "She will most likely have news of her own to announce, if things continue with Lord Haversley."

Mr. Lacy nodded. "Yes, true. I shall look forward to our own," he whispered as he saw Anneliese coming toward them.

"I am sorry it took me so long to meet you," said Anneliese in a quiet voice toward Suzanna. "And Mr. Lacy, it is a pleasure to see you out of doors!"

He nodded toward her. "I needed the fresh air."

Suzanna tilted her head and said nothing.

"Now, Mr. Lacy," said Anneliese, "this must mean you will join us for all of the Christmas festivities tomorrow?"

"I would hate to impose, and I am not sure how I will be feeling . . . "

"Oh, but we all expect you!" Anneliese came closer to him, pleading. She smiled in his direction, her lightly freckled, straight nose wrinkling into a smile. She was always so warm and pleasant.

He leaned on the railing. "Truth be told, I think I do have it in me to celebrate tomorrow, even if it causes me to return to my bed for the week after."

"Now that's the spirit," said Anneliese. She clasped her hands together and made her way closer to him, engaging him in easy conversation. He watched Suzanna take a turn through the gardens but was so involved in Anneliese's current story, he did not know when Suzanna left them.

It was still dark the next morning when Suzanna threw on her simplest dress and tugged her thick, unruly hair into some semblance of a bun, planning to return to her room well before anyone else awoke. She shuffled downstairs through the dark hallway and past the moonlit drawing room.

Lighting a candle, she edged into the kitchen. She entered through the servants' door and retrieved some wood to stoke the oven fire. She opened the larder and removed a bit of butter. Everything was well stocked and readily available, waiting for the staff to start preparations for Christmas morning. She opened the door once more and found the flour and other necessary ingredients and began to make a few small loaves as a Christmas surprise.

She had brought small Christmas gifts for the women but needed two more for the men. She had not planned on Mr. Lacy being there, and now she felt she ought to have something for Lord Haversley if she were to give a gift to Mr. Lacy. She knew Mr. Lacy and Anneliese would silently understand her contribution, and the others would think she had made her way to the bakery.

After fifteen minutes of measuring and kneading, she placed two doughy mounds on the long wooden paddle she found hanging just above the oven. Suzanna sat at the great table and rested her head in her hands. She would let the dough rise for a half hour and then put it in the oven. At least she had made the recipe before and felt confident in the end product.

She nodded off, head bobbing, for what seemed only a minute. It must have been well over a half hour when she was jolted awake by the sound of the larder door closing. The bread had almost over risen.

A large figure—so large it had to be male—turned, half disappearing into the shadows.

"Hello?" Suzanna hesitated, standing and backing up toward the entrance to the main part of the house. How long had she slept? The servants were granted a few hours of respite on Christmas morning, and she did not think anyone would be up this early.

Whoever it was cleared his throat and leaned on something. He shuffled slowly toward the servants' table, moonlight showing his face.

"Sorry to startle you, Miss Spencer," said a familiar voice. She probably should have had more sleep, because she thought she saw . . . no it couldn't be him . . . sneaking away from the larder.

Suzanna stepped back further, her hands bracing herself on the long counter, eyes squinting. "Lord Haversley?"

The tall man pulled himself to his highest stature and attempted a ceremonious half-bow. "At your service," he said, and Suzanna noticed he lacked his usual self-important tone. "Although," he said, clutching his half open nightshirt in a failed attempt to close it and wrapping his dressing gown tighter, "it looks as though *you* are already serving."

"Um, yes, I suppose." If the light had been stronger, Lord Haversley might have seen the red on her cheeks. "Forgive me, Lord Haversley, you have found me out. I thought a few French rounds a suitable gift for my friends, although I must admit I *am* using your ingredients."

Lord Haversley nodded. "And I am the one sneaking into the larder for much less noble reasons." Lord Haversley attempted to hide whatever he was holding behind his back. With his other hand he gestured toward the bread on the table. "Miss Spencer, I am rather impressed that you have *any* cooking skills at all. A gentleman's daughter like yourself? How did you come to learn?"

Suzanna bit her lip and turned to hoist her puffy loaves into the oven behind her. She realized he had asked a direct question, so she answered shyly, "I have always liked cooking. Especially baking. I know you think it beneath someone of my status, but I have snuck into the kitchen more than once and tried to learn a thing or two."

Lord Haversley looked at the long servants' table and sat down. "On the contrary, your skills would be welcomed in this house, especially if you keep up such hours. Those loaves look delicious."

Suzanna came to the table and sat across from him. She baked because she liked it, not because she needed to. Was he teasing her? Or insinuating that she ought to be part of his staff? That he thought her no better than a servant? Perhaps he meant it as a compliment, for the bread they had eaten for breakfast yesterday did seem quite hard. Regardless, what a remark for a gentleman! He had forgotten his manners twice in the last few days. First he had asked her to dance, and now he was commenting on her baking.

He still had not explained his presence. She would not let him off so easily.

"Excuse me, sir, but why were *you* traipsing about the servants' area before dawn?"

Lord Haversley's eyes shifted briefly. "I had a few items to prepare for Christmas and have not slept much." He quickly placed a small amount of something on the table and then rubbed his hands together, which were covered in dark smudges. "I must admit when I have trouble sleeping, I often make my way here. Bad habit, I suppose. But our cook seems to know to keep the fruitcake well stocked."

"So," said Suzanna, examining the food he put on the table, "you survive long nights with fruitcake?"

Lord Haversley chewed his lip. "It would appear so," he said sheepishly. This enigma of a man was caught. Since when did the lord of a place sneak around the kitchen? Suzanna raised an eyebrow at him.

"It started when I was seven. My groundskeeper told me when I was grumbling for food that most cooks kept a small stash of ready foodstuffs in the larder, and since then I have made good work of sneaking food every so often. It helps that now I am tall enough to find it."

Suzanna smiled, surprised by the informality of Lord Haversley. Gone were his perfect manners, his ability to woo every lady, and his pompous air—not to mention his over-frilled ensemble. His lack of cravat did him credit.

He grinned in her direction and broke off a piece of fruitcake. "Want to try some?"

Suzanna, whose stomach had been growling since she awoke, accepted. After a few bites she tilted her head to the side.

"Your cook makes quite the fruitcake. Best I have ever tasted. Much better than her bread."

Lord Haversley chuckled as he nodded, and Suzanna joined in.

"She and I have never talked about it, but she never questions where it goes, and every new batch seems a bit tastier than the last."

If only Suzanna's cooking could merit such praise. She hoped the French loaves would at least be edible. And now he knew her secret. He had caught her asleep at the table. What did he think of her? He seemed unbothered, but it was early and Christmas morning, so he might just be feeling charitable.

She knew the bread had longer to cook, but the fruitcake was finished between the two of them, and Lord Haversley looked ready to go. As he moved to leave, Suzanna thought of how surprised she was that she enjoyed his company. Perhaps a good question would keep him there a bit longer. For the second time in the past week, she did not wish their conversation to end.

"May I ask you about Miss Grysham?"

Lord Haversley settled deeper into the bench. "Yes?"

"Is she always so social here? She seemed rather quiet in Elmbridge."

"I should be asking you, Miss Spencer," Lord Haversley said, "for I have never seen her so willing to talk to gentlemen. She is a new creature! I thought it your influence."

"Oh, surely not mine. But most young ladies do come into this phase, I suppose. How else is one supposed to catch a husband?" Suzanna knew of at least *one* other way to catch one but did not mention it at the moment.

"You declare yourself beyond this phase? Or perhaps not entered it yet?"

"I am twenty-one years old, Lord Haversley, so I am well aware of the stage. But it is not my nature to flirt and socialize like most ladies do."

"Ah, I see. I have witnessed *that* firsthand. You commit to being rather stoic, especially during quadrilles."

Suzanna pressed her lips together, trying to stop her cheeks from turning up into a smile and give her away. "I fear, in that case, I was simply allowing my partner to concentrate on his next dance steps."

Lord Haversley shifted his eyes at the ruse. "Miss Spencer, you have found my faults yet again!" He crossed his long arms across his chest. "Is there any hope of keeping these secrets quiet between us? First the fruitcake and then dancing. If this information gets out, I will be positively ruined!"

Of course he would worry about his reputation. He always seemed a bit too preoccupied with it. But he did not seem angry. His smile was wide. If Suzanna had known any better, she might say he was enjoying the banter between them. Suddenly she realized every part of her felt warm. Perhaps the bread had cooked too long.

She scooted out the side of the bench and turned toward the flames. Raising the large wooden paddle, she pulled the bread out to check its progress. One of the loaves held a tiny charred spot, but that was the only blemish. A little bubble of triumph spread across her face as she laid the bread on the table. Lord Haversley's eyes followed her motions.

"You seem quite pleased with yourself," he said.

She lifted her eyes to meet his gaze. "And now, we are almost even, for you have found my secret." She shook her head and brushed her hands together. "I think I have perfected it, and I *am* a little proud."

She drew herself up and lifted her chin. "But since you have only found out one secret about me and I know two of yours, I trust you shall remain silent."

He nodded solemnly, but his eyes twinkled. The moonlight made their color deeper than she had remembered.

He cleared his throat. "Now I must return to my room before anyone else learns of my secret penchant for fruitcake."

"Right." She curtsied and watched him as he went back to the hall door that led into the main house. After he left, she looked to the side and smoothed her hands on the apron she had borrowed. That whole conversation had been so . . . pleasant. And easy.

She hastily walked to the larder to examine exactly what else she had missed among its shelves. After finding butter and cinnamon, she filled two small jars. This would be the final touch. And the missing items would probably be unaccounted for, added to what Lord Haversley had already pilfered.

Matthew woke, the ache in his leg and hand nothing compared to the tightness in his heart. It was Christmas, and he had not been able to procure gifts for anyone. How ungrateful he would seem in a few hours. Perhaps it would be better to remain in bed. Surely he should have arranged for a servant to buy a few items in his stead, but every bit of money had been stolen off his person. He relied completely on the kindnesses of the Haversleys.

A few moments later he heard the quick triple tap on his door, customary of Lord Haversley.

"Do come in," Matthew called, turning on his side.

"Happy Christmas," said Lord Haversley as he walked up to the bed. "Feeling well enough to join us in an hour or so?"

Matthew debated whether to speak his concerns, for it would take swallowing his pride to address such a petty worry. But this man had seen him at his lowest, so perhaps it would be possible to explain.

"I had planned on it, but I am terrible at gift giving, and I did not realize until yesterday that I should have something for each one of you. To be honest, I have contemplated feigning severe leg pain in order to avoid the ladies especially."

Lord Haversley pursed his lips and raised his eyebrows. "You cannot be serious. You would cower in bed and avoid them? Really, come now. "

"I do not know why I am admitting any of this to you, but I feel like I am such a charity case. I have not a shilling with me!"

"I am aware," said Lord Haversley with a grin. "If I cared about paying for your bills by now, I would have suggested your removal days ago."

Matthew furrowed his brow toward his friend. "And why exactly have you not cast me out?"

"It is a good question. Dr. Willows charges something monstrous, you know. Especially for broken bones."

Matthew felt almost sure his friend spoke in jest, but part of him began to worry just how much he had overstayed his welcome.

Lord Haversley laughed and walked over to the mantel, resting his head on his raised fist.

"Now look. I am glad to have you here. You may think me ever so altruistic and gracious, but I assure you I have my reasons beyond simple Christian charity for helping you out."

Matthew let out a curt chuckle. "I see. What are your more base reasons?"

Lord Haversley turned and looked him in the eye. "I do believe I shall be linked to Elmbridge for the rest of my life. If my mother has anything to do with it, I shall marry Lady Florence within the year. If that happens . . " He lowered his voice. "She *is* a fine match with a splendid family, but I might need the occasional respite from . . . from her and her mother. "

"Ah."

"Yes. And I need someone with a sound mind to discuss matters of real importance. Like what I wish to do with Parliament. I cannot do *that* with a lady."

"Perhaps you could speak of those things, if you found the right kind of lady."

Lord Haversley stared at him a moment, then shook his head. "*That* would be like finding a needle in a haystack."

Matthew thought about his own engagement. Suzanna understood serious subjects. He still loved her, though yesterday's talk had frightened him. What if he lost her to smallpox? And then, there was that look in her eyes. What if she really didn't wish to marry him? What if she felt just as duty bound as Haversley did to marriage?

What had happened to the light, easy way Suzanna spoke to him?

He felt Lord Haversley studying his face and looked up carefully. "Right. Well, I am glad I can do my part of the bargain. I am happy at any time to relieve you of any unwanted female company."

"Perfect. Now get out of bed and make your way downstairs. I figured you did not have any gifts, so I bought three bracelets for you to give to the ladies. Please give them as though they were from you."

Matthew smiled as he shook his head. "I will never climb out of this hole. I shall forever be indebted to you."

"I intend to keep it that way, so you will feel obligated to do as I wish."

"Touché," said Matthew. Lord Haversley's valet came in to help Matthew prepare. He would be facing the women after all.

"I am sorry, Miss Spencer," said Kate after a loud knock, "but if I do not start on your gown and hair, you will miss the midday Christmas meal."

Suzanna nodded as she rolled out of bed.

"I am rather surprised, miss, for you are usually such an early riser. Are you feeling unwell?"

If only Kate knew the night—or rather early morning she had had. "I am just fine, only a bit sleepy."

Within thirty minutes Suzanna was dressed and wore a multifaceted braided bun.

Suzanna smiled at Kate. "I believe there is not a more efficient lady's maid in all of London. Which is excellent good luck when one wishes to maximize sleep and beauty."

Kate's cheeks turned rosy and she curtsied. Suzanna pulled her white muslin shawl over her ebony dress as she descended down the stairs. She had carefully wrapped the cooled loaves and placed them in the basket, along with the other small gifts.

"Happy Christmas!" said Anneliese as soon as Suzanna entered the drawing room. Next to her sat a few wrapped packages. Suzanna looked to her right and saw Lord Haversley already standing and Mr. Lacy rising to his feet.

Suzanna recalled then how much she loved intimate gatherings of friends. As soon as Lady Haversley appeared, Lord Haversley turned to the group and said, "Before we enjoy the meal, let us exchange a few gifts. Shall we start with you, Mr. Lacy?"

"I would be honored." He shifted more weight onto his good leg. "For the ladies, I have procured a few baubles that the storekeeper tells me are quite in vogue." He gave a nod to Lord Haversley, which Suzanna thought was odd, and then turned back and held up three bracelets with small stones set in metal prongs, handing the most ornate one to Lady Haversley and then one blue and one green to Suzanna and Anneliese, respectively. Suzanna wondered if he meant to match their eyes.

The room was silent for a moment, and Suzanna noticed the color on Anneliese's cheeks start to rise. "Thank you, Mr. Lacy. You did not need . . ." Anneliese sputtered.

Suzanna smiled toward her. "Nonsense! Of course he would think of us *all* on Christmas. They are truly beautiful. Thank you so much, Mr. Lacy."

Lord Haversley stood next. He held three flat rectangular packages and handed them to his mother, his niece, and Suzanna.

Suzanna stared down at her package, turning it over before opening it.

"Oh, Jacob," said his mother, "you have captured him perfectly." She hugged the gift to her heart.

Anneliese walked to her uncle and gave him a brief hug around his middle. "It is just the way I remember them."

Suzanna finally tore the corner off the wrapping and looked down at the paper. It was not as elaborate as the other two. It was a simple black and white piece instead of a painting, of an older man in a rector's hat, sitting and reading in his garden.

"How did you . . ." said Suzanna as she looked up at him.

"I saw him like that once when I was passing by on my horse. The thoughtfulness of his pose struck me."

"This was his favorite place."

She willed back a tear. The room went silent for a moment.

Lord Haversley was an artist?

Suzanna looked from Lady Haversley to her son, who quickly glanced down.

"You painted these?" she asked quietly.

"Well, yes. Painted Anneliese's and my mother's. And sketched yours, in ink. I am sorry it is not in paint. I did not have enough time for more."

Suzanna ran her fingertips reverently over the edge of the drawing. She looked again at her father, the lines of his face and hands so perfectly represented. Did Lord Haversley know how much this meant to her? The whole world had moved on since her father's death, but she constantly felt the pain of losing him. Lord Haversley had taken his time to make this—to think of her and to choose such a perfect subject and setting. She had never expected such a thoughtful gift, nor had she ever been given something so dear. Suddenly his dirty palms and late night made sense.

"It is perfect." She smiled toward him. "So very, very thoughtful." Her words could not do it justice.

She thought then of the master bedroom where Mr. Lacy convalesced. Those paintings must have been by Lord Haversley himself. How she wished now she could go back and examine each of the brushstrokes.

The room stayed quiet as the ladies admired their pieces, until Lord Haversley changed his tone and addressed everyone.

"And my gift to Mr. Lacy is a new horse, although I could not fathom a suitable way to wrap it and bring it inside." He let out a chuckle.

Suzanna and Anneliese let out a gasp simultaneously. Mr. Lacy's mouth dropped. "Haversley, you do not need to do such a thing. I was going to ask to have one brought up from my family."

"I insist, my dear friend. A gentleman should never be without his horse, and I have met few gentlemen as agreeable as you."

Mr. Lacy shook his head as a slight grin covered his face. He paused for a moment and brought his hand up to his chin. "Well, then, my friend, you will have to accept my gift, although it is at my father's estate. I wish you to have my German Dreyse rifle. You will put it into much better use than myself."

Lord Haversley nearly fell into the mantel he stood next to. "You own a Dreyse? Goodness, man, I underestimated you. I cannot take *that* from you."

Mr. Lacy smiled. "You will do much more with it than I ever will. I shall bring it to the fox hunt in Elmbridge in a few months, and you may have it there."

Lord Haversley smiled from ear to ear. "I would like that very much."

Lady Haversley handed out a few gifts next, followed by Anneliese, who gave each man a new stick pin, a hair comb to Suzanna, and gloves to her grandmother.

Suzanna felt rather bashful about her gifts, especially the bread, but it had fallen to her turn.

"I know men generally respond well to food." Suzanna pulled out the loaves and small glass containers of spread and gave one to Mr. Lacy and Lord Haversley. "A necklace for you, Anneliese, as a thank you for inviting me here and a shawl for you, Lady Haversley."

"Why, thank you!" exclaimed Lady Haversley. "So finely woven. And I do say that color is quite complementary to my complexion. I cannot wait to wear it!"

Mr. Lacy unwrapped the paper and pulled a bit of the loaf apart, dipping it into the cinnamon butter. "It is the best bread I have ever tasted. Not a bit too salty, and the consistency is perfect!" He smiled at her widely. She thought he must have supposed it was she who cooked it, but true to form he did not say anything that would give away her secrets.

Then Lady Haversley asked, "What bakery did you go to here? I did not know we had such fine bread so close."

Lord Haversley's eyes shot toward Suzanna. They narrowed a bit in the corners, showing concern. He must have suspected she did not wish to explain all.

"There is a bakery just down the street that specializes in these sort of savory loaves," said Lord Haversley as he pulled at the bread and put it in his mouth. Suzanna watched eagerly as Lord Haversley nodded in approval of his bite.

Suzanna looked back at Mr. Lacy and paused, a large smile overspreading her flushed cheeks. He cleared his throat.

"Yes, there is a bakery . . ." She gave a vague nod.

"Well, they are excellent," said Mr. Lacy toward Suzanna with a smile.

Suzanna sat across from both men as her eyes went back and forth between them. Each thought he had kept a great secret only he knew. It was exceedingly kind. She appreciated such sentiment, amused that both seemed rather inclined to help her out.

That night Jacob sat alone in the drawing room in front of the crackling fire. Mr. Lacy had turned in, quite fatigued after so much movement, and Suzanna and Anneliese had just dismissed themselves to the breakfast room to enjoy a cup of hot cocoa. As they left, he knew something had changed within himself.

His mother came near and sat across from him in a matching club chair.

"It has been a lovely holiday." She released a contented breath. "I would have thought perhaps you wished to celebrate it with the McCallisters, though."

Jacob crossed his arms. "Mother, I know what you are implying with such a comment. I wish I could tell you that I am convinced I ought to marry Lady Florence, but it is simply not the case. I thought that in coming here perhaps I would miss her, but I have hardly thought of her." He stretched out his long legs and folded one over the other at the ankles.

"She would be an agreeable match, Jacob."

"Yes, you are right." He looked steadily into the flames.

She let out a compassionate sigh. "She is not getting any younger, and Lady Chalestry made it *quite* clear that they all expect an answer by the spring fox hunt. She is to have a ball the next day, and they would like to announce your engagement there. Remember, we did have an agreement that by next summer . . ."

"Yes, Mother, I remember. I promised you I would be engaged by then." He stood and walked toward the fire. "I will announce my engagement by the fox hunt—or at least the Hunt Ball. I promise." He jabbed at the flames with his prong. "If you will please excuse me."

He bowed and retired, remembering something he had to do. He opened his desk drawer and withdrew his small leather book. He needed to adjust an entry. He filled his pen and began. First he searched for her original mention and drew a line through it. Then, on a new page, he wrote:

Suzanna Spencer—21. Exceedingly pretty—mesmerizing blue eyes, hardworking, and a surprisingly good baker. Quick with words. Cares for the poor families in her parish. Rather skilled at dancing, especially at the quadrille.

He paused for a minute and rubbed his hand against his slightly stubbled chin. He dipped his pen again and added:

Possibly the woman I want to marry.

He closed the pages and wound the leather strap around the book. He would have an engagement to announce at the fox hunt. With any luck, it would not be to Lady Florence.

Chapter 13

The morning after Twelfth Night, Suzanna waited in the foyer as two servants brought down her trunks and loaded them in the carriage. Mr. Lacy met her there before anyone else. "I shall come visit Norling Place when I return to Elmbridge," he said looking at her, barely leaning on his crutch. "In the meantime, please stay safe."

"Of course. We will be fine," said Suzanna. She was not concerned for her health. She could help those fallen ill and in turn fill her solitude.

Anneliese came in next, with Lord Haversley at her side. Mr. Lacy backed away a few steps as Anneliese embraced Suzanna.

"My uncle"—she looked up and smiled toward him—"informs me that perhaps he shall need to visit Berkeley again in a few weeks. If so, perhaps I can visit you!"

"I would love that!" she said.

"You will travel there despite their bout of smallpox?" asked Mr. Lacy.

Lord Haversley took a step toward them. "Indeed. Even more reason to visit. I always have need to travel to Berkeley." He looked pensive, and Suzanna wondered exactly what he meant. Did whomever he had courted there . . . had she fallen ill?

"Please visit, then. You are *both* most welcome," said Suzanna, glancing at Anneliese after she said it. She intentionally meant to emphasize Anneliese's visit over her uncle's.

By the look on his face, Lord Haversley took her meaning to be pointed toward him. His eyes wrinkled and he smiled as he said, "I wish you a pleasant trip, Miss Spencer."

She curtsied, realizing that all of his bravado and falseness had vanished. She stole a look at Mr. Lacy, who eyed Lord Haversley warily.

She nodded toward a bundled-up Kate just outside the doorway and walked quickly to the coach, afraid to make eye contact with either of the men.

Once in Berkeley, Suzanna made her way to the Nobbs' house.

"You will come, won't you, Kate?"

Kate's eyes looked fearful. "Aren't they sick, miss, with smallpox?"

"Why yes, but that is why we are going. You and I have been vaccinated. We are protected."

Kate swallowed, pursing her lips together. "Shall I prepare some linens then?"

"Yes," said Suzanna. "And we should bring some hearty broth."

They took the carriage to the Nobbs' thatched-roof cottage on the edge of town. As they arrived, the smell of soiled linen and human waste met Suzanna's nose. Mrs. Nobbs, covered in dirt and blood, held a lifeless child in her arms. Suzanna had been here once before. The child was the woman's youngest, not yet one year old.

"Edward is gone, died just this morning," the woman cried, clutching the poor babe to herself. Suzanna hugged the woman as tears filled her eyes. She then looked over Mrs. Nobb's shoulder. Her next youngest two children lay side by side, both their faces full of red sores. One slept fitfully while the other kept touching his raw skin.

"Mrs. Nobbs, I am so sorry about Edward." She held the woman a long moment, running her hand over her hair, trying to still her.

"Kate, take these coins and go fetch something suitable for . . . for us to lay him in."

Mrs. Nobbs burst into tears at these words, understanding Suzanna meant a casket.

"You just sit right here," said Suzanna, ushering the grieving mother to the only chair in the room. "I'll tend your little ones."

She gathered water and dipped a cloth in it to try to help the children's fevers. Their sad, glazed eyes made Suzanna's heart ache. "There, there, little ones. It is going to be all right." She hummed a song to them, but the more she took stake of their arms and faces, the more she understood the severity.

"Are they going to pull through?" said Mrs. Nobbs as she rocked herself back and forth wildly, trying to soothe her mind.

"I . . . I can't say. I will change the linen. Keep them away from others, so no one else falls ill, if possible. None of you have had the vaccine, right? Most in Berkeley have been protected here."

"We are new to Berkeley, miss. We did not know, and it scares me so . . ."

Suzanna stood and put a hand on Mrs. Nobbs, trying to quell her wavering, elevated speech. "I understand."

Kate returned an hour later, and they stayed to bury the baby.

By the end of the next week, Mrs. Nobbs had lost three of her six children to the dreaded smallpox.

Suzanna helped her bury them all.

After nearly four weeks of arguing with some of the most old-fashioned men in England, Jacob determined attending Parliament was worthless unless he could help the bill pass. Though a few people were on his side, several of his peers demanded more evidence in their deliberations to prove his case.

He could not help but agree with them in some respects. They were talking about lives and an illness that killed. People, he knew, feared the unknown. What he really needed was Mr. Phipps to come to London. Although only a working man, his testimony of what had happened with Dr. Jenner could convince just about anyone.

Jacob now tumbled toward Berkeley in his carriage. It was far too cold to ride Sylvester, and he needed to review all of his notes as he traveled. He had invited Anneliese, but she thought it rude for both of them to leave Mr. Lacy alone, so she chose to stay behind.

As he rifled through the stacks of paper in front of him, his mind started to wander. It felt strange, for he usually stayed so studiously on topic, but he assured himself as he looked out the window that it was only because he had entered Gloucester County, and such proximity made him think of her. Why had he not been more direct with Miss Spencer when she had left Lysetter Hall? He could have called on her, had he asked, but it was only under the guise of Anneliese, who had not come after all.

By afternoon he would reach Berkeley, and Miss Spencer would be so close. He knew before he arrived he ought to stop at Chalestry Manor to see Lady Florence, but thoughts of Miss Spencer kept running across his pages. As he passed Elmbridge and came closer to Berkeley, he even thought he caught a glimpse of her out the window. He suddenly remembered her flour-dusted hair and tiny aproned waist and wished that he was back hunting for fruitcake.

Mr. Phipps would receive him that evening, and Jacob tried to strategize exactly how he would convince Mr. Phipps to go to London. He had attempted before, but Phipps declared he would not leave his wife and family. There must be some way to persuade him of just how important all of this would be—that his presence could change everything.

"There must be more I can do," said Suzanna to Kate in late January. "I can comfort those—like the Nobbs—who grieve, but I want to stop this! Just yesterday Mrs. Eves asked me if I had talked with James Phipps, the man who Dr. Jenner first tried vaccination on. She thinks I could learn from him—that he would share his knowledge, and then I could administer the vaccine. Then I could actually save people."

Kate's face went pale. "That seems like a dangerous idea, miss. I, for one, think his 'medicine' cursed."

"Oh, don't be foolish. It has saved us all! Grab your cloak. We will call at the address Mrs. Eves gave me yesterday."

Within fifteen minutes Suzanna rapped the door and watched great clouds of breath come from her mouth in the cold air. After what seemed like several minutes, a young woman opened the door.

"Hello," said Suzanna. "I wish to speak with Mrs. Phipps. Is she at home?"

"Do come in."

She and Kate walked through the door, waiting silently. A moment later a middle-aged mother shushed a child behind her as she entered.

"Mrs. Phipps?"

The woman nodded.

"I am Miss Suzanna Spencer, lately moved from Elmbridge. I wanted to make my acquaintance with you and possibly talk with your husband about his experiences with Dr. Jenner."

Mrs. Phipps smiled. It seemed it was not her first time someone had asked the question. "He is currently in the barn, working on some repairs, but I shall see if he is available."

Suzanna thanked her, and the servant reappeared and ushered her and Kate into a modest sitting room. Apparently they employed two servants, for suddenly another maid bustled in and upon seeing Suzanna tried to tidy the room as discreetly as possible. She must have been in a great hurry to clean, for the servant swept and adjusted every item before Mrs. Phipps returned.

"My husband is finishing a few last-minute preparations for another guest this evening. Is there something I can help you with while you wait?"

"Perhaps I should come back another time. If you are receiving other visitors, I do not wish to intrude."

That explained the whirling maid.

Mrs. Phipps held her child by the hand, whom she directed toward a short wooden chair next to the fire. "No, please have a seat. My husband wishes to talk to anyone who has an interest. He said he should be just another few minutes or so." Mrs. Phipps turned to her child and whispered, "Now, Thomas, let us practice sitting still for dinner tonight."

Suzanna smiled at the mother and child. The latter seemed he could not control his little squirmy body long enough to even make it to the chair.

"Mama, why do we always have so many guests?" whispered the young Thomas.

"Because your father is a remarkable man," said the mother. She picked up a basket of knitting and looked at Suzanna expectantly.

Suzanna sat on the edge of the padded bench and clasped her reticule. "Thank you for allowing me to stay. You see, my father owned a home here, where I have recently taken up residence due to his passing. He was the rector of Elmbridge, and I have always been interested in helping those in need. So when I helped a family here in Berkeley with the smallpox, my friend mentioned Mr. Phipps' life and his great part in the discovery of the vaccine. I must know more." She paused and then continued. "And I am particularly interested in hearing the story of his childhood and learning how to administer the vaccination myself."

"My husband is no physician, miss. Such a task is not generally given to women, let alone a gentlewoman like yourself. We will have to see what he says . . ." Mrs. Phipps trailed off as a heavy door opened at the back of the room.

"Good day. You must be Miss Spencer," said the man, wiping his hands on his work apron. His hair was not yet completely grey, and although of average build, his muscles were still tight. "I shall be with you in one minute," he said as he turned to his wife. "Do you have the rooms in order? There is room in the barn for the carriage, and the extra groom has been given instructions." Suzanna watched Mr. Phipps take off his apron and check around the sitting room, seeming pleased. The Phipps had apparently gone to great lengths to prepare for their visitor.

"Yes, love. Heaven knows it is all much better than last time you brought him here *unannounced.*"

Mr. Phipps rolled his eyes and pursed his lips. "Miss Spencer, I am so sorry to keep you waiting."

Mrs. Phipps excused small Thomas, who gladly ran out, and Suzanna shifted slightly on the couch.

"How may I help you?" he asked.

Suzanna drew in a deep breath. "I wish to learn about your past, Mr. Phipps, with the smallpox. Specifically how to administer the remedy, if you will let me." She added the last sentence quietly, not sure how he would take the idea.

He tilted his head and raised both eyebrows. "First tell me what you know about the vaccine."

"I have had the procedure—been vaccinated. I believe that is the correct term. Why did Dr. Jenner call it that?"

Mr. Phipps nodded slowly. "He coined the word. *Vaccine* comes from the Latin root for *cow*, because Dr. Jenner used cowpox as an alternative to directly infecting the patients."

Suzanna settled eagerly into her seat. "I have heard it is much safer than using actual smallpox residue for the procedure."

Mr. Phipps scooted to the edge of his chair and rubbed his hands together. "Yes. You are correct. I am glad you have a basic understanding. Now, to answer your first question. When I was eight years old, Dr. Jenner, who employed my father as his gardener, used me to test his theory. He took some residue from a milkmaid named Sarah, who had recently milked a cow who had cowpox. Sarah had a few sores on her hands, and Dr. Jenner scraped the pus off and placed it in a cut on my arm."

"Were you scared?" asked Suzanna, fixing her eyes on him.

"Of course. But Dr. Jenner himself had experienced the awful smallpox transfer, often customary in those days, and he assured me that I did not want to experience that—you know, the old way. Give someone actual smallpox from another, and then leave them in a barn and hope they survive? Such agonizing horror still haunted him. He just had to know if cowpox would be less terrible than giving someone smallpox.

"And so, I fell a bit ill, but nothing like those given actual bits of the smallpox. He then exposed me to smallpox, which was the scary part, but I did not fall ill! You see, Dr. Jenner solved the mystery. Cowpox gives you immunity without dying or nearly dying from smallpox. And it does not make you contagious like the smallpox transfer, possibly infecting others until the infection passes. Dr. Jenner checked his work by exposing me to smallpox several times, but I have never, ever fallen victim to the speckled monster. Finally, he had a solution. He hoped to annihilate smallpox from everyone someday."

Mr. Phipps paused, reflecting on his last statement. "I am honored to have known and helped Dr. Jenner."

Suzanna looked down at her skirts, which she had unconsciously been wrinkling together in her hands. What a miracle. And to be talking with one of the men who made it possible.

"It is incredible. How fortunate we are to have your sacrifice," said Suzanna.

Mr. Phipps simply tilted his head and walked to a small cabinet and removed a bottle. Inside were several long bird feathers, which looked like pen quills, the shaft seemingly filled with some kind of liquid. He turned, raising it aloft. "Are you quite sure you wish to know how to administer it? There is always the chance for illness, and as a gentlewoman . . . " His explanation was interrupted by a loud knock on the door. Mr. Phipps paused, lowering the jar a bit as his servant went to answer it. Mr. Phipps quickly straightened his vest and ran a hand through his hair.

Suzanna did not wish to intrude. She stood to leave, but Mrs. Phipps patted her back down. "If it is him, he is quite early." Suzanna wondered how to excuse herself, but the door opened before she had time. She saw the servant take the man's coat, hat, and gloves as he turned into the room. The size and visage looked familiar, and as soon as he divested his large scarf, Suzanna could not believe her eyes.

She watched as Lord Haversley's gaze met Mr. Phipps, who sat directly in his line of sight. She sat in the far corner, and he did not look in her direction at first, but she recalled his familiar voice as he began.

"Ah, Phipps, my dear friend. Already preparing your quills? I do love your enthusiasm for our cause." Lord Haversley was perfectly unaffected, and he looked and sounded like the best version of himself.

Mr. Phipps cleared his throat and smiled, glancing toward Suzanna. "I actually was about to explain vaccination to a new acquaintance. Please allow me to introduce Miss Suzanna Spencer."

Suzanna stood and curtsied. She watched his eyes widen as his arm crossed his middle and he bowed. She bit her lip, trying to hide a smile. She usually did not have the upper hand in situations such as these, and she quite enjoyed the surprise on his face. She realized she had never seen him in such plain traveling clothes, but she remembered his wide smile and broad stature just the same. She thought for a brief moment that he looked more handsome here than in an overcrowded ballroom. How did he know Mr. Phipps? From his salutation they somehow seemed long-time friends.

Lord Haversley cleared his throat. "Miss Spencer! I did *not* expect to see you here. What a pleasant surprise!" He seemed a perfect mix of confusion and amity, like a child's face when he received an unexpected gift.

"You know the lady?" said Mr. Phipps to the pair.

"Why yes, she is a dear friend of my niece," said Lord Haversley, attempting to steady his eyes. He looked toward Mr. Phipps. Suzanna felt hurt for a moment that she was only an acquaintance of his niece's, not of his own.

The offhand way he told of their acquaintance caused Suzanna to feel as though she was intruding on Lord Haversley's space yet again. A minute ago she thought they shared a serendipitous moment, and now she was only his niece's friend. Why did she always feel so unintentionally out of place? Just like after their dance at the Yule Ball. How did he always get his way?

She did not wish to stay any longer, so she gathered her things and took a step toward the door.

"I was just leaving. Forgive me. Mr. Phipps, perhaps I could come tomorrow and learn more about your process."

"Oh, of course, Miss Spencer. I can see you truly wish to learn." He started to place the glass jar back in the cabinet. Suzanna attempted to shuffle past Lord Haversley, who followed behind her. She pretended not to notice as she donned her gloves.

He bowed his tall head. "I am so sorry to have interrupted your time. Are you sure you will not stay?"

Suzanna lowered her voice as she moved toward the door. Lord Haversley was still close, so she said, "I came unannounced, and it is quite clear the Phipps were expecting you. It is no matter. I live a close distance away and shall come again."

"Then allow me to call on you at . . . at . . . Norling Place, is it?"

Suzanna tilted her head and gave a half-smile. He remembered the name? He had only gone there once for his niece. Perhaps Suzanna was not *so* much of a bother as she assumed she had been. He had listened and remembered something.

"Yes, Norling Place." *And I shall be quitting it soon, when I am married,* she added silently to herself.

"May I call on you tomorrow?"

Suzanna's eyebrows drew together. Surely he meant to visit out of obligation to his niece. Anneliese would expect him to go, now that Suzanna knew they were in the same town.

"Oh, yes of course. I shall prepare a letter for you to take to Anneliese." She was trying to avoid him as gracefully as possible.

Lord Haversley's eyes shifted back and forth, but he gave another short bow. Suzanna grabbed her cloak and nodded toward Kate.

She turned and opened the door. As she left she felt the stare of Lord Haversley's eyes following her every action, although he said no more.

Chapter 14

Jacob awoke early. He normally slept through anything, but last night his mind would not quiet, and it had nothing to do with little Thomas Phipps' kicking feet in the next room. Today he would visit Suzanna. Did she think he would visit her out of obligation? Anneliese *would* be glad to hear he chose to call, but he wished to see her of his own accord.

The sun had finally started to rise as he viewed his reflection in the mirror. He looked a bit like he had slogged through mud, his eyes drooping, his hair disheveled. He pulled the bedclothes up to tidy the room and looked around. This room was the master, especially made up for him each time, but he pretended along with the Phipps that it was their guest room. Tasteful yet simple curtains hung over the window that looked over the farm. For a farmer, Mr. Phipps had a good life.

Jacob tried to ignore the tired lines under his eyes and brushed the hair over his temples forward in an attempt to disguise the silver streaks starting to emerge. He was glad he woke early, for without his valet he would need ample time to prepare and leave directly after breakfast. He only hoped Suzanna would think highly enough of him in his simple attire.

Mr. Phipps told him over breakfast the general direction of Norling Place, and Jacob feigned he had never been there. He began walking but stopped in town to purchase a few hothouse roses. He wanted to make his intentions clear, and somehow roses seemed the fastest route to do so.

The brown and grey stone cottage was covered with vines on one side. There was a second story, and Jacob wondered if Suzanna sat behind the curtained window he saw. He glanced down at the small bouquet in his hand and debated if he ought to toss them into the bushes. Giving her flowers was a rather bold gesture. But before he could analyze more, he forced himself to knock on the door.

The servant seemed to be expecting him and ushered him directly into the drawing room. Jacob checked his pocket watch. Twenty minutes to ten. Perhaps too early to call on a lady, but like the roses, there was no turning back now. Suzanna was nowhere to be seen. Of course she liked roses, right? What young woman didn't? But what if the flowers made him appear too forward? Maybe he should have waited for a subsequent visit. Wincing, he dropped the flowers behind the couch that sat perpendicular to the mantel. He thought briefly about hiding *himself* behind it as well, but he was not as easily hidden.

He looked around the room, which was plainly outfitted. The curtains and furnishings were simple but tasteful, and beside a small glass vase on the mantel, the only other decoration was a black and white drawing in a frame on the small end table. As he looked closer, he realized it was his drawing of Mr. Spencer that he had given her for Christmas.

After what felt like half the morning, Suzanna walked into the drawing room, leaving the door wide open. Her lady's maid came in behind her and sat in the corner with a basket of mending.

Suzanna's honey-colored hair was pulled back in a simple bun, accentuating the sharp line of her jaw that drew him up to her sky blue eyes. Those eyes held his for a minute, until he looked purposefully down to his pocket watch. Only three minutes, not thirty, had passed.

"So sorry to keep you waiting," said Suzanna as she spied the pocket watch. Jacob looked up sheepishly and stuffed it into his waistcoat.

"Oh, do not apologize. I was looking at the time because I fear it is a bit early to call."

A simple smile spread across Suzanna's face, like a flower blooming at daylight's first ray. "People do wake up earlier here in the country than in London, I suppose." She gestured to him to sit down, and he shuffled to the closest chair and settled himself.

"Right. Most definitely," said Jacob as he strummed his fingers on the leather arm. Suzanna seemed to wait for him to speak next, and although he wished to compliment her in some way, he decided against it just yet. He had the tendency to come on too abruptly and tried to rein himself in. After an awkward pause, he let out, "I was surprised to find you at the Phipps' yesterday evening."

Suzanna folded her arms and looked at him squarely. "You mean you were surprised that I would be visiting with someone such as Mr. Phipps?"

Jacob stiffened for a moment. She seemed defensive. This was not exactly how he had planned his visit going, having thought this was a safe topic of conversation. "Well . . . I suppose so, now that you mention it. I did not think you would have any business with Mr. Phipps."

He watched Suzanna delicately adjust her perch, tilting her head. She reminded him of a beautiful songbird. "It was my first time meeting him," she said. "His story fascinates me. And with so many people ill around us, his business ought to be everyone's business." She thought exactly as he did.

"Have you always been interested in his work?"

Her beautiful voice chimed, "I have always thought smallpox the most horrid of diseases. I want to help where there is the most need."

"I see. Is helping the needy a new interest?"

As soon as he said it, he knew his choice of words was bad. He meant to sound interested, but instead the quick succession of questions seemed like an interrogation. As a rector's daughter, surely she had always been generous toward the poor.

Her voice dropped. "New? I daresay it is not. There were several families who I helped in Elmbridge. Perhaps you might ask your niece. Anneliese came with me on a few visits during her stay."

How had he not noticed all the service she had rendered? Had he really been that self-concerned to miss it all? Jacob ran his tongue over his teeth and studied his boots. Her tone of voice did not seem as though she enjoyed him being there. It was a rather good thing he discarded the roses behind the couch.

Suzanna clasped her hands together in her lap. "But seeing you has helped me solve one mystery. I had my suspicions as to why you came to Berkeley so often. I thought perhaps someone here competed with your Lady Florence, and so you secretly stole away to court both until you could figure out who you preferred most."

Good gracious. Now she thought him pursuing two different women? If *she* were counted now with Lady Florence, that would not be too far from the truth. And *his* Lady Florence? Oh dear. Should he set her right? Should he tell her that he actually wished to pursue her?

No. Not yet. He rubbed his hand across his chin.

"But now I suppose"—her voice softened two degrees, and she brought her hand up in suggestion—"that you wish to know what Mr. Phipps knows, just as I do."

Lord Haversley blinked and opened his eyes wide. So she did not think him a complete blaggard. He felt a smile pull at his cheeks, a small shimmer of hope whistling through him.

"Why yes." He tugged on his cravat. "I did not come here to pursue any young lady." It was mostly true, until that morning when he had called at her house. "I came to Berkeley originally because I wanted to learn more about the smallpox vaccinations and meet Mr. Phipps. Now I need his help—his testimony in London."

Suzanna seemed to relax. "Help *you*?" she said, raising her eyebrows. "Are not men of your status persons who help people like *him*?"

"A man of my status does generally look out for the farmers on his land. But in this case, I need his knowledge, life experience, and verbal testimony to convince the rest of Parliament that it is absolutely vital that we pass a law about vaccination."

Suzanna smiled as she studied him. Her look sent a thrill through him.

"I am glad to know you were not pursuing another lady. I did see you riding with some woman in a carriage towards Elmbridge, though, a few months back."

"That was Mrs. Phipps! I promised to take her—and her husband, who you must have missed—to the doctor in Elmbridge." He shook his head as he watched a small laugh escape Suzanna's mouth, which she covered with her petite hand.

"I am glad to hear it," she said when her laugh stopped. A serious look crossed her face, and Jacob watched her go quiet for a moment. She was contemplating something. He reached over and picked up the framed picture of her father, the one he drew for her at Christmas.

"I need to thank you for that," said Suzanna. "I did not have a good picture of him except for when he was young, so I will forever be indebted to you. It is a very accurate likeness."

"It is no matter," said Jacob. "I meant what I said when we were dancing at Christmas."

Suzanna shot him a confused look. Perhaps she did not remember. He was bordering on forward, but maybe he could connect with her on this point.

"I said then that I understand your grief. And I do."

Suzanna relaxed a bit, her perfect posture softening in her seat. "How is that, sir?"

"The true reason I am so interested in Mr. Phipps' work is that my sister died when she was ten from smallpox. We were the best of friends, and her death changed me forever." He stopped, debating if he should tell what he had never told anyone.

"Go on," she said quietly, perfectly reading his countenance.

"I . . . I blame myself for her death. For not insisting on the vaccination."

He watched her eyes snap shut. What must she think of him now?

He hurried to speak, unable to bear silence or her reaction. "Since then I have wanted nothing more than to save others from a grief like mine. Mr. Phipps and Dr. Jenner's knowledge is the way to saving others."

When she opened them, tears flooded her perfect blue eyes.

"I am so sorry," she said. A deep silence stretched between them. Finally she said, "You painted her, did you not? I recall seeing a few portraits in your master suite when Mr. Lacy was injured."

"Yes, I painted them all. It soothes the heartache, I suppose."

She leaned forward toward him, an understanding frown punctuating her mouth. She paused and nodded, her eyes full of compassion.

"I cannot imagine your grief—to lose so many."

He simply nodded, hoping she would say more, but she seemed to fall into a contemplative silence.

After a long moment, Suzanna stood and quickly moved to the writing desk in the corner. "Now, I must thank you for your visit. I do have a small note for Miss Anneliese if you would be willing to take it to her."

Jacob wondered exactly what had changed and why she suddenly seemed so distant. He stood, acquiescing to the obvious clues that meant she wished their visit to be over.

"I would be delighted." He must save face. "I do have a few more people I wish to call on today."

It was best to seem quite occupied. She signed her final flourish and sealed the letter, walking with it in hand toward the door. "Thank you for your visit, Lord Haversley."

"It was my pleasure," he said and then added, "and perhaps another time we might talk more about our mutual interest concerning smallpox."

"Perhaps," she said evenly. She had moved close to the door, but for one instant, Jacob thought she seemed to linger.

Why was she so distant? He could not leave like this.

"Anything else you wish to accuse me of?" he quipped.

Her subdued, even demeanor broke briefly. "Not particularly, although I must say that your simpler cuffs suit you well."

Her eyes sparkled, and she swung her arm toward the open door and gestured outside.

Lord Haversley tugged on his jacket sleeves. Why did everyone seem to notice his tailoring? Were his cuffs truly that ostentatious?

Miss Spencer cocked her head slightly toward the entryway.

"I will have a discussion with my tailor when I return home."

"And I will stop accusing you of pursuing the ladies of Berkeley."

He could not help the large smile that spread across his face.

Kate picked up her mending, gave a quizzical look, and remained silent as she went upstairs. Suzanna sat again on the couch, strengthening her resolve to keep her distance from Lord Haversley. He should not have spoken of his family that way. She had no idea he was so involved in anything—let alone keeping people safe from smallpox. He cared so deeply. He cared about *exactly* what she cared about.

How had he become so feeling, so genuine, so selfless? This was not the man she thought she knew a few months ago.

No. But maybe he had always been this way. He masked his goodness—his caring nature—behind parties and money and heaven knows how many frilled shirts. But this version of him was the *real* Lord Haversley. The real Jacob.

Perhaps his name did fit him.

She stood and walked to the window. No matter how much she had felt of his goodness, no matter how impressed she'd been with him, she *must* think of him no longer. She had been informal, vulnerable, and perhaps slightly flirtatious. She had badgered him about his cuffs, and such behavior was unacceptable and appalling for an engaged woman.

Though she *had* shooed him out the door well. Once she realized she had done wrong, she immediately tried to make him leave. He seemed a little confused, but it had to be done. Her loyalty, her word, her promise was to Mr. Lacy and to her father. She had agreed to an engagement, and although no one knew, she ought to still act above reproach.

She sighed and closed her eyes for a moment. She stood to leave the room when she noticed something behind the couch. Reaching over the back, she lifted a bouquet of half a dozen hothouse roses, tied with a crimson ribbon.

It couldn't have been. Lord Haversley did not *almost* bring her flowers. And yet they must have been from him. No one else had been there, and they were quite fresh. Something like this did not just show up at one's house, behind one's couch.

She inhaled their scent and then gathered them in her arms and sat again, silently remembering his form across the room, strumming the arm of the club chair. He meant to bring her roses? That seemed quite a bit more involved than paying a visit on behalf of his niece.

Her heart pounded for a moment.

No. She must stop this. She ought not to think or dwell on it more. It was more than her heart was able to give.

She swept up the roses and picked the empty vase off the mantel, setting the flowers inside. She then walked upstairs, where Kate stood airing a gown.

"I wish you to have these," said Suzanna as she thrust the flowers forward. "As an appreciation of being a most excellent lady's maid. I know since coming here you have had to function as so much more than that. Not to mention you are my closest friend and companion as I live here alone. Thank you."

Kate's eyes opened wide, and she curtsied. "Why thank you, miss," she said. "It is so kind of you."

And much too kind of Lord Haversley, Suzanna thought as she grabbed her cloak and walked toward Mr. Phipps' cottage. Lord Haversley had declared he would be visiting others, which meant he would *not* be at Mr. Phipps'. She simply could not bear to run into him again.

Three hours later, Suzanna left Mr. Phipps' home with a small bag of instruments, a few quills full of the vaccine, and a renewed sense of life. She had assured him of her sincerity, convincing him it did not matter that she was a gentlewoman. He had then shown her the procedure and taught her the importance of vaccination in lieu of variolation, reiterating that administering cowpox proved much safer than giving someone a small amount of the smallpox from another infected person. She now knew how to help those around her, more than just delivering baskets of goods and tending fevers. The ability to perform the procedure had long-term effects to improve lives for good.

She thought then of her father and mother, who had made such contributions to the people around them. She had always wished to follow in their legacy—to do something with a true impact. Maybe that was why she finally felt closer to her father. She was honoring her parents' memory. Somehow, in learning to serve others, the sting and weight of their deaths felt a little less heavy. Thank goodness for James Phipps.

As she neared her home, her mind could not completely shut out Lord Haversley. Being in the Phipps' house only made her remember him more, along with the recollection of the discarded flowers from that morning. Mrs. Phipps was soft spoken but proved to be quite cheerful and talkative upon closer acquaintance. She even ventured questions about Lord Haversley to Suzanna, which she tried to gloss over as quickly as she could. Suzanna knew she ought to dwell on thoughts of that man as little as possible.

The next morning, however, Lord Haversley called on her again.

Suzanna shuffled nervously at the top of the stairs, straining to hear the conversation below.

"Lord Haversley," said Kate, and Suzanna knew she was trying to gather courage to speak to such an intimidating man, "Miss Spencer wishes me to say that she was not expecting any visitors quite so early and wonders if you would call back later."

There was only a hint of a pause, and it sounded as though he was smiling when she heard, "It is no matter. I am prepared to wait."

Blast! Why was he so persistent? Kate turned and scurried up the stairs, wide eyes meeting Suzanna's.

"Thank you for trying," said Suzanna in a grateful whisper as Kate made swift work of her hair and dress. As Suzanna prepared to walk downstairs, she chose to be on the defensive, speaking only of pertinent matters.

She curtsied briefly and then began, "I visited Mr. Phipps again yesterday. I trust you plan to make clear to Parliament the importance of vaccination versus variolation."

Lord Haversley was still standing, and his confused countenance conveyed that he did not expect the conversation to start so abruptly. He seemed to swallow whatever he was going to say as he rubbed his chin.

"Why . . . yes, Miss Spencer. He has impressed that importance upon me, especially as of late. But you need not trouble yourself much about Mr. Phipps. He has agreed to come to London with me when I return."

She watched his confident, strong jaw tilt in her direction but gave it no heed. "How wonderful! I am glad that he has agreed. Are Mrs. Phipps and Thomas coming as well?"

"No, they will remain here. He will not visit for long." He shifted his weight and glanced toward the couch, but Suzanna did not invite him to sit. "Unfortunately I will remain in London until just before the fox hunt." She felt him study her face, following her every movement. He said it as though his removal back to London would be a great loss to her, but it actually made things much easier. For both their sakes, it was truly best that he leave Berkeley as soon as possible. She did not wish to give him any semblance of encouragement.

He moved his feet together but did not quit his gaze. Then he said, "Perhaps you might visit London again."

This was exactly the conversation she had tried to avoid.

"Oh no. Not at this time. I am best situated here, I assure you." Suzanna clenched her fists and walked quickly to the writing desk. "The Nobbs on the edge of town lost three children to smallpox just a few weeks ago. I witnessed it firsthand. I must make sure everyone here and in Elmbridge are safe."

He simply nodded and she continued. "I was actually thinking it would be appropriate to return the favor to Miss Grysham to invite her here for a few weeks, though." She walked to the small desk and dipped her pen. "I am sure that several young men are seeking her hand already, but even still, perhaps she would enjoy the trip."

Lord Haversley, who had not taken a seat during the whole conversation, paced back and forth a few times.

"I am sure she would be delighted," he said, throwing up his hand. His pleasant words did not quite match his tone. "Do issue her an invitation, and I will take it with me when I return home. I only wish I could be the one to deposit her back here, but I am already looked down upon for the days I have missed during this session." Then, although she had purposely not invited him, he finally plopped himself into one of the chairs across from her writing desk.

Suzanna waved a hand toward him. "Naturally *you* could not come. You are far too busy!" She penned another line and then fanned the paper. She wondered if she had been too direct, but it was best to be straight forward. She would throw him off this chase with another diverting question.

"I have been meaning to ask, how is Mr. Lacy's leg healing?" She had received a letter from him three days before but did not disclose such information. "He shall be leaving your home soon, I would imagine?"

Lord Haversley's brow wrinkled, his perfectly set eyes clouding for a moment. With an even tone he stated, "Why yes, within the next week, I believe. The doctor says he will walk normally very soon."

"Then that is just the thing! Anneliese and her lady's maid could travel *with* Mr. Lacy. I am sure your mother would come as well, at least to Elmbridge in preparation for the hunt. Then I shall see my dear friends again!"

From her vantage at the writing desk, Suzanna could sense Lord Haversley's body tighten as if he were tugging against jesses that suddenly tied him down. He crossed his ankles and his strong arms, and peered into the fire with a scowl. She did expect that he felt a bit jealous of Mr. Lacy, but it was just the line she needed to stop any further conversation. She was sure Lord Haversley understood the direction of her words.

"Yes, of course." He looked away. "You should write your letter. I am sorry I keep interrupting you."

Suzanna nodded and penned steadily, grateful for the prospect of visitors. She blotted it, folded the sheet neatly, and sealed it, with no conversation in the interim. She did notice, out of the corner of her eye, Lord Haversley spying behind the couch as he stood to prod the fire.

She said nothing of the roses.

"I wish you a safe trip," she said as she handed him the letter.

"Thank you, Miss Spencer." He tucked the letter into his waistcoat. She noticed then how simply he was dressed, not a single frill anywhere to be seen. She liked him best that way but thought better than to mention it.

He drew himself up to his full height, as though pushing his shoulders back would save face against her pointed words. Perhaps she had gone too far. He bowed, adding finally, "I shall see you again at the fox hunt, I hope."

"Indeed, Lord Haversley. I would not miss Lady Florence's Hunt Ball for anything."

She had promised she'd be there. Promised Mr. Lacy, that was—and she had promised she would be out of mourning.

Her promises had nothing to do with the man she shut the door on.

Chapter 15

D r. Willows had come to visit once per week since his injury. Mat-thew had started to heal well, but an infection in his leg had set him back considerably. Finally, after several weeks, he seemed to be turning a corner and felt well enough to meet the doctor today in the lavender-hued sitting room.

"I have done all I can," the doctor said and gathered his things. "I believe it will be uncomfortable, but you should be able to travel."

"Thank you," said Matthew. The doctor turned to go as Anneliese came around the corner and stood in the doorway.

"Yes, thank you, Doctor," she said with a curtsy as he walked passed her.

"Hello, Miss Grysham," said Matthew politely. "It is pleasant seeing your bright face in this room."

He appreciated the visit, for when she did not come around, it was quite lonely in the house. Lord Haversley had been gone for nearly a week, and Lady Haversley kept mostly to herself.

"Thank you," she said with another soft curtsy. She moved quite gracefully, like a swan on water. Matthew had seen enough of her now to know she was always refined.

"Lord Haversley's valet wished me to show you this crutch." She pulled it out from behind the door and took it to him. The wood was dark with a beautiful grain, finely carved and quite smooth. "He says it works much better than the one you have been using. He claims it is much more comfortable."

Why hadn't the valet brought it himself? He thought it odd she carried it but did not mind.

"It looks like quite an improvement!" He gestured toward the rough apparatus he had been using that lay on the floor. "How does his valet know as much?"

"Apparently Lord Haversley broke his ankle when he was fifteen, and this is his. It took some effort to find it in the back groom house."

"I see," Matthew replied. "And Lord Haversley does not travel with his valet?"

"No, he said he could manage himself. He prefers to travel simply when it is not to a fine lady's house. He should be back within the week."

Matthew nodded, not knowing what else to say. Anneliese did not move, and it seemed she had more she wished to speak of, so he waited patiently, looking in her direction.

She nervously fingered her gown, pursing her lips.

"I thought," Anneliese began, "you might want to start walking more. The doctor advised that it would be good to keep using your muscles. I am happy to assist as your walking partner anytime you feel up to it."

Matthew thought for a moment, wishing Suzanna had not left so quickly. After all, *she* should have been his walking partner. Anneliese was a sweet girl, and it would not do to turn down the offer from his host's niece.

"That is very kind of you. I shall start this afternoon. Since there has been very little rain as of late, should we try the garden?"

"Of course," said Anneliese as Matthew noticed her straight, wide smile. "That sounds easy enough."

Matthew felt her gaze on him another moment longer, until she looked away quickly and said, "I had better be going. I hope your crutch is an improvement."

"I suppose we shall find out this afternoon," he said pleasantly as he watched her disappear.

Suzanna woke to the sound of a loud scream coming from the servants' quarters. She hurried through the kitchen to find Kate writhing in her bed, a violent fever causing great beads of sweat to run down her face.

It was the beginning of smallpox.

First, fever. Then blistered pox would come, followed by sores, then scabs. There was no mistaking the signs.

"My dearest Kate!" exclaimed Suzanna, taking stake of her friend as she felt her burning head with her palm.

"I . . . I am sorry, miss," Kate whispered, her eyes rolling back, almost incoherent. "I must admit I never . . . never took the vaccine. The day your father had all his servants receive it . . . I hid and then ran the cook's errand because I was too afraid."

Suzanna's hands shot up and covered her face. "No. No." She started to sob. "All this time, I didn't even ask you. I thought you had . . . I assumed you would be fine . . . taking you to the Nobbs, having you touch their children . . . and you said nothing."

Suzanna crumbled to the floor and whispered to the ground. "So you will have the worst of it, then."

She stayed there for several moments, until she realized her terror and heartache would only scare Kate more. She finally sat up and tried to look brave, to not let on just how bad it would be. How . . . fatal . . . it very well could be. At this moment, how could she stay strong?

"You can make it through, Kate," said Suzanna taking her hand, but the girl had already fallen into another bout of delirium. "You must fight," she said, doubting if Kate could even comprehend her. Kate's head moved back and forth, her eyes shut in pain. "Pray and fight."

Then Suzanna closed her eyes. "I won't let you die."

Jacob looked across the coach as Mr. Phipps snored loudly. They would reach London that evening, and Jacob had just finished rehearsing his argument toward Parliament for the second time. He willed himself to analyze the points he and Mr. Phipps had discussed at length that day, but as he reviewed it, all his thoughts turned wayward.

Again.

She had been standoffish, cold, and dismissive the last time they met. So why did thoughts of Miss Spencer continue to plague him? Perhaps it was the chase. Nearly every young lady he even talked to fell at his feet. It *used* to amuse him, but now it felt pathetic. It had taken him nearly ten years to know what he wanted—a girl with a little spunk, especially when it was directed toward him. A girl just like Suzanna, who served people such as the Nobbs. A girl not afraid of smallpox, a girl who might actually want to discuss serious things. He must pursue her—and make it known what he now valued in a woman.

There was the problem, however, that she and Mr. Lacy had both mentioned each other. They did have the acquaintance and connection of her father, but could there be something more? Jacob would have to watch closely.

A few hours later, Mr. Phipps and Jacob tumbled out of the carriage.

"You both must be quite famished," said Lady Haversley. Anneliese and Mr. Lacy also stood in the entryway to greet them.

"Yes. Our supper last night and meal this morning were awful." Jacob cleared his throat. "Allow me to introduce you, Mother, to Mr. Phipps of Berkeley."

"A pleasure to meet you," Mr. Phipps said as he took her hand.

"My son has, of late, made quite the habit of collecting acquaintances at this house." She smiled, raising her eyebrows toward Jacob.

"Only the finest of men, Mother," he said. "Now what did you say about that supper?"

"Right this way," said Lady Haversley. Several candles lit the entry-way, and Jacob's boots clicked as he turned down the hallway.

"And how are you, Miss Anneliese?" He put his arm around her as they walked down the hallway toward the savory smells of a meal. "I saw your dear friend, Miss Spencer, in Berkeley. I had the pleasure of visit-ing with her, and she sends you these two notes." He pulled the missives out of his waistcoat pocket and handed them to his niece. How she had earned two notes and he had not received much goodwill after two meet-ings was beyond him.

"Oh you did! How fortunate," said Anneliese with her ever-present smile. Would she ask him exactly how he had met with Suzanna? She unfolded the paper and read the letters quickly.

"She wishes for me to come visit!" Anneliese exclaimed, taking her uncle's arm. "And suggests I come whenever Mr. Lacy travels back to his post, which she seems to think is quite soon."

Mr. Lacy, who had been hobbling slowly just in front of them, stopped and slightly raised his head. "I do intend to return to Elmbridge within the week."

"A hopeful guess on her part," escaped Jacob's lips. "She must really believe you are healing quickly after your infection."

"Yes . . . Miss Spencer is always quite hopeful, and I know she wishes the rectory to have someone constant again as soon as possible."

Walking a pace behind Mr. Lacy, Jacob rolled his eyes. He seriously wondered if the rectory was the real concern.

They entered the gold-trimmed dining room, and Anneliese stood between Mr. Lacy and her uncle as she asked, "Grandmama, what say you to traveling to Elmbridge next week? Shall we go with Mr. Lacy?"

Lady Haversley took her seat, and the rest then sat. "Next week? I thought you were enjoying your time here in London. Are you sure you wish to quit it so early?"

Jacob watched his niece pause for a moment, as though she were purposefully trying to seem nonchalant.

"It would only be until the fox hunt, which is not so very far away," she said. "And if Mr. Lacy would consent to two women traveling with him, I *would* like to see Miss Spencer again."

How lucky Anneliese was to have an invitation to see Miss Spencer. She had not been so gracious to extend one to himself.

Mr. Lacy gave his comfortable, customary grin. "I would be delighted to have you both join me."

Lady Haversley looked from Anneliese to Mr. Lacy. "Perhaps we shall go early. I will write to Lady Chalestry tomorrow and see if her schedule is agreeable."

Chapter 16

———— ❧ ————

"**M**y respected associates gathered here," said Jacob as he situated his stiff sleeve inside his jacket. He stood in the middle of the long rectangular room, casting his gaze to both sides of his seated colleagues. He tried to command the attention of every man.

"Allow me to paint a picture for you." He gestured toward his peers. Mr. Phipps stood silent, yet close to him, as he continued. "Gentlemen of Parliament. Imagine with me three of your dearest friends. The first contracts smallpox and succumbs to its vicious grasp and dies two weeks later. The next friend is variolated—with some of the same infection from the first victim. Being exposed to just a small amount might help, right?" A few men nodded in assent. "Wrong. He fights the disease for some time but eventually is weakened until he dies.

"Now your third friend—or may I say family member, as the case may be—is given what Dr. Edward Jenner coined a 'vaccine.' Your friend is purposely given a small scratch on top of his skin on which is placed a bit of cowpox—*not* smallpox, mind you—taken from the pustual of an infected animal in your town. This is in lieu of an actual smallpox remnant. You see, cowpox, or this vaccination, is similar in form to smallpox but with much less risk. He will develop a resistance to the sickness but not die from it. He may be sick for a few days or weeks, but he will eventually recover, so much the stronger. His body will be able to fight against smallpox. He is immune."

"But some still die!" yelled one of his most vehement opposers, the spray of his words visible to Jacob. Jacob swallowed, clasped his hands together, and paused a moment. Another voice rang, "It is unnatural! It comes from a cow! It is not guaranteed success."

Jacob nodded but continued. "Yes, it is true. It does not always work. And some live through the smallpox. But how many people die every year because of the dreaded speckled monster? I have brought someone with me today whom I wish to have speak with you."

Mr. Phipps stepped forward as Lord Haversley gestured to him. He wore his best dark suit, which was still quite simple, and if one looked closely enough they might notice his right leg trembling. But he raised himself as tall as his frame would allow and began.

"Gentlemen, I am honored to speak today. My name is James Phipps. I was but eight years old when Dr. Jenner first gave me the procedure of vaccination as Lord Haversley has just described. Dr. Jenner was a brilliant doctor. He even worked for His Majesty, King George III, in his later life. Many years ago, Dr. Jenner heard that milkmaids seldom succumbed to smallpox. Indeed, have we not all heard the milkmaid's refrain,

"Where are you going, my pretty maid?"
"I'm going a-milking, sir," she said.
"What is your fortune, my pretty maid?"
"My face is my fortune," she said.

A few of the men slapped their thighs and the back of their chairs in approval. It was not hard to follow Dr. Jenner's logic. Mr. Phipps then continued. "Through Dr. Jenner's brilliant research, we know that milkmaids were often spared from smallpox because they were exposed to cowpox when milking. That is how they kept their pretty faces. This disease is similar enough that our bodies fight it the same way. I urge you to listen to Lord Haversley. You must do as he says and pass a bill. Variolation is not safe and should be disregarded in lieu of vaccination. I have been exposed to smallpox twenty times in my life, and it has not killed me yet. Oh, how I wish every soul in England could be treated. I wish you could have seen the lines of people coming to Dr. Jenner's Temple of Vaccina, as he called it."

A tear welled in Mr. Phipps' eye. "There is much we can do to fight this disease. I assure you, passing this bill is the first step."

The noise of stomping feet and fists pounding their chairs sounded throughout the hall, coupled with the voices of several in agreement. Mr. Phipps continued to recount exactly what Dr. Jenner had done over the course of his life and how he helped others.

Jacob watched many members listen intently to all he said. After several minutes, he rubbed the sweat off his brow and exhaled heavily. Perhaps they might be persuaded, thanks to the simple testimony of James Phipps.

The next three days Suzanna hardly slept. Kate turned and twisted and vomited so much that her face looked ghastly pale, and she became extremely fragile. Her fever had lessened, but the sores all over her body had begun to rise and fill with fluid.

Suzanna sat the whole day near her dear maid, trying everything she could to comfort her, but there seemed almost no change.

The hours were filled with silence and fervent prayers.

Jacob returned from his sessions of Parliament a few days later with great progress toward a bill. "I think your explanation of the importance of vaccination was quite beneficial. You really should have been a statesmen or an orator, for your narrative is quite compelling."

Mr. Phipps looked down at his hands. "Thank you, sir. I have no fear of smallpox. How could I with what I have experienced?"

"Well, thank you for all you have said and done. I am sorry the House of Lords still has more questions for you," said Jacob as they exited the carriage. The sun was setting, and although the air held a chill, it was quite pleasant after a long, stifling carriage ride back to Lysetter Hall.

"Would you care to join me for a bit of fresh air, Mr. Phipps?" Jacob asked as he made his way toward the side gardens.

"Thank you," said Mr. Phipps walking toward the entrance. "But I ought to write Millie a note to tell her we will be another week."

"Please feel free to use my desk in the study."

Jacob made his way around the side of the house. As he approached the first bend in the hedges, he saw Mr. Lacy walking beside Anneliese. He could only see his niece's face from his angle and had never seen her countenance more aglow.

He paused a moment and then made his way to a tall, thick hedge closer to the pair. Mr. Lacy and Anneliese had stopped walking, both sitting on one of the marble benches in the garden.

Neither had noticed his approach. He shouldn't be eavesdropping, but his curiosity won over in the moment.

"Have we walked too far?" said Anneliese, worry in her voice.

"No, indeed. I am quite all right."

"I do hope that our strolls have been enjoyable and not too much of an exertion for you."

"Yes. I most definitely do enjoy them and am glad you suggested walking. I sometimes need someone to get me going, and this was just the trick."

If he liked a girl who spurs people to action, it is no wonder he likes Miss Spencer, thought Jacob.

"I am looking forward to visiting Miss Spencer," said Anneliese next.

"You will not be sad to miss so much of the Season?"

"No," she said, and her deliberate pause was not missed by her uncle. "It was quite diverting at first, but with so many people on show all the time, I find it exhausting. I know now that the country is much more appealing to me."

Jacob could not see the look in Mr. Lacy's eyes but knew by the hopeful tone in his niece's voice she meant more particularly the area of the country that included Mr. Lacy.

How long had Anneliese had feelings for him?

Mr. Lacy paused for a moment, and Jacob wondered what exactly he was thinking.

"There is beauty there to be sure."

Anneliese nodded and looked into Mr. Lacy's eyes for a long moment. It was then that Jacob realized how wrong he had been about Mr. Lacy's feelings. Had Mr. Lacy seemed excited about returning to Elmbridge because Anneliese would be traveling with him? Traveling with her to Berkeley meant several hours—days, actually—of concentrated time with her. Had their affection for each other bloomed while he was away? It seemed too perfect a way to remove Mr. Lacy's interest from Suzanna.

"It is getting rather late. Shall we head back?" said Mr. Lacy.

"Yes, of course," replied Anneliese. She stood and stepped away from the bench, her eyes suddenly meeting Jacob's through an opening in the leaves. He tried to crouch lower, but it was of no use. What would they think of his eavesdropping? He should have come out and openly mentioned his presence when he first came near them. A grown man like himself ought to act better. He prayed she would conceal her surprise.

He held his breath and, taking a gamble, thrust his finger to his lips and with his other hand motioned her to walk a different way out of the garden away from himself. After quite a bit of pointing and gesturing, Jacob heard Mr. Lacy say, "Miss Grysham, is everything all right?"

Jacob froze as he watched Anneliese answer. "Yes, forgive me. Perhaps we ought to walk back through this path. I think it will be easier with your crutch."

As soon as they were out of sight, Jacob hurried through a shortcut into the house. He knew he also had the advantage of two good legs and no romantic desire to walk slowly, and he made it easily to the back door before the other two entered.

He sat snugly in the drawing room and feigned great interest in the closest book he could find when Mr. Lacy and Anneliese entered.

"No doubt you are quite fatigued," he heard Anneliese say. "Would you like to return to your room? I can tell one of the servants to bring you a bit of refreshment."

"You are so good to think of me," he said. "That would be delightful."

As soon as he started up the stairs, Anneliese sidled up next to Jacob.

He furrowed his brow and continued to read *Grazing Habits of Sheep in Scotland* when Anneliese leaned over the top of his page.

"Oh, come now," she said in a whisper, "do not go on reading as though nothing happened. Why on *earth* were you snooping around the garden just now?"

Jacob gave a dramatic eye roll. "I would think *you* the one who would not want to talk about it. I was willing to give you complete discretion, but if you wish to bring up such an obvious subject, I suppose we can." He added a large shrug to drive the point home.

"What do you mean, Uncle? If it is not too bold to say, it is not every day that a distinguished Member of Parliament sneaks through the hedgerows and listens to conversations in his own garden."

Jacob finally raised his eyes to meet hers. "I mean . . . that I just witnessed an exchange that clearly proves that a certain niece of mine has feelings for my crippled guest."

Anneliese's cheeks blushed as she covered her mouth with her petite fingers.

Her voice was almost too quiet to hear. "Is it that obvious?"

Pursing his lips and raising his eyebrows, Jacob nodded in mock solemnity.

Her eyes went wide. "You mustn't tell anyone!" she said.

"As I said," he replied, covering his heart with one hand, "I am the model of discretion."

She looked around the room to be sure no one heard them and leaned closer. "Do you think it is possible that he could care for me? Not necessarily right now. I mean, in the future, if we were to be much in one another's company . . ." she trailed off and sat bouncing her hands lightly in her lap.

"It is entirely possible, Anneliese. Should we ask him?"

"Oh, heavens no!" Her palms shot up to the sides of her face.

Jacob chuckled quietly, until she realized he meant it as a joke.

Anneliese seemed to be studying the floor, and after tracing her slipper in a circle a few times said, "Although you *are* his close friend. Perhaps you could ask him if he has any inclination toward . . . myself." She grabbed her skirt. "Did he seem interested, Uncle? I guess that is the real question I should be asking. Just now in the garden." She gestured a flapping hand as if Jacob wasn't already completely aware of what they were talking about. "Do you think I have a chance?"

Jacob reached across the couch and placed one hand on her shoulder, giving a soft smile. "I could not see his face, my dear, but the fact that he went walking with you is promising. At the very least he did not seem to *hate* it," he teased.

Anneliese dropped her hands into her lap as Jacob sat back and folded his arms. She gave him a long, stern look and slightly shook her head.

"You are insufferable," she said with a smile.

Jacob took up the book again. Anneliese waited a few moments more on the couch and then finally stood, smoothed her skirts, and turned to leave.

"I will ask him his thoughts next time I get the chance," Jacob said with dancing eyebrows as she stood in the doorway. She turned, and as she exited the room he could see her profile shift into one of utter glee.

Chapter 17

Kate was not improving. If things continued like this, she would die. Suzanna had felt warm and weak for the last few days, almost as though she had a fever. But it was nothing, especially when she looked at her listless maid. She had to take action to help Kate.

She stared at her friend's limp body, so still she must be near death. What would Dr. Jenner do if he were here? What would Mr. Phipps do if he weren't in London with Lord Haversley?

She returned to Kate's bedside, supplies in hand, and drew out her knife. There was no time to ask for permission. She rolled up Kate's sleeve and slit her arm. Then she took her knife and made a small incision on her own forearm near the crease of her elbow, enough so it bled, and let some of her blood drip into Kate's arm. People often experienced blood-letting, but could blood *giving* help Kate? She didn't know if it would work, but something told her to try. Her body had learned to fight the pox. Maybe somehow, by some chance, it would work.

"Now to pray for a miracle," she said as she bandaged her arm.

Matthew wrapped his small bundle of sermons and letters Lord Haversley had saved as he prepared for his journey with Miss Grysham.

Lord Haversley entered his room and said, "I expect you to take home all of the clothing and shoes I have lent you during your stay here." He walked to the armoire and opened the top drawer, thumbing through a few items.

Matthew laughed and shook his head.

"Why thank you, but I do not intend to do so. Everything I wore was from you, Lord Haversley, and nearly two months of imposition was enough, without stealing your wardrobe."

"On the contrary," said Lord Haversley. "I have more than I'll ever need, and every clergyman ought to have a few items he could wear to events that do not involve church. That is *exactly* why you ought to take them."

Matthew chuckled. Perhaps Suzanna was right about Lord Haversley's clothing particulars. "You certainly are known for your unique fashion choices."

Lord Haversley stopped and shot a glance toward his friend.

"Why does everyone keep saying that about my wardrobe? Is there something wrong with it?"

Matthew turned and smiled, thinking of Suzanna's often exasperated comments.

"People do notice that you dress well," said Matthew with a shrug, trying for a relaxed tone.

Lord Haversley swiveled toward him. "Colonel Unsworth once told me that dressing well gives one confidence in situations with women."

Matthew could not suppress a low hiccup of a laugh. "With all due respect, I do not know if *he* is the best source for wisdom. He seems to adore every woman who comes into his path. I have found that genuine women appreciate someone who is real, and ruffled cuffs have never led a lady to believe a man is sincere." *At least not any women worth paying attention to*, he silently added.

"Perhaps you are right. No one has ever been so blunt with me before, and I believe it is just what I needed to hear. Stupid of me, really, to listen to Unsworth."

Matthew watched his friend swallow, lost in thought.

"Perhaps, but I know he is your friend. You did save my life, which makes us friends as well . . . I suppose," added Matthew after a moment, raising one eyebrow.

"Right," said Lord Haversley, catching his humor. "Well, as a friend, might I ask you one more question before you leave my household?"

Matthew rolled his hand, gesturing for him to continue. He did feel quite comfortable around this man. "Ask me anything, if you are prepared for a straightforward answer."

Lord Haversley stood and wandered away from him. "I have noticed in the last week that you have taken quite a few walks with Miss Grysham. Now I know she is my niece, but as an unbiased friend, I must say she would be quite the catch."

Matthew felt a weight settle in his gut. He did not, for once, have the ability to answer openly. He agreed Miss Grysham would be a very desirable wife. He had objectively noticed her good qualities. But it was not his prerogative to divulge his engagement with Suzanna. Not until she was out of mourning. Furthermore, he did not wish to slight Lord Haversley or Miss Grysham in any way.

"Indeed, she would. If only she did not live in London."

Lord Haversley kept his back to him but turned his head over his shoulder. "The distance could be easily overcome, if you desired."

Matthew cleared his throat. "Yes, I suppose you are right." The distance was not the problem. He felt his palms start to sweat. The heat of the room seemed to rise, as though a fire had just been stoked. He cared for Suzanna and was obligated to her. They would make a perfect match. Perhaps he should just tell Lord Haversley of their engagement. He would understand.

Lord Haversley turned and looked at him with a raised eyebrow.

Mr. Lacy felt his Adam's apple bob as he swallowed. "She is a wonderful girl. I shall make sure she meets up with Miss Spencer safely." It was all he could offer. He gathered his bundle, leaving behind all borrowed clothes, and headed toward the stairs.

"Thank you again for all you have done for me these past weeks," he said as he limped to the landing. "I am forever indebted to you."

He saw Lord Haversley nod from his periphery, rubbing his hands together as though he were thinking. Matthew hoped his disinterest was clear. He did not wish to mislead Miss Grysham—or her uncle—in any way.

The carriage ride was no easier. Miss Grysham sat across from him, the model of civility. Her maid dutifully knitted for most of the journey, never looking up, and Lady Haversley employed herself with a book, although it quickly sent her to sleep. Miss Grysham looked at him often, smiling softly, pursuing a steady dialogue.

"Mr. Lacy," she began, "why did you choose the clergy?"

Matthew smiled at such a question. Anneliese seemed quite genuine in her inquiry. "Ah, Miss Grysham, I am sure you do not wish to hear the whole of it as it is rather boring."

"On the contrary, Mr. Lacy, I am sure it is an insightful story, and we have plenty of time before us."

Amused, he exhaled. She did have a point. "I am a third son, Miss Grysham, which means, I am afraid, that I am rather dispensable. Fathers keep their first son around, tightly underwing. And perhaps their second, God forbid, should he be needed. But the third . . . well, I have the luxury of inheriting little and also having few parameters put on myself by others." Matthew chuckled lightly, watching Miss Grysham nod as her eyes drew up merrily.

"As a boy, I thought the army sounded gallant, but the more I learned of anger and bloodshed, the more I realized it was not for me. I was fifteen when I realized perhaps I could do more good as a teacher. I thought teaching religion might yield a more positive and lasting effect on the souls of men. "

"To be sure," said Miss Grysham. Mr. Lacy noticed she leaned closer as they spoke. He shifted in his seat, trying to increase the distance between them.

"Luckily my father had the means and declared I had the brains to attend Oxford. I suppose the rest just fell into place."

Miss Grysham clasped her hands together. "Miss Spencer told me they sent the brightest vicar, so your father must have been right."

Matthew looked at the floor. Her compliment was so genuine. It did remind him of Miss Spencer, whom he would see in a few days. He was glad Miss Spencer thought so highly of him to mention it.

Perhaps he ought to turn the focus off of himself.

"Miss Grysham, do you have very many memories of your parents?"

"Yes, actually. They did not pass away until I was nine. I count it a blessing that I remember so much of our time together."

Matthew nodded. "And did you know your grandfather very well?"

"Oh, yes. My father was the first son of the late Lord Haversley. Consequently," she said, a teasing tone entering her voice, "he was not dispensable to my grandfather." Her eyes turned more serious. "However, in our case, it is rather fortunate my father did have a younger brother."

Matthew immediately felt foolish for his earlier comment. He had always assumed the Lord Haversley he knew to be the eldest son.

"Miss Grysham, I am so sorry. I did not mean what I said about brothers to cause pain in any way."

His eyebrows furrowed as he looked into her face. She leaned even nearer and exhaled gently. "Mr. Lacy, I assure you there was no offense taken."

Matthew was grateful for her kindness. She was always unassuming, and he appreciated that about her. They would have two days until Elmbridge, and he hoped their conversation would continue in the same open way.

After a few hours, Matthew realized he knew more about Anneliese Grysham than any other female in the world.

What amazed him the most was the ease of the conversation. She was not the chatty, fast-talking type but spoke with more reflection. In fact, she asked him several questions, as one topic seemed to flow into another. After they discussed why he chose the clergy, they talked of their families' preferences in literature, gardening, parts of England he had visited, and where she wished to visit. Before he knew it, they had come to the inn for the evening.

Matthew took care of all the arrangements, securing two rooms at the end of the hallway. The accommodations were quite nice as traveling inns went, and they turned in early.

After he heard Miss Grysham's door latch, he sat, candle in hand, analyzing the day. It had passed so swiftly and pleasantly. Anneliese Grysham was one of the most interesting and easy people he had ever met. But surely he did not have feelings for her. It was merely a product of Lord Haversley mentioning her that made him even think about Miss Grysham for more than a moment. Perhaps it was the close proximity for such an extended period of time. By this time tomorrow, they would be in Elmbridge, and the next day, Miss Grysham would travel on to be with Miss Spencer.

As they settled into the carriage the next morning, Matthew hoped for a more alert Lady Haversley, who might keep the conversation between herself and Miss Grysham. Lady Haversley did talk for the first two hours but then settled into sleep. And although she did not sleep, Miss Grysham's maid offered no more than three syllables. Today she held a handkerchief she was embroidering, and her gaze never left the fabric.

Miss Grysham, however, continued to be talkative.

"I am ever so excited to see Miss Spencer tomorrow! What a true friend she has been to me."

"Yes, she is quite loyal," offered Mr. Lacy.

"You two have been friends many years, I gather?"

"Oh, no," Matthew said as he looked out the window. "I only met her last summer, when I was a vicar and Lord Chalestry wished for someone to help Mr. Spencer and prepare to take over the rectory when the time came. "

"Well, that is longer than I have known her." Miss Grysham looked again at him with her piercing light green eyes. "I have been trying to figure out how I can repay her for her great friendship to me and was hoping you might have some insight."

Matthew did hold a few secret insights about Miss Spencer but none that he was willing to divulge. He had turned to the window but found he must look Miss Grysham in the eye once more. For one trying to stay removed, the closeness of the carriage was making it difficult.

"I assure you that as a female, you know much more than I do about Miss Spencer."

A shy grin spread across Miss Grysham's face. "Come now, Mr. Lacy! I know the two of you to be like brother and sister. Surely she has confided in you. I keep wondering if she cares for any particular gentleman. I wish nothing more than to see her married to someone wonderful! Possibly with someone my family knows. My uncle has so many connections. If only I knew who she might find agreeable. She has said nearly nothing during her mourning, but that is almost over."

Matthew pulled deeper into his corner and played with the half-drawn curtain, feigning great interest in the outside. He did not answer for several moments.

From the corner of his eye he could see Miss Grysham bite her lip. "I am so sorry. I can see I have made you uncomfortable." He looked back at her, watching her eyebrows furrow as she glanced at her hands. "Perhaps I should have said nothing about it." She looked nervously at her grandmother, as though she were checking to see if she was still asleep.

Matthew took a deep breath, grateful for Miss Grysham's awareness of the situation. Normally he would have been put off by such open dialogue, but Miss Grysham's sincerity felt different.

"Your concern for your friend does you credit," he said at last. "Miss Spencer is lucky to have you."

After a pause, and avoiding his eyes, she said, "I think she must be quite lonely in Berkeley. I hope that when she comes out of mourning she might consider marrying."

"I am sure she will choose someone when she is ready and the offer is presented to her. Having her well settled was her father's dying wish."

"I see," said Miss Grysham. She became quiet and inspected her maid's needlepoint dutifully. "This is beautiful weather for traveling, is it not?"

She gave him a large smile and continued to chatter for quite some time about the unusually warm month they had experienced.

As the day rolled on to the rumble of the carriage, Miss Grysham finally fell asleep, and Matthew was left with his thoughts. It was high time Suzanna stop mourning. It felt harsh to think such a thought, but things were becoming too confusing. People wished to find a match for Suzanna when she already had one. People wished to find him a match, although *he* already had one. How much longer must they endure an engagement that neither could not speak of? Since they had become so familiar with Lord Haversley and his family, things had become decidedly more complex and frustrating.

He began to wonder, with much less humor, what Suzanna's true feelings were toward him. If she had not even hinted to Miss Grysham, or mentioned him to her, what did that mean? Miss Grysham, he knew, was observant enough to figure out that perhaps he and Suzanna ought to be together. Why did she not think that a possibility? She thought them like brother and sister? That was not exactly the feelings he wished for in a marriage.

The more the carriage drove on, the more he felt uncomfortable. Miss Grysham's presence did nothing but remind him of the predicament he was in. If he could only see Suzanna again and sort things out with her. Perhaps he ought to ride on to Berkeley the next day with Miss Grysham, under the guise of business with its curate. Then he could speak with Suzanna again in person.

Why were women so complicated?

Chapter 18

It had been nearly two weeks since Kate's fever began. Now the deadly smallpox ravaged her body, the rash covering her face and limbs in sores that had started to crust over. In the beginning, the vomiting, writhing, aching Kate needed constant attention, and Suzanna hadn't even thought to write and tell Anneliese to stay away. And now if she were to write a letter and Anneliese had already left, the McCallisters would learn of it all, and they must not know.

Suzanna had felt unwell for several days but pushed through the relatively minor pain and fatigue. Finally, after days of terrifying bouts of unconsciousness, Kate's eyes had fluttered open for the first time. She took water and broth. Somehow, between prayers and Suzanna's blood-giving, maybe she would pull through.

Suzanna wanted to hope, wanted to say all was well.

But it was too early to tell.

As soon as she heard the carriage the next day, Suzanna ran out to meet it.

"Anneliese," she shouted, taking hold of the carriage door. "Oh, and Mr. Lacy!" She had not expected him, but continued forcefully, "I must urge you to leave this instant and return to Elmbridge. My lady's maid, Kate, has contracted smallpox. Some people here, even some who have had the vaccination, seem to be experiencing the symptoms. For your own safety, you cannot stay!"

"But what about you?" said Anneliese.

"Yes, you cannot be safe," Mr. Lacy pleaded. "You should come to Elmbridge at once."

"I cannot leave her. If I am not here, who will attend to her? Norling has a cook and one other servant, and I told them to stay away."

She watched as both of her friends' brows furrowed. "But surely you will fall ill," Mr. Lacy said.

Suzanna tried to appear easy. "I will be fine. I have helped many others, especially lately."

Mr. Lacy stared at her.

"I insist, and you know you can't change my mind." She gave a soft smile afterward, but Mr. Lacy lowered his shoulders in defeat.

"Please don't mention any of this to the McCallisters. Lady Florence will consider Kate and me pariahs forever."

"Naturally. But if you can, please still come to the fox hunt. Lady Florence expects you," said Anneliese, trying to be hopeful.

"My first obligation is to Kate. I must see that she pulls through this."

"When will you know if . . . if everything will be all right?"

Suzanna closed her eyes slowly. "By next week."

Anneliese nodded, looking thoughtful. Suzanna motioned to their driver to return to Elmbridge.

Inside the house, she went to Kate's makeshift bed in her own room and placed a cool cloth on her head once again, silently pleading Kate would make it through the next day, and the next. And somehow past next week.

Chapter 19

On the way back to Elmbridge, Matthew and Miss Grysham formed a plan. Miss Grysham would go back to Berkeley by the end of next week. By then, the risk of infection to herself would be lessened, but Suzanna could desperately use the help and the company. They spoke as if Kate would live. It was too painful to imagine otherwise.

Then, after a few more weeks, Miss Grysham could help Kate and Suzanna travel back to Elmbridge. Suzanna was expected there, and Kate could easily be hid among Matthew's servants and convalesce in peace. Suzanna not going by then for the fox hunt would stir too much suspicion.

Matthew felt awful that the person he was supposed to watch over, the person he was to let no harm come to, was alone and grieving, trying to fight the speckled monster all by herself. He was left to his fervent, frequent prayers.

"Tell me at once," Anneliese said as she stood in Suzanna's doorway more than a week later. "Is Kate still alive?"

Suzanna had tears in her eyes. "Yes. By a miracle from God." She tugged the long sleeves of her dress down as she leaned against the door-frame. "You'll see the craters that cover her cheeks and arms. Almost all of her scabs have crusted and fallen off and turned into the ugly scars they will always be. She will never look the same again." Suzanna wiped another tear. "I fear how many people will shy away from her. I know you and I will not." She patted Anneliese's hand. "I wish the scars where the whole of it. She will forever be blind in her left eye."

Anneliese's hand covered her mouth, but Suzanna continued. "We must be grateful she can still see partially."

Anneliese nodded soberly. "I cannot imagine what she has been through . . . and yourself. You look weak." Anneliese patted the sleeve of Suzanna's forearm, but she pulled back suddenly.

"I am just a little tired."

Anneliese nodded. "Of course you are. Now I am here and wish to help you however is best. I will stay with you a few weeks more until she gains more strength to travel. Then in Elmbridge, we will feign you did not bring your lady's maid, and mine will help us both. We can hide Kate at Mr. Lacy's, for he said she may stay with his servants and you can sneak away and visit her or send for one of Elmbridge's superior doctors if needed. You and I will still stay at the McCallisters', and it will work out quite smoothly."

Suzanna could not believe she saw her dear friend before her eyes— and with such a plan. She truly was an angel sent to her in a time of need.

"Her illness still remains. She is healing, but I do not want to cause you any harm. Perhaps you should leave."

"I did *not* come all the way here to have you turn me away."

Suzanna stopped and nodded, even more amazed at her friend's courage. "For someone who less than a year ago had never come to the country, you are becoming quite the traveler."

Anneliese smiled. "I think it is less the countryside and more the company."

Suzanna nodded. "Come get settled, my dear friend. You are too good."

"You know," said Anneliese a few days later, "me coming back here was all Mr. Lacy's idea. He is such a wise man."

"To be sure," said Suzanna as they sat taking their dinner. She had known few men as good as he. Even now, he had sent this angel to her. Suzanna wondered if she appreciated enough how fortunate she was, that in just a few weeks, she could announce their engagement. Yet she still wished to avoid thinking of her future and changed the subject.

"Did anyone strike your fancy, this first Season of yours?"

Suzanna watched Anneliese's eyes dart to the floor and then back at her. Perhaps she had feelings for someone, but she was far too shy to say anything.

"Well, if not," Suzanna continued, feeling lighter than she had in weeks, "I have been thinking that it is absolutely requisite that you marry a man who allows you to be close to me, so we might continue this friendship! What do you say? Who shall we pick for you, Anneliese?"

"Oh dear." Anneliese blushed.

Did she not wish to talk about eligible men?

Anneliese chewed on her lip, her eyes looking to the side. "I really haven't met too many men around here, and not that many in London."

Suzanna tilted her head and thought a moment. She nodded. "I fear you are right. Having a friend who is still in mourning is not exactly a recipe for high social interactions."

"I did not mean it like that," said Anneliese, swallowing.

"Oh, I know," said Suzanna, giving an easy smile. "I was just thinking perhaps there will be someone for you at the spring fox hunt. The McCallisters have promised to invite people from all over the county!"

"Is that right?"

Suzanna stood and poured more tea. "If only Mr. Lacy knew more of the men around. He could surely introduce you."

Anneliese cupped her saucer and almost sputtered her tea. "Introduce me? Do you not think he is keeping best acquaintances for you, Miss Spencer? Surely, as a friend of your father he wishes you to have the best match." She paused. "When the time is right, of course."

Suzanna chewed slowly on a biscuit and thought a moment of the most honest way to answer. She knew exactly why he wasn't looking but could not tell that to even her closest friends.

"I am sure he has several acquaintances who would be delighted to meet you," Suzanna said quietly. She looked down at her dark gown. She was still in mourning and did not need to say more. She missed her father terribly. Somehow, for the moment, wearing black seemed to keep him close to her and shield her from the outside world. From her future.

Anneliese drew her out of her thoughts as she placed a hand on Suzanna's gloved hand. "You are too kind, Miss Spencer, for if they are anything like Mr. Lacy, I would be a lucky woman. Men of his caliber seem rather hard to find, don't you think?"

"Why yes, he is the best sort, to be sure."

Of course Anneliese was right. Suzanna knew she would do well to remember this more herself. Yet, if he were the perfect match, why did she not find herself always thinking of him?

Suzanna stood, brushed a crumb from her dress, and pulled down her sleeves. "I must get back to Kate."

Two weeks later Kate felt well enough to sit up on her own. Her arms and legs were now scarred, but she had adjusted to her limited sight remarkably fast.

Suzanna thought they still ought not to travel.

"She is not well enough yet," she said to herself as Kate slept. "I know the ball is approaching and Lady Florence expects us, but I cannot leave her. It is not wise to move her."

Kate's eyes fluttered open. "You have given me every comfort, miss. I wish to go wherever I am needed. I am strong enough to make it to Elmbridge, I promise."

"She does improve every day, and I know she will be comfortable and well hidden at Mr. Lacy's," said Anneliese. "But I will write and say we are quite enjoying ourselves. Another week? Or two?"

"Two weeks," said Suzanna. "The weather will be even more in our favor by then."

Kate offered a soft smile. "I will be strong enough, I promise. I'll give you no more trouble."

It had never felt like trouble.

Toward the end of March, Suzanna stepped down from the carriage as it deposited her and Anneliese. Kate had first been taken to Mr. Lacy's, tucked right into bed in an extra room, and given a maid to wait on her night and day. She was healing and no longer contagious but still quite frail.

"It is ever so good to see you both! It has been ages," said Lady Florence to the young ladies once they started to walk inside. "How are you liking

Norling Place, Suzanna? I wish to know all about it. When I am not completely occupied by so much company, perhaps I will call. Miss Grysham seemed to love it there. What a long visit! And Miss Grysham, I need to hear everything about your time in London, for I did not hear all before you *had* to see Miss Spencer. Is your first Season to your liking? I am amazed you would choose to spend so much time in the country! Is there not someone in London? Who do you have your eye on? He will be a lucky man!"

Suzanna walked next to her two friends, taking in the grandeur of Chalestry Manor once again. Spring suited it well—the hardy snowdrops and crocuses full, with the tips of tulips just starting to emerge. The inside of the tall residence was no less breathtaking as they crossed the threshold. New intricate white and pink floral curtains hung in the main hall, looking quite fresh and ethereal.

Lady Florence must have noticed Suzanna's sweeping gaze. She turned to Anneliese and continued talking. "We have changed our tapestries since you came last. We are preparing, as I am sure you have gathered, for the spring fox hunt. It is to be the biggest event of its kind, to finish out the hunting season! Oh, and Miss Grysham, I could have participated more in London this year too, but I did not find it necessary, if you know what I mean." Lady Florence gave a knowing look toward Anneliese. "Might I ask, are your *uncle* and his friends in good health?"

Suzanna assumed Lady Florence included his friends only for good measure.

Anneliese smiled, barely acknowledging the obvious. "Oh, yes, they are doing quite well. Lord Haversley has mentioned the fox hunt a few times, to be sure."

"Of course. I had heard he might even come a bit early," said Lady Florence, prodding for information.

"Depending on Parliament, I believe," said Anneliese.

"Naturally," said Lady Florence as she looked across the room. Suzanna wondered if Lady Florence knew anything about Lord Haversley's work in Parliament. She used to think them perfectly suited for each other, but his serious pursuits suddenly did not match her superficial level of care toward the world around her.

Lady Florence turned and faced Suzanna, studying her dark, long-sleeved gown for a moment. She had always been critical of others' tailoring, but Suzanna hoped she would not notice more. Suzanna clasped her hands behind her and moved back toward Anneliese.

"Well," said Lady Florence after a pause, "I am sure you wish to see many of your acquaintances while in town, so I have invited Mr. Lacy to dinner."

Suzanna tried for a half-smile, remembering how Lady Florence had insinuated months ago that she and Mr. Lacy would make a perfect match.

"How thoughtful," said Suzanna as she watched Anneliese agree with a large smile and quick nod. His coming to dinner would be the first of several social interactions Lady Florence would subject them all to.

Dinner consisted of nine large courses, which exceeded anything Suzanna had eaten at Chalestry in all her years of friendship with the McCallisters. It was the presence of Anneliese that caused all of the show, most likely in the hopes she would relay it all to her uncle.

As Lord Chalestry and Mr. Lacy came through that evening, Suzanna gave a purposeful nod to Mr. Lacy. He seemed to understand Suzanna's need for secrecy around Lady Florence. As he approached the women, he said, "Lady Florence, I wonder if you could do us the honor of playing the piano. There is simply no one who plays as well as you."

"Oh, Mr. Lacy, you are too kind." She paused an obligatory moment, a delicate hand perched on her sternum. "But if you insist, then I shall!"

Within seconds the room sounded with a Beethoven sonata.

Suzanna grinned and leaned toward him as he took his seat near her. "You are brilliant," she said. "How does Kate fare?"

"She seems quite comfortable. The doctor said it is miraculous how well she has healed. I, too, thought she looked much better than I had expected."

Suzanna reached over and squeezed his hand. "Thank you for sending Miss Grysham. She was so wonderful. And thank you for all of your help."

He nodded humbly, a small smile pulling up on one side.

When the sonata came to an end, everyone clapped and Lady Florence walked over and joined them.

"Do you have secret subjects to discuss? I am intrigued by what I am missing!"

If only she knew, on several levels, how many secrets existed between the two of them.

Anneliese now sat on the same chaise as Mr. Lacy, who replied, "Not in the slightest! You know how Suzanna is always inquiring after the needy in Elmbridge. It was nothing more."

"I see," said Lady Florence with a distrusting tone.

"Oh, yes," said Anneliese hastily. "We surely ought to make some visits while you are in town."

"She is a perfect friend to have, is she not?" said Suzanna. "Miss Grysham is always willing to serve others. I think she loves it as much as I do."

Mr. Lacy nodded. "Yes, you two make quite the pair. I believe you will have the whole town healed and mended in your short visit."

"Now, not too many visits," crooned Lady Florence, "for tomorrow we shall attend Mr. Lacy's sermon, of course. Then Monday, I was thinking a garden picnic would be just the thing, for the weather is warming nicely. What say you?"

Suzanna smiled, knowing Lady Florence always desired a full social calendar. "Both sound perfect."

Before five minutes passed, Lady Florence had tried to outline every day before the fox hunt, with Suzanna secretly planning ways to disappear so she might check on Kate.

Chapter 20

A few days later, around noon, Matthew pulled up to Chalestry Manor, knowing his invitation to picnic came only because Lady Florence wished for yet another event to impress Miss Grysham. Lady Florence had never taken particular interest in him, which suited him just fine.

"Good day," said the butler. "The ladies are assembled out back."

He was led through the great doors toward the rear of the house and down a few steps toward two ladies holding parasols.

"Good afternoon," he said with a bow. Lady Florence and Miss Grysham curtsied in return. Matthew paused a moment, noticing Miss Spencer's absence. So it *had* been her in the passing carriage on his way here. Gone to check on Kate, no doubt.

Lady Florence cleared her throat and quirked an eyebrow toward Mr. Lacy. "As you can see, Miss Spencer is not with us. I am sure she informed *you* where she went?"

It was rather insufferable how she oozed nosiness into every question, assuming he would have an answer. He would not let on he knew about Suzanna's true plan.

"I have not the faintest of ideas," he said, looking around. "She has been staying with you. Perhaps *you* could tell *me*."

Lady Florence gave an icy smile, but Miss Grysham laughed openly.

"You *do* have a point, Mr. Lacy," said Miss Grysham with a pleasant grin. Lady Florence looked away as Mr. Lacy gave Miss Grysham a nod, mouthing the words, "Thank you."

"Well," said Lady Florence, "she is always disappearing. She says she must call on old friends, but how many must she see?" She huffed a little as she swished her skirts. "We, however, will carry on without her."

The three made their way down the steps and began walking, Lady Florence hurrying ahead of the other two, leaving Matthew in her wake.

"I appreciated your sermon yesterday," said Miss Grysham to Matthew. "The Ten Commandments provide a wholesome reminder to us all."

Matthew turned his head toward her as they walked over another hill. "Why thank you. It is refreshing to know that someone actually listens to what I teach. It is quite disheartening how many people I see asleep during Sunday service."

"Oh, you do not say! From your vantage point, I am sure you see everything," said Miss Grysham. Lady Florence slowed as they came to a small stream. Mr. Lacy moved quickly to the water, extending his hand to help Lady Florence cross, and then to Miss Grysham. A small flutter ran through his fingertips at her touch, but he credited it to the cold water that splashed against his leg at the same time.

"You know," Miss Grysham said, "it is not your delivery. I am sure every rector in the county experiences the same thing."

Lady Florence had finally slowed her pace to match them and threw her head over her shoulder. "Which is why, in my opinion, you ought to employ a bit more fist-pounding, fire and brimstone moments in your speech."

Matthew adjusted his coat. "Forgive me, Lady Florence, but I do not believe God speaks to us in such heated terms. And if He does not, nor should I."

Miss Grysham looked at Lady Florence and then at him. She seemed to feel the tension and added, "What a noble sentiment. I, for one, am glad to know you think so."

He found himself giving another thankful smile to Miss Grysham. It was easier to endure Lady Florence's condescension in the presence of friends, and Suzanna had always been an excellent buffer in that regard. If Suzanna had to be away secretly visiting Kate, at least Miss Grysham served as that buffer.

As the three walked back up the steps later that afternoon, Lady Florence declared herself "quite fatigued due to the long walk" and rushed inside and up the stairs, without so much as a good-bye to Matthew, although she did offer one to Miss Grysham.

He did not think it appropriate to stay long with Miss Grysham downstairs alone but did wish to speak for a moment.

"I must thank you for your presence this afternoon," he said quickly. She gave a deep curtsy, her head buried low.

Matthew dropped his voice. "I fear Lady Florence and I have never been easy companions, and the way you smoothed out the conversations today did not go unnoticed. You are a true friend."

"It was my pleasure," she said. Matthew thought he noticed her high cheekbones a bit more pink than usual. Was she blushing?

"Please visit us again," she said in a hurry, "for I am sure Miss Spencer will return soon."

He tipped his head toward Miss Grysham with a knowing look and thanked his stars that the afternoon still passed so amiably without her.

"We are almost here," Jacob's valet said, just before they pulled into Chalestry Manor.

"What good time we have made," Jacob replied.

A few days earlier, when they had left London, Jacob had walked around the carriage, inspecting the horses. He lamented he had to take his valet and so many changes of clothes, but he was visiting Chalestry Manor, after all. He made sure his prized Sylvester was tied behind the carriage to accompany him on the journey. A man should not go into a lady's territory without his trusted companion.

He had just lost the vote in Parliament to pass the Vaccination Act. Jacob had thought it secured, after all Mr. Phipps had done. It should have been easy, but at the last moment, one of the assents had turned to a "no." His frustration and sadness at such a decision had weighed on him, and only the prospect of seeing Miss Spencer in Elmbridge brought him a little excitement.

As soon as he arrived at Chalestry Manor, his mother came out to greet him. Her singular presence surprised Jacob, thinking perhaps more of a party would notice his arrival.

"Perhaps you and I ought to take a turn around the grounds," she said.

Jacob untied Sylvester and nodded as they walked toward the stables.

Immediately Lady Haversley began her speech. She glanced to the side, with what Jacob surmised was attempted ease, but the look on her face belied her calm demeanor.

"Jacob, at the risk of getting my hopes up, I wish to ask you what your intentions are for the Hunt Ball."

He should have guessed she would ask him about this again.

"I assume you are asking about Lady Florence. I do not know if I will ask her, Mother."

His mother continued to look away, trying to continue the point despite that comment.

"Not Lady Florence, per se. I know nothing is official, and the McCallisters understand you have also been very social in London this season, which I noticed as well. If it is not Lady Florence, I am just wondering if *any* young woman has piqued your interest enough in the last few months . . ."

Jacob cut into her brief pause. "To ask them to be my wife." There was a finality in the statement that had never been anywhere close to final in his mind.

Lady Haversley finally looked at her son. "I think it is about time, Jacob."

She was right. He continued to walk with her in silence. Ten years of bachelorhood ought to be enough time to find a wife. And he *had* found her, but she had absolutely no idea he wanted her. Anneliese had mentioned in her last letter that she and Miss Spencer were already in Elmbridge. In that moment he confirmed what he wanted. He admitted he had known since Christmas, since writing about her in the book, but now was his time to act. She had brushed him aside in Berkeley, but perhaps there were moments when he thought she *did* like him. She had teased him, ever so slightly at Lysetter Hall. There also was her drive to eliminate smallpox. What lady of breeding would learn to administer vaccines and spend time with deathly ill people? No one was like Suzanna.

He imagined her tiny aproned waist, flour dusting her face in the moonlight. How many times had that image danced before his eyes? He had developed a more robust appetite for fruitcake—and baguettes— since then. And a penchant for Miss Spencer.

Now he would go straight away to her, tell her of his intentions, and they could be engaged within the week. Why should anything stand in his way? For the first time, he felt sure about a woman, and all that lacked was Miss Suzanna Spencer understanding his feelings for her.

A cool calm washed over Jacob, as though he had just taken a large draught of a refreshing drink. He smiled and placed his free hand on his mother's arm.

"You have spurred me into action." He could not quell his growing smile. "I will propose to someone before we return to London, I promise." He lifted her hand and kissed it as they walked inside.

She looked a little perplexed at the word *someone* but nodded as her shoulders relaxed.

"Well, then," said Lady Haversley, dusting off her perfectly groomed skirt, "that was much easier than I thought."

She clicked her tongue and smiled down at her hands.

Jacob only hoped she would not be too terribly disappointed when she learned it would be Suzanna Spencer and not the daughter of her dear McCallisters. He was sure Lady Florence would find another beau to throw herself toward within the week.

Less than an hour later, Jacob found himself walking to the stables, just as he had upon his first arrival, this time with his mother furiously on his heels.

"Jacob, you have *just* arrived. Lady Florence and your niece are having a picnic. You must not leave."

He turned and stopped for a moment. "I have a short errand to run."

"Can it not wait?" Lady Haversley came two steps closer. "Please do not go. It will look bad to Lady Florence."

Jacob suppressed his desire to roll his eyes. "Mother, she always has an ample number of guests here and loves to entertain them all. She will not even notice my absence." He bent down and kissed his mother on the forehead. He wondered if his mother would ever notice that Lady Florence would like any man with money or a title.

Lady Haversley opened her mouth, as if to say something, but stopped.

"Mother," said Jacob steadily, wide shoulders square and stance firm, "I *must* go. There is no changing my mind."

She smiled wanly and nodded, as if defeated.

Jacob attempted a forced smile and turned his riding boot deeper into the gravel.

He knew his mother thought it was because of Mr. Phipps. Pursuing anything regarding smallpox would have been worthwhile, but he had learned from Anneliese's whispers in his few moments inside that he had to only make it to Mr. Lacy's house to find Miss Spencer alone. So he would go, even if that meant riding out now, despite having just arrived.

The same towheaded groom as always greeted him when he walked into the stables. "Have you brushed down my horse?" said Jacob with a smile.

"I can tell your journey was a strain for him." He gave the straps a firm yank as he finished tightening up the saddle. "Clearly, a long ride. Are you sure you will take him?"

"You of all people must know how a man is with his horse."

The groom nodded, a faint smile on his lips. "I guessed you might need him quickly, like last time. He is watered, fed, and brushed, sir."

"I am glad we have this understanding," said Jacob, patting the young man on his shoulder.

Jacob mounted the horse and thought he heard the man mutter, "Always in such a hurry."

And he was. The faster he found Suzanna, the faster he could win her.

Suzanna could not remember the last time she had been so completely covered in flour, and it felt more than right. Kate was upstairs and had mentioned maybe a bit of fresh bread would do her good. She was nearly healed now, and Suzanna did not need any more excuses to come to the kitchen—her old kitchen, the one she had learned everything in.

She had snuck out of Chalestry early that morning and spent the whole of the afternoon, while Mr. Lacy had been out, at his house.

She had two loaves complete and had just started on a second batch when she heard the clang of the door behind her. The current dough was rather stubborn in coming together, so she continued kneading as she said, "I used to keep the finest wheat here. But this does not knead properly!" She gave a few whacks to the bread. Once she was married and living here again, she would see this remedied.

"I have never met Mr. Lacy's cook, but I will be sure to let her know."

The deep voice, although familiar, caused Suzanna to jump nearly out of her apron.

She turned quickly, flattening the loaf with her palm, and let out a small gasp. She hastily pulled down her sleeves as she held her breath.

A tall, smiling figure stood in the doorway, one arm behind his back.

"Lord Haversley? What in heavens' name are you doing here?"

"I might ask you the same. However, dear Anneliese has told me of Kate. I am ever so sorry."

She let out a pent up gust of air. If anyone knew that she was sneaking away to the home of an unmarried bachelor, she would be ruined. But she had to help Kate, so the risk was worth it. She appreciated he knew the name of her servant and treated her like an equal. Lord Haversley's tall head almost touched the frame and he leaned against the wood, as though he were completely at ease. Apparently *he* did not seem at all alarmed that she was in Mr. Lacy's house.

"There is a rumor that the vicarage is in dire need of a baker, and I came to inquire after the opening."

Suzanna, still a bit trembly, attempted to brush the dust off her hands and face, while shaking her head.

"You must think you are very funny, sir. Have you come to mock me?" He should not be here. She felt a bit unnerved by how informally he had barged into her kitchen.

"Not in the slightest. I see the position is already filled." He took three steps in and removed the hand from behind his back, exposing a meager bouquet of what looked like fledgling wildflowers.

"To . . . um, brighten your favorite working space."

He brought her flowers—again? Perhaps it was something he always did when visiting women. Had she ever noticed hothouse flowers for Lady Florence? She racked her brain.

"Thank you," she said as she rummaged in the cupboard to find a vase. As she stuffed the stems down into the opening, she looked up at him and asked, "Did you by chance try the front door, or are you fond of going through the servants' entrance?"

"To be candid, I did knock upstairs, and a servant insisted I wait inside. But I dismissed myself, saying I would try back later, having an inkling where you might be."

He knew her that well? He guessed she was baking? Surely she ought to be more careful about *who* knew that secret. And to be in his presence, alone. This was not appropriate for anyone, especially a lady of privilege who lived on her own and who, she might add, was engaged.

One of Mr. Lacy's servants came through the door, carrying a bundle of firewood.

"You will never believe who just called."

The wood tumbled to the ground with a few noisy clangs as the maid's mouth dropped almost to the floor. Her eyes shot directly to Suzanna, a small, upturned hand barely pointing toward Lord Haversley. She quickly righted herself and curtsied. "Lord Haversley, I see you have found Miss Spencer on your own."

His warm chuckle filled the kitchen. "Is there anyone else I can startle today?"

Suzanna smiled back. "Some of Mr. Lacy's other servants have gone to town. Otherwise I am sure they would be willing to oblige."

He nodded and turned toward the maid.

"Miss Spencer, I wonder if this skilled maid could finish your bread and you and I could talk in the drawing room."

Suzanna did not exactly know why Lord Haversley had come to call and did not wish to be alone with him, if in fact his flowers were a sign of his affection. What would she possibly say if he asked her something personal? She knew the best defense was not letting him have a chance to ask any questions in the first place.

"Oh, that will not be necessary," said Suzanna with tight lips. "A lady should always be in the presence of a chaperone, and this maid will serve as just that for the time being."

Suzanna watched Lord Haversley kick a small pebble across the flour-speckled floor.

"Then perhaps we might *all* move to the drawing room." His face was serious, his eyes steady. She looked away swiftly.

"Oh, no." She cleared her throat. "I need to finish this bread, you see." She knew she was bordering on rudeness, but she could not bear a more formal setting with him. No one knew she was engaged. It would be so awkward to talk of it now, especially in Mr. Lacy's own kitchen. She turned toward the bread and pounded it more fiercely than she had ever done before. At this point, she was sure it would be ruined, but the loaf was the least of her worries.

And . . . if he did ask . . .

No.

She was getting ahead of herself. He did not come here to ask her anything. She would not let him.

She was still in mourning. Could he *never* remember such a fact?

Also, she was engaged.

She could not let her heart think more.

She must change the subject. "Mrs. Phipps told me you pay for all of her husband's supplies. That you pay people to procure the cowpox. She said every related expense in the last half year has been paid for by you. Is it true?"

A slight smile came across Lord Haversley's face. His eyes shifted back and forth, and he turned toward her, all frustration absent.

"Mrs. Phipps was not supposed to mention that. But yes, I have, for I am very committed to the cause, as I believe you are. We need widespread access for everyone. We have even tried passing laws about it, you know. We were so close in Parliament this last vote. Just at the end, one of the people who had agreed to pass the bill switched his vote. Some of them are still afraid of the practice and do not understand the benefits of a vaccination act. They fear it 'unnatural.' We lost by one vote. One vote!"

For a moment the room went silent. The maid seemed to have faded into the farthest corner of the kitchen, and Suzanna stared at Lord Haversley. Who was this man before her? She had once thought him so foppish, insincere, caring only about trivial matters. Months ago he had come off that way, but not now. She recalled his story of his sister and why, exactly, he cared about smallpox and vaccinating others.

She knew in that moment she had misjudged him. Behind his cuffs, cravats, and stilted language stood a man who had a deep sense of right. He had taken it upon himself to change all of England. To save people from further pain, suffering, and death, and in turn save their loved ones too. Legislation, monetary backing, time, resources—his actions showed just how much he cared.

Before her stood one of the most noble men she had ever met. In the kitchen, no less, and bearing flowers. He must be there to further their relationship, and she thought for one moment she might be able to accept him. She wondered if a seed of love had sprouted within her, but it was all ridiculous. When would it have started? She was engaged, and in one week's time he would know it.

She had to get him out of this house as fast as possible.

He disrupted the silence and her thoughts. "I know you have done much to stop the spread of smallpox, too, Miss Spencer. You saved Kate's life. And Anneliese told me you gave the vaccine to many others in Berkeley."

He reached down and grasped her left arm. She had tried to pull down her sleeves, but there had not been time to button them tightly. She had been meticulous about long sleeves and gloves the last month, wrapping her bandages tightly underneath her dress to keep them hidden. But she had needed bare hands for the bread.

He slowly turned her forearm over so her palm faced up. He pushed up the dark sleeve, studying the visible scars and stared at the bandage, just below the elbow. Then he took her right arm in his hand and examined it too.

Now he would know. Surely he supported smallpox, told people of the vaccine . . . but he would never wish to be this close. He would run away.

"You've . . ." His voice trembled, but he did not drop her hands. "You've had it. These scars are very recent, Miss Spencer."

Still he stared at them, and Suzanna realized she should be filled with dread. But his touch felt compassionate, understanding, as if he actually wished to know.

"I . . ." She gathered her courage and lifted her eyes to his. "I had been vaccinated years ago. But I think for some, the immunity might lessen. I think I was so close to Kate, even gave her some of my blood, that I did contract a few symptoms. No real sickness, just fever and these sores on my arms. Though all my scabs are healed, I still wear this bandage as a precaution."

She did not add how lucky she felt. She would probably never wish to bare her arms again, but she had been spared the brunt of it.

He lifted her right hand up to his mouth and kissed it. "Miss Spencer, I have never known such a woman. You are so brave, so selfless. I am honored to know you."

He still held her hand. She gracefully withdrew it as she stepped closer and interrupted him. "What I have done is hardly anything compared to your great service. *Everyone* is indebted to you." She tried in vain to button her sleeve and edged away from him.

She had to remove him from her presence. He could not stay any longer. She took the crook of his arm and deliberately walked him toward the door, dragging him along with her. "Perhaps we ought to speak of your involvement with the vaccine another time."

They stood at the doorway, and Lord Haversley looked perplexed. "We could go for a walk now." He looked deliberately at her hand on his arm.

She shut the door a little. "Oh, well, no. I have a very pressing engagement I must get to."

In truth, she did not need to go anywhere. She only needed to be rid of him. The way he looked at her . . . the words he had said. He should stay no longer.

And if she were merely talking semantics, her engagement to Mr. Lacy *did* press on her.

She withdrew her arm and curtsied toward him. She smelled the scent of horse hair and wildflowers on him. As she looked up the few steps, she spied his horse, the same light brown color she remembered, a bit of sweat glistening on its coat.

"Thank you for your visit," she said with a smile, nearly closing the door on him. His brow furrowed as he looked down at her, a mix of confusion and frustration.

"You will be coming back to Chalestry?" he said, trying to step a bit toward her.

Her head filled the closing width of the door as she said, "Of course. Before I am missed."

He let out a great gust of air. "Good day, Miss Spencer." He turned and walked hastily toward his horse.

"Good-bye," she whispered as the door latched shut.

She relaxed her body against the wall and breathed a few shallow breaths. What had just happened? She had all but cast him out of Mr. Lacy's house, and he did not even state why he had come. Why was she so afraid of what he might say?

More startling, what did she wish he would have said?

She felt her knees buckle as she slid down the door into a collapsed bundle.

He had not recoiled at the sight of her scars.

Did she care for him?

Did it matter?

He would just be a scar left on her heart.

Chapter 21

Jacob pushed his heels deeper into Sylvester, racing toward Chalestry faster than he could ever remember riding. Sylvester seemed to understand his sentiment. No complaint or defiance was present in his smooth gait. At least someone in the world understood him.

Jacob had not even declared his purpose for calling before that stubborn, hard-headed Miss Spencer had shooed him out of the kitchen. A lord, a Member of Parliament had called at her servants' entrance with flowers, and she had the audacity to send him on his way? Such manners were inexplicable.

But then the sight of her clear sky blue eyes came before his mind. Her dusty apron, once again cinched tightly around her tiny waist, which billowed out nicely over her full skirt . . . and her scarred arms. Her perfect, scarred arms. Most women would not sacrifice so much, especially for a servant. But Miss Suzanna Spencer was different.

Perhaps she was the prettiest girl he had ever met, so it must purely be her perfect face that drew him in. But the more he tried to convince himself of this, the more he knew he had met many an equal beauty, and it was more than her looks that won him over. His hand reached back and felt the small satchel that held his notebook. Why, among so many entries, did Miss Spencer trump them all?

It didn't matter, he reminded himself, because she would not give him more than five minutes. He wished to declare his feelings, and yet he said less than a half-page of words! He kicked his heels deeper into Sylvester's flanks.

What an idiot he had been for thinking she would have him, for skirting the issue and beginning with banter. How could he have been so daft? Next time, he promised himself, he would march into her presence and declare his intentions unequivocally, and quite clearly, before her perfect rose-colored mouth could utter anything that could derail the conversation.

Maybe he ought to turn his horse around and set things right. He pulled on the reins, coming almost to a complete stop. He looked at the open road and paused a moment, then thought better of it. He had been too hasty last time. Perhaps he needed a better plan. Maybe she really did have some pressing engagement. Or maybe she was embarrassed by her appearance—by her scars—while caught baking. She needn't be.

He could wait until the ball. He had that much self-control. He gritted his teeth, telling himself it was true.

Would she say yes? He would ask her just before. She would have to be daft to turn him down.

He tugged at his cravat as he tightened the reins with his other hand. He headed toward the open field. He was close to Chalestry, but his mind needed to ride a bit longer.

He shuddered at the memory of her door inching closed over her face. How humiliating! What could be her reason? Did she really disdain his presence that much?

But she was never self-important. Surely she was one of the most selfless people he had ever met. So what was it? Why did she always end their conversations so flippantly? Perhaps there was something he did not understand.

There was less than a week to the fox hunt. He could seek her out sometime before then. They were staying in the same house, after all. He could make his feelings known. And maybe she'd listen this time.

Maybe.

Suzanna gathered up the rest of her things as she handed a warm loaf to Kate. "You are looking so much better," she said. "Enjoy the bread."

"Thank you again, for everything, miss." Then she stopped and put her hand on Suzanna's arm. "What is on your mind?"

Suzanna came out of her thoughts and looked at Kate. "What do you mean?"

"Your eyes look like they are covered by a dark storm, if you don't mind me saying."

Suzanna relaxed her furrowed brow and tried to attempt disinterest. "Oh, no, perhaps it is the glare of the sun. I shall return tomorrow."

She stood in the doorway, lost in thought. She could not get Lord Haversley's surprise meeting off her mind—or the fact that she would announce her engagement in less than a week. Her thoughts vacillated between the two ideas until she nearly felt sick. If she didn't wish to be married to Mr. Lacy, why did she now find herself thinking about being the lady of the house with increasing frequency? It didn't seem right. Kate looked at her a long while, sensing something was still wrong.

A few more days, and the full weight of her secret engagement would explain all.

"Miss Spencer, I wish to come to Chalestry before the ball," said Kate to Suzanna.

Suzanna stared at her.

"I want to help you in your first day out of mourning. I am feeling much better. I doubt the McCallisters even remember which of their guests have brought which servants. And if anyone asks, I shall say I had a cold but you finally sent for me to relieve Anneliese's lady's maid."

Suzanna peered at her friend. Her wounds were nearly all healed; just a few red pox scars stood visible on her face. But several people had scars—herself included, she realized—and she doubted how well any of the McCallister servants knew Kate.

"I'll wear my bonnet and long sleeves. No one will know or be scared of me." She pleaded with Suzanna. "I insist. I am going mad here alone."

Suzanna could believe that.

"All right then, the day before."

Suzanna did her best for the next five days to avoid Lord Haversley. In turn this meant she avoided nearly everyone, continually finding ways to make excuses to Lady Florence that she must visit her old friends, then actually steal away and visit Kate. It was convenient, too, that Lady Florence invited Mr. Lacy over so often so Kate was alone. But Suzanna's list of necessary visits was nearly running out. Today she took the carriage back to Chalestry Manor, grateful tomorrow was the fox hunt. Kate was by her side, looking well. Suzanna reviewed their explanation, if they needed it, for her absence once again.

As they drove through the long park, she spotted Mr. Lacy and Lord Haversley practicing archery atop the hill. She thought she saw a strawberry-blond head turn over his shoulder and drop his bow, say something to his partner, and walk toward the front of the manor.

Lord Haversley stood for a moment longer, his tall, toned frame releasing an arrow. Suzanna was not sure, as the carriage rounded the drive, but it seemed the arc of the arrow landed it in a perfect bullseye. It looked like he muttered something, threw down his bow, and plodded heavily after Mr. Lacy.

She had tried to say nothing to Lord Haversley in the past five days. Hopefully he would not question her now—or heaven forbid divulge Kate's secret. She continued to gaze out her window, the ever steady and ever faithful smile of Mr. Lacy coming closer to view. He really was the best sort of man.

When the carriage stopped and the groom lowered the step, Mr. Lacy was there to hand her out. As her foot met the gravel, she looked across to her right, noticing Lord Haversley stood exactly opposite of Mr. Lacy, keeping a good distance, wearing a decided glare. She gave a short curtsy toward him and turned back to Mr. Lacy.

"Good afternoon, gentlemen." She kept her gaze toward Mr. Lacy. "It seems a fine day for archery."

"Yes," said Lord Haversley. She avoided his eyes and looked back in the carriage.

"I finally decided Kate ought to join me from Elmbridge, since she is over her cold," she said, "and I have put too much strain on Miss Grysham's lady's maid." Mr. Lacy knew of the plan, and she only hoped Lord Haversley had not told Lacy of their meeting in the kitchen. This way, everyone knew her backstory.

"I'll be in the servants' quarters when you need me again, miss," said Kate. She knew it was best to blend in rather than wait until someone else questioned her.

Suzanna stood alone, now flanked by Mr. Lacy and Lord Haversley on either side. She did not know if observing their archery was for the best or if she should come up with a reason to leave them.

But Lord Haversley stepped closer. "My niece has been asking about you all day. Perhaps I could take you to her." He extended his arm and came close enough that his coat sleeve brushed Suzanna's traveling cape.

Suzanna looked at Mr. Lacy, whose brow puzzled into a wrinkled *V.* She stood frozen for a moment, until she realized she needed to act nonchalant. "Oh, yes, I have been meaning to talk to her. Let us go straight away." She hoped it would be brief and he would not try and speak to her again. She had almost taken his arm when Lady Florence came shuffling briskly through the front door toward them.

"Miss Spencer!" she called, the layers of her gathered soft pink skirt bouncing. "So glad you are back." Lady Florence took Suzanna by the hands, all smiles as her eyes flitted between her and the two men. Lord Haversley dropped his proffered arm, clenching his jaw and narrowing his eyes, looking off into the distance.

Lady Florence did not stop talking. "And still wearing black. I am sorry about your father as ever." She smiled at Suzanna, pulling her a bit closer.

"Thank you. I miss him dearly."

Lady Florence nodded and conspicuously eyed the two men. "Of course, you must be weary, always leaving to visit everyone in all of Elmbridge." She cleared her throat. "Mr. Lacy, perhaps you ought to lead Miss Spencer inside for some refreshment."

Lady Florence laced her arm through Lord Haversley's and began immediately speaking of the archery. Suzanna thought she saw his eyes harden as he capitulated to the artful siren.

"My mother sent me out here, saying I *must* see your target. Would you show it to me?" said Lady Florence's honey-sweet voice as they walked away, the tone Florence most often employed when talking to Lord Haversley. Suzanna was sure Lady Florence—or at least her mother—imagined Lord Haversley having his true target set on making a match with her.

Mr. Lacy chuckled and eagerly offered his arm to Suzanna. She took it, and they walked toward the house.

"Suzanna," Mr. Lacy said as soon as they were out of earshot, "what did you do to Lord Haversley? He seemed quite on edge as soon as I told him you were arriving. And so visibly miffed just now."

Suzanna gave out a nervous laugh. "I haven't the faintest idea," she said, fiddling with her skirt, "but maybe he is self-conscious of that dastardly cravat. If it were any bigger, a bird might nest in there!" As soon as she said it, she felt she had gone too far.

"You might actually be right," said Mr. Lacy, eyes twinkling. "Lady Florence seems to like it that way. I heard her compliment him on it in front of his valet, and that surely did not help."

"Do you think they are well matched?" said Suzanna. She was not sure they were, but when Lady Florence was near, it seemed a bit more believable.

Mr. Lacy shook his head. "No. Definitely not. He is a good man. She is polished, wealthy, talented, beautiful . . . but lacking his level of substance."

"I see," said Suzanna as they reached the main staircase. "I think I am safe to say that to people of sense, substance *does* actually matter. Would you agree?"

He lifted her hand as though to kiss it but lowered it suddenly. "Of course." They were now at the door. He smiled and bowed as he said, "I think I owe it to my friend to continue our game of archery before Lady Florence gets the best of him."

Suzanna curtsied. "You are a good man," she told him with a chuckle.

As she walked inside, she knew she meant it. If only the same couldn't be said of his friend.

Chapter 22

The men started their fox hunt early the next morning, leaving the ladies in the drawing room.

"The hunt today, the Hunt Ball tomorrow. It is *so* obvious you have attended to every detail," Suzanna said to Lady Chalestry.

"Indeed I hope so! We love to serve our guests. The men shall enjoy their sport, but tomorrow you will see the true festivities! And how lucky we are to have you here, Anneliese. So many of our friends have expressed a great interest in the Haversley family—many mothers and sons." She gave a purposeful wink toward Anneliese. "You shall not want for a partner! Of course the daughters aren't as fixed on your uncle, for they know he will most likely . . ."

Lady Florence, who had been reading a letter just delivered to her, delicately placed a hand on her mother's knee and whispered, "Mother, you must not say things so flippantly. He has made no such promise."

Florence quickly closed the letter and turned her angular chin away from her mother, crossing her arms. Clearly Lady Florence wasn't sure Lord Haversley would ask her, though her mother depended on it. Did Lady Florence not wish it to be so?

"Well," Suzanna said, edging toward the door, "I think a bit of fresh air would do me good. If you will excuse me." She waited for Anneliese to make some excuse as well, but her grandmother gave her a look that meant she was *not* to leave.

"Oh, Miss Spencer, I meant to ask you, " said Lady Chalestry toward Suzanna as she reached the door, "do you plan on dancing tomorrow?"

156

"Yes, I will come out of mourning tonight. It has been six months, and I feel my father would wish me to return to society."

"Splendid!" Lady Chalestry clapped her hands. "I shall be pleased to show you off too tomorrow. Think of all the superior dancing and breeding Elmbridge has to offer!"

Suzanna nodded, curtsied again, and then turned and headed for the door. She made her way through the back gardens and walked quickly down the hill.

Her father's grave was just at the other end of the McCallister estate, and it would be about a half hour's walk through some of the prettiest woods in the county. About ten minutes in, she heard a rustling off the small dirt path she walked through. Startled, Suzanna hid behind a tree. It dawned on her that taking a walk this deep into the woods during the hunt was a poor idea. The sound of two horses breathing noisily met her ears. From behind the large trunk, she could see Lord Haversley and Mr. Lacy perched atop their respective mounts.

"What an incredible chase," said Mr. Lacy. "Lord Chalestry's dogs are so dynamic. Wouldn't you agree?"

Lord Haversley's warm laughter rang in Suzanna's ears. He had a particularly delightful laugh.

"The running of the hounds is magnificent." He sighed and looked at his friend. "But perhaps now is a good time to admit that I do not particularly care for killing the fox."

Mr. Lacy's eyes went wide. "You don't?"

"They are such beautiful animals. Believe me that my Sylvester could have been at the forefront. But toward the end I do tend to intentionally lag behind."

Mr. Lacy shook his head. His fingers raised to his temples. "So that is why you wished to take a different way back?"

Suzanna smiled. Lord Haversley surprised her yet again. He was such a kind man at heart.

Lord Haversley looked over the top of the trees below them and pulled on his cravat. "I had to have some excuse for why I slowed. But yes, let us at least take the long way home. I would not mind being away from the ladies a bit longer."

Mr. Lacy nodded. The horses walked slowly into the thicket of woods, and Lord Haversley said, "Now that we are away from the group, I thought I might ask you a question."

Their walk had brought them even closer to her, and Suzanna's cheeks immediately felt red. She really ought not overhear their conversation, but she could not pull herself away.

"You may ask anything," Mr. Lacy said, pulling the reins to a stop. Suzanna could see both faces from her hidden alcove, the noonday sun beating down on both of them. She wedged closer into her tree trunk.

"Have you thought any more about my inquiry regarding Miss Grysham? She would undoubtedly make a splendid companion." Lord Haversley had also stopped, and both men looked intently at each other.

Suzanna had to hold a hand over her mouth to stop from gasping. So many questions raced through her mind. Was Lord Haversley matchmaking? And what did Mr. Lacy think of it? He had always seemed so loyal to her.

The clearing of his throat interrupted Suzanna's thoughts. Mr. Lacy patted the horse's withers and looked down.

"I have not told you everything, as it was not my place to do so," he began. "But I believe you shall find out soon enough, and frankly I cannot bear not speaking of it any longer."

Lord Haversley adjusted his riding coat and ran his fingers over the edge of the Dreyse rifle Mr. Lacy had given him. He narrowed his eyes. "Whatever do you mean?"

Mr. Lacy cleared his throat and swallowed hard.

"I . . . am engaged to someone else."

Suzanna clamped her eyes shut for a moment and then opened her left eye in time to see Lord Haversley's reaction.

"Engaged? Congratulations, my friend!"

Lord Haversley wore his most robust smile—his genuine one. Not the one he employed when he tried to impress Lady Florence. The one he had worn when he first called on her.

How did she know his different smiles?

Lord Haversley seemed to wait for more words, but Mr. Lacy remained silent, so he gestured for more details as he rolled his hand. "Why did you not say so in the first place? Miss Grysham will have other opportunities; there will be other men." He swished his hand in the air. "But might I ask who the lucky young lady is?"

Mr. Lacy's horse pawed at the ground, as though he felt for his rider.

Suzanna clenched the sides of her dress, wishing she could shrink into the moss below her feet.

"Miss Suzanna Spencer."

Suzanna watched as Lord Haversley straightened, his smile vanishing. A very uncomfortable pause followed.

Lord Haversley's tone dropped a few notches. "So all this time," he said, his eyes steady, "you had already caught the fox."

Mr. Lacy raised his eyebrows and then nodded. "I suppose that *is* one way of saying it. Her father had one dying wish—that she be settled, that she have someone."

"And you are that lucky man?"

"Yes." Mr. Lacy removed his hat and ran his hand through his hair.

Suzanna knew both men before her to be wise and calculating at times. What exactly was going on between them? She watched Lord Haversley open his mouth. "And you love her, more than anyone else in the world?"

Mr. Lacy's horse took a few paces, distancing himself from Lord Haversley. Mr. Lacy sighed before answering. "I do not know how to say this, and it must never leave this grove." He looked around himself, his gaze glancing over the spot where Suzanna hid. "Suzanna was the first girl I cared for in any way. She is the best friend I could have ever wanted, and she is, as I am sure you have observed, quite beautiful." Lord Haversley nodded, waiting as Mr. Lacy continued. "But I feel as though sometimes she does not love me as one should love a husband."

Suzanna watched Lord Haversley's Adam's apple bob low and then return before he spoke.

"But she said yes to you."

Mr. Lacy rubbed his hand up and down the arm of his riding jacket. "Yes, and we are to announce it tomorrow."

"I see," said Lord Haversley. He sat taller, straightened his shoulders, and looked his friend square in the eye.

"Tell me that you love her."

Mr. Lacy did not hesitate.

"I did. I do."

Lord Haversley raised a brow and stared hard at Mr. Lacy.

"From the first I thought I loved her. But I think it was so sensible, and she was my first love. It is different now. There is some sort of mutual acceptance between us, which does not feel much like love to me. But what do I know? It does not matter. I will, of course, be faithful to her and her father's wishes. Our love will grow, with time."

Lord Haversley studied him like it wasn't enough.

"Do you feel for another?" Lord Haversley pressed.

Mr. Lacy steadied his eyes and did not answer.

"Good grief, man! Out with it!"

Mr. Lacy looked down. "There has always been the hope that the love I feel for another would be reciprocated. But even when we are alone, Suzanna does not increase her attentions."

Suzanna did not know how much more she could bear. What he spoke was too true, and it pained her that she had caused him such grief. How long had he known this and carried the burden of obligation? And to know that all this time, or at least lately, perhaps he did not love her, that he was just keeping his oath to her father?

Lord Haversley rubbed his thigh, his eyes turning serious. "Well, then, if this is how you feel, have you considered breaking the engagement?"

Mr. Lacy's eyes shot open, the whites clearly visible from Suzanna's vantage. "You know I would never do such a thing. Miss Spencer expects us to wed, and I could never harm her. Someone *must* take care of her. It would be inexcusable. I cannot. I gave my word to her and her father, and I will not use Miss Spencer, or her father, ill."

Suzanna watched as Lord Haversley's eyes bore into Mr. Lacy's person. She had never beheld such a serious, genuine look from him. He finally exhaled slowly. "She deserves to be loved fiercely, with one's whole heart, as do you, my friend. The alliance of husband and wife is not to be entered into lightly. It should not feel like only friendship! With her, the most mundane moments should feel . . . miraculous."

Mr. Lacy dropped his head. "Of course you are right. But no matter how she loves me, or how I feel toward her, I will not break my vow."

Suzanna could take no more. She stepped away from her tree and heard a large twig snap beneath her foot. Both men looked in her direction. She hunched down for a moment and then raced through the thickest part of the forest. As she ran, she listened behind her, terrified that if anyone gave chase, she would need to come into the open immediately. But after a moment, with no sound of dogs or men on horseback coming after her, she knew she was in the clear. She did not stop running until she reached the back of Chalestry Manor.

Why had she chosen to go walking during a hunt?

Clearly she was not thinking straight. It took several minutes for her heart to slow its beating, but it wasn't because she ran.

It was interesting that neither man had called out when they heard her move. Perhaps they saw her, which she thought unlikely, or thought it was an animal. Or, they were both so absorbed in the conversation that they *chose* not to move. She thought she knew what Mr. Lacy was thinking. He did not love her. All this time, she thought it would break his heart if she did not seem to love him. And now she wondered if perhaps he was acting just as much as she had been. When had he changed? Did he never love her? Was it merely out of duty all this time?

No, surely not. At one point he did. When he asked her to marry him, she was sure it was real love. But no longer. Whatever the reason for the change, she knew she must break off the engagement. No matter what she had promised to her father, she could not live with herself if she subjected Mr. Lacy to such a fate, not now that she knew his true feelings.

And her own.

For the rest of the afternoon Suzanna waited near the stables. Mr. Lacy would come back before dinner, and she must do what her conscience told her to.

Finally he came to return his horse, and thankfully Lord Haversley was no longer at his side. Suzanna rose from her shaded bench and moved to stand directly in his path.

Mr. Lacy's strawberry-blond hair curled a bit in the heat. He stopped immediately. His green eyes met hers, and they held each other's gaze for a long moment.

"I must speak with you," said Suzanna.

"Good day, Miss Spencer," said Mr. Lacy, with the same tone he had used so many times before. "It is a pleasure to see you."

The hardest part of hearing it was knowing everything he said was completely heartfelt. He would always be good to her.

"Please do not say anything else." She thrust her gloved hand out toward him. "And perhaps, for my sake, we should sit down."

Mr. Lacy's eyes filled with worry as he took a seat next to her on the bench.

"Miss Spencer, are you unwell?" he asked in a whisper.

"I am fine, but please say no more." She took a long breath and continued. "I . . ." She turned her head away for a moment. "I . . . have decided that no matter what we promised my father, I wish to release you from our engagement."

Mr. Lacy's body stiffened, and he placed his hand on top of her quivering one. "Miss Spencer! What has come over you? Why would you wish to do that? Surely you are unwell." He bent his head so that his eyes found hers. "We shall be a splendid pair."

Suzanna looked at him, her eyes filled with tears. He did not exactly reiterate his love for her, and she knew she had crushed his feelings gradually, until nothing was left.

"Thank you. You have always been so kind to me." She pursed her lips together and began again. "I just have realized you deserve more than I can give. I, too, agree we could be happy and would work well together, but you deserve someone who loves you—in every way."

"You must think about what you are saying." He wiped his brow. He was sweating, and Suzanna suspected it was no longer from the hunt. "I do not wish to break my promise to you or your father."

"Please do not worry yourself about that. I have Norling Place, and my father has left me a few hundred pounds per year. I shall live a wonderful life. Since I learned how to administer the vaccine, I have a new passion, and helping people fight smallpox will be my quest. It will be my life's work."

Mr. Lacy removed his hand from hers. He sat still for a long time.

"But we could be happy together," he said again.

Suzanna shook her head. "Not as happy as you might be with another."

Mr. Lacy held her gaze for a long while and then looked down. The two sat together in the silence of their own thoughts. Suzanna knew he understood. It was better this way.

After several minutes, his voice came, just above a whisper. "Your mind is quite made up?"

"Completely," she said, attempting to smile but coming up short.

He nodded and rubbed his hands along his trousers.

She did not know what to say next or how to leave the conversation. He stayed a few minutes more. She may have ruined his plans, his idea of marriage, but there was some way she could yet help him. She turned to face him on the bench and looked him in the eye.

"I have it on good authority that a certain Miss Grysham would not mind you seeking her attentions."

Mr. Lacy sat straight up, his eyes going wide. Finally he shook his head. He sat still for another minute longer. "Suzanna?" His voice turned up at the end. "What would make you think that?"

"My own eyes, Mr. Lacy!" *And Lord Haversley's suggestion.* She decided against adding the second part. He already knew what his friend thought. "The walls of Berkeley seem to be as thin as anywhere," said Suzanna as she cocked her head.

He laughed. "I hope you do not think I was unfaithful. I just fear we were much thrown together."

She put out her hand, silencing him. "You were and are perfectly noble. You don't need to explain anything to me." She wiggled her eyebrows. "I understand it *perfectly.*" She stared, and he returned the sentiment. Their friendship was suddenly as it once was. She felt a smile creep across her lips—a real one. It had been a long time, but she finally felt free.

Jacob had stayed behind, claiming Sylvester needed an even longer ride, and that far away he might finally shoot the Dreyse Mr. Lacy had brought him. Mr. Lacy had nodded and had headed toward the stables.

Ride Jacob did—and shoot at quite a few trees for another hour. The hunt was successful, and the men were to gather together to celebrate with some refreshment, but he would not return. Not yet.

Too many of his hopes had been shattered this day. To know Suzanna was gone, completely out of reach, was more than painful. He had tried to ignore her, tried to seek her—in vain, for she was always flitting about—and then he almost confronted her after archery. If only Lady Florence had not wedged her way into their party then. As it was, he had planned to stroll through the gardens tonight, after he washed up, and somehow draw Suzanna away from Anneliese. But now—now he would do nothing.

He swallowed hard. He had promised his mother.

Why?

His mother wanted his happiness. She wanted one of her children to settle in marriage, to have a family, to live a long and happy life. All she wanted was for him to have those things his siblings were never able to experience.

He should be grateful. At least he had his health, and he might someday make a difference in the world if he tried hard enough with smallpox.

If he could not have love, at least he would work to convince Parliament of what was right. Lady Florence, he supposed, could be by his side. He was sure she was more kind, gentle, and level-headed than she appeared when trying to impress a gentleman.

He finally dismounted Sylvester, who glistened with sweat. He had come to the same spot on the edge of the estate he stopped at his first time on the grounds more than six months ago. If he had known then how twisted and convoluted his heart would become, would he have ridden right on to Berkeley and skipped Chalestry Manor all together?

Surely.

But sometimes, even as a lord of a great estate, one did not get what one wished for. He kicked at the ground and removed his cravat. He crumpled it in his hands, ignoring the chastisement his mother had always given him as a young boy that he would ruin the fabric.

Finally, after walking several more minutes, he again mounted his horse, shook his head, and tried to erase all thoughts of Suzanna and cling to every amiable quality of Lady Florence.

Lady Florence was the first to notice. She clutched Lord Haversley's arm as she pulled him along with her toward Suzanna.

"Miss Spencer! How beautiful you look. I had become so accustomed to your black that I am struck again at how becoming you are in color! Any young man will be glad to dance with you."

Lady Florence looked toward Lord Haversley, who only humored them with a slow dip of his head. Suzanna was sure that she blushed. She thought of how that very afternoon, she had released herself from the only man who had seemed to once love her. Mr. Lacy came in behind her, giving a bow to the general room, and approached Suzanna. When Lady Florence and Lord Haversley looked to be in conversation, he leaned toward her and whispered, "Are you really sure?"

"Quite," Suzanna said with a smile.

He looked down for a moment and then met her eyes. "I do hope we shall always be good friends."

He took her hand and kissed it.

"Most certainly," she said as she noticed Lord Haversley watched them. She realized then she wished to stare back at Lord Haversley but told herself to turn away.

Anneliese entered and came to her side whispering, "You look lovely."

Suzanna smiled and followed Anneliese as the party made their way into the dining room. Lady Florence sat next to Lord Haversley, who had Anneliese on his other side. Lord Chalestry sat at the head of the table, with Lady Haversley in the place of honor to his right. Suzanna took her place next, with Mr. Lacy to her side, and a few others of the hunting party sat around the table.

The rich meat should have lulled Suzanna into a stupor, but for the first time in months she laughed and talked throughout the entire meal. She spoke most to Anneliese and Mr. Lacy on either side of her. Suzanna marveled at how different she felt. She had come out of mourning, and the memory of her father still felt dear, but the pain had lessened a few degrees.

She was not obligated to Mr. Lacy. He had become her esteemed friend once more, offering several witty remarks, and Anneliese thought anything either of them said was quite funny. The air felt light again, as though a cloud had blown through without releasing any rain.

However, Suzanna did feel bad for Lord Haversley. He sat across from the Master of the Hunt, whose bragging knew no end. Even when Lord Haversley turned toward Lady Florence, who simpered at his every comment, his gaze swept around the room. Perhaps some of the food did not sit well with him, for he seemed to grimace every time he looked in Suzanna and Mr. Lacy's general direction.

What *was* it in his eyes? And why was she noticing them at all?

She cared for him. All this time, she had ignored her feelings, tried to hide them. But now, free to act, she knew her heart.

She thought of his visits—the fruitcake, the roses behind the couch, the wildflowers, the offer to go walking. Could he feel the same now?

He thought she was still engaged. He sat next to Lady Florence. If this was his choice, she should not interfere. And what if she did not really have the capacity to love him? If she had not fallen for Mr. Lacy, could she really love Lord Haversley?

Or was her mind playing a cruel trick on her heart?

Chapter 23

The next morning Suzanna set off early again toward her father's grave. The uncomfortable memory of why she hadn't made it there yesterday played in her mind. Now as she walked, she reflected on what she had heard. Mr. Lacy was all politeness at dinner, and Suzanna had felt happier and lighter than the past several months. She knew both she and Mr. Lacy honored their engagement for her father and not for themselves. They had tried, they had remained faithful, but their union was not meant to be.

However, she couldn't shrug off one lurking thought. She ought to feel secure as an independent woman with a clear future and her own living. But somehow she felt a little empty. Was it the prospect of loneliness? She would stay busy with vaccinations. She did not wish to draw pity from anyone.

But there was more. Mr. Lacy had intimated to Lord Haversley that he did not feel loved by Suzanna. The very realization caused her to shiver. What if she lacked the ability to truly love someone? Was it indeed possible? She loved her father; she felt she loved her friends. But was she incapable of reciprocating a romantic love?

There were not many men better than Mr. Lacy, and yet she knew she did not feel toward him what some described as love.

And if *he* did not love her, was it possible for any man to love her and have it last past first infatuation? If she had driven away Mr. Lacy's love, would she somehow do that again with someone else?

Of course, maybe it did not matter. She had decided she ought to be content to remain single for the rest of her days. She could and would do much good on her own.

Her thoughts continued to circle as she came to her father's grave.

Suzanna looked at the life around her—the budding flowers, the green-leafed trees. It all seemed so alive. Yet she felt sullen. She turned to her father's grey headstone and began to speak as though he could hear.

"I have much to confess," she said out loud. "I do not love Mr. Lacy as a wife should love her husband, and so, we are not getting married."

Somehow it felt better to explain it to him. Standing there, looking at his headstone, she felt relief and despair at the same time.

The wind tugged at her hair. "No, there is not someone else who has asked," she continued. "And there may never be someone else." She sighed and reached down to wipe a bit of dirt from his stone. She wished for a moment that the someone else might be Lord Haversley, but that would never be. Last night at dinner he barely spoke to her. He had chosen Lady Florence.

"I could not force myself, or Mr. Lacy, to go through with the marriage. He does not love me either, at least not the way a husband should."

She looked at the ground and started to cry. The grass was thinner on top of his grave than the space around it. Her heart felt the same way—only partially filled with patches still left empty. She longed for her father, but that was only part of the reason for her tears. She ought to feel relieved, but she felt so completely empty. And alone.

Suddenly she realized part of her yearned for something she did not have.

"I fear," she said again, "that I shall never marry. I had never thought it a fear, Father, but now I do. I cannot go back to Mr. Lacy, for my heart will not change. But can I love anyone in that way?"

The shade from a nearby tree started to fall over Suzanna as the sun moved in the sky. It chilled her. She had lost her father, and now she felt she had lost more, a part of her she never knew existed. How could she feel so lost when a true love was something she never possessed?

An unsolicited picture came to her mind: the tall, handsome figure of Lord Haversley. She shut her eyes and turned, pushing away the thought as soon as it materialized. Why did she keep thinking of him? He had all but secured Lady Florence's hand, and she was sure that would happen by the end of the ball tonight.

She stood in the silence and listened to the trees around her, looking back at her father's headstone. "What would you tell me if you were here?"

Her father had always possessed great wisdom. If only he could speak to her now.

More than ever, she felt utterly alone.

Lord Haversley paced angrily in his lush green suite. Everything, even the walls, seemed to scream at him. *You have chosen Lady Florence,* they seemed to say. Why did he promise his mother he would make a decision? She wanted his happiness and had waited so long for the only person left in her family to have happiness. If he did not choose someone, she would be devastated. He had never seen her this happy since before her husband died. For that reason he could not bear to leave Elmbridge without an engagement.

Of course Lady Florence was the polite choice. The political choice. She was a wonderful match—if one were forming connections by familial friendships and financial alliances. But had he not just declared yesterday that one should truly love and be truly loved in a marriage? Should he not subscribe to his own maxims?

If he couldn't have Suzanna, what did it matter? All he had seen in her—all that he hoped he could call his wife—was promised to another.

Over the past few weeks Suzanna had repeatedly shut him out, but it all would have been nothing, had yesterday's information not made it so incredibly final. Miss Suzanna Spencer was engaged to Mr. Lacy.

No amount of hunting, persuasion, roses, or dancing could help him if that were the case. And it was. Mr. Lacy was not the sort of man to overstate anything. He had said it simply. He was bound to duty.

Jacob had no chance.

He tossed his leather-bound notebook across the bed. Lady Florence was now the best choice. At least his mother would be in raptures. Their financial situation would improve, and everything would be perfect, except his perfectly broken heart.

A knock came at the door.

"Come in," said Lord Haversley with no attempt to hide his agitation. His valet cowered slightly upon entering.

"Sir, I have instructions to remind you that this once, you should not be late to the ball." He said it hesitantly, as though he could feel the tension in the room.

"Yes, of course," said Lord Haversley as he pointed to the vest and waistcoat he wished to change into for the ball.

"You are sure, sir? Both pieces seem a bit simple for such an event as tonight."

"I am quite certain," Lord Haversley replied. Never again would he be the flashiest man in the room, no matter how much everyone expected it.

"As you wish."

Jacob entered the sparkling ballroom, one of the first guests to arrive. If it were possible, there were even more decorations than the last ball the McCallisters had hosted, and there stood flowers and candles enough to match the extensive guest list.

Lord Chalestry greeted him. "Hello, Lord Haversley. I did not have the opportunity to ask yesterday, but how does Parliament fare?"

"If only I could get them to listen to me," said Jacob. "They were close this last time, but I must keep working on some."

Lady Florence entered next, wearing a light blue gown that exactly mirrored her eyes. Her hair was curled perfectly around her face, her waist drawn in tight. Jacob had to admit he had never seen her more beautiful. "Hello, Lord Haversley."

He bowed low, coming up slowly.

"Good evening, Lady Florence. You are looking well this evening."

She smiled wide. "Thank you."

"Might I ask you for the first dance?" said Jacob. His mother smiled at them both.

He knew he ought to stay by Florence's side and talk more with her. He had done the right thing, methodically going through the motions, but it brought him no joy. Against his better judgment, his eyes darted around the room, searching for Miss Spencer, but she was nowhere to be seen.

At least twenty more guests had joined the already crowded ballroom when Mr. Lacy made his way through the entrance.

"Mr. Lacy!" Anneliese's cheery voice sounded in Jacob's ear as she took her uncle by the arm and pressed toward Mr. Lacy.

As soon as they came within a comfortable speaking distance, she continued. "My uncle assures me that your leg is completely healed. He said you were marvelous on the hunt yesterday."

"Your uncle is kind," said Mr. Lacy, looking from Anneliese to Jacob. "We were actually in the back of the party, riding slower than some. It was rather uneventful."

In the way of foxes, Jacob knew his friend was correct. But the information he learned yesterday was ironically useful and completely heart-wrenching and life-altering.

"What I mean," Anneliese said, bashfully batting her lashes, "is that he declares you are now able to dance." She ended her speech so quietly, Jacob could sense her nerves.

"Right. Well that is *quite* true." He pulled down the edges of his coat. "Would you do me the honor of the first dance?"

Anneliese beamed. Jacob looked around, wondering exactly why Mr. Lacy had not asked Miss Spencer for the first dance. She had declared her mourning over. She had even appeared in a beautiful light teal dress last night, which he had noticed brought out her eyes.

Now, as he looked around for the second time, he noticed she had not come down to the ballroom yet. Surely as soon as she did, she would be at Mr. Lacy's side, their engagement clear to everyone.

The first dance passed, and Jacob noted that Lady Florence's dancing and beauty did not disappoint. She really was a distinguished young woman, polished in every sense of the word. Talented, well-known, and at that moment, quite thirsty. He had just finished getting her a drink when Mr. Lacy passed him.

"A word?" Lord Haversley asked him.

"Of course."

The two walked to the edge of the room. "Is this not to be your day of triumph with Miss Spencer? Where is she tonight?"

"I did notice she has not yet arrived," said Mr. Lacy as he looked around.

Jacob did not understand how his friend could be so dismissive. "Really, Lacy, I do think . . ."

A beautiful young lady with dark curls and a plum dress walked up to them.

"Miss Blair, how could I have forgotten? I promised you the waltz. Excuse me, Haversley," said Mr. Lacy as he bowed and walked off.

Jacob had to will his mouth shut. Mr. Lacy did not deserve Suzanna. How unfeeling of him to not care about his own fiancée.

If only Miss Spencer were here, Jacob would make sure she was noticed. They could have danced together, and it would have been splendid—perfect. He might even consent to dancing a quadrille if she were free. He might not be able to marry her, but at least he could enjoy her as a dance partner one last time.

As it was, he ended up watching the next set. As a few minutes more passed, he found himself, instead of chatting with Lady Florence as he should, prowling around through the different crowds and even taking a quick turn in the gardens, looking for Miss Spencer. He was obligated to dance the next set with a cousin of Lady Florence's but could not keep his mind off Miss Spencer. Where *was* she?

After that dance he noticed that Lady Florence seemed to have disappeared as well. He had watched her walk into the garden but said nothing as she passed him, and he did not see her again.

Finally he decided he must ask Anneliese about Miss Spencer. But as he came up to her in between sets, he thought the McCallisters must have rubbed off on her. She did nothing but chat his ear off.

"Uncle, is not this the most splendid event? I am having the best time! Oh, and Grandmama wishes me to remind you to ask Lady Florence for the supper dance so you may be seated close to her, although I have heard a few people whispering about her absence. No one has been able to find her. After your dance, she seems to have disappeared. I thought her with you . . . "

"She is not with me," said Jacob through his teeth. "And you may tell Grandmama that I know what I am doing."

Anneliese grew quiet and brought herself up to her full height. "I will say nothing of the sort." She looked at him with disapproval, her head angled to the side. "Are you feeling well?"

He should not have been so short with her. Miss Spencer's absence had driven him to complete distraction. "Forgive me, Anneliese. I should not have been so rude." His brow furrowed as he scanned the crowd once more. Then, with the easiest tone he could muster, he added, "By the way, where is your friend Miss Spencer?"

Anneliese leaned slightly toward him. "It is just the most ironic thing! Here she was, excited to attend, and then this afternoon, she told me she needed to leave. She made it sound rather immediate."

His eyes riveted on his niece. He tilted his head to the side and tugged on his perfectly tied cravat. Anneliese continued to speak. "I am ever so disappointed. We were going to have such fun together, now that she can actually dance."

Jacob cleared his throat. "And where did she say she was going?"

"I do not know! I was so shocked that I did not even think to ask her until it was too late."

Jacob rolled his shoulders back and heaved a great sigh as he tried to remain calm. "How interesting." He bowed and headed directly toward Mr. Lacy.

Mr. Lacy was in the middle of three women, who all seemed quite enthralled by his speech. What had happened to all of his dearest acquaintances? Anneliese and Mr. Lacy seemed uncharacteristically jovial, and Miss Spencer, who was always around—tormenting him with her presence—had fled!

"Excuse me," said Jacob, remembering to tighten his cravat as he wedged his way between a lady and Mr. Lacy. "But you must know something about Miss Spencer. Where is she?"

Mr. Lacy's face dropped. He seemed to have been enjoying himself thoroughly, and something about Jacob's question took all happiness out of his countenance.

Mr. Lacy excused himself from his new friends. Walking toward the edge of the room, he placed his hand on Lord Haversley's shoulder. "After she did not come I began to wonder the same thing. And not five minutes ago, one of the servants brought me a note that said she decided to return to Berkeley. She thought things would be better that way. I am quite sad that I did not get to say good-bye to her myself, although I think she thought it would cause me grief to come to the ball."

Grief?

All of this made no sense.

"So," said Jacob, taking his friend by the sleeve and pulling him close, "tell me if you are still engaged."

Jacob could feel his face getting warmer as Mr. Lacy pursed his lips and motioned them to the large door at the back of the ballroom. Jacob hurried him through the corridor and into the crisp air until finally Mr.

Lacy stopped, inhaled, and started. "I should have never mentioned any of that to you." Mr. Lacy looked down and kicked at the gravel. "She has chosen . . ." He paused a great while, tugging on his waistcoat and shuffling his feet. "It was entirely her idea . . . she insisted . . ." He broke off once more, squirming as he scrunched his face together. After a long silence, he finally turned and faced Jacob. "We broke off our engagement." Mr. Lacy's eyes met his friend's. "Yesterday, after the hunt."

Jacob's heart stopped for two beats as he processed the information. Then with a violent rapidity it began again, sending sheer happiness through his veins. "She does *not* love you then, as you had suspected?"

Mr. Lacy shook his head and stepped away from him. "*That* is your question? Goodness." He paused and shook his head, his eyes rolling toward Jacob. "I thought I made that clear yesterday. I did not think she loved me, and it turns out, she did not. Not more than a friend. But thank you for bringing it up again."

Jacob put his palm to his forehead. "I am sorry. I did not mean to make it worse. I did not mean to cause you more pain. I just meant . . ."

Mr. Lacy turned around slowly. He placed his right hand under his chin and rested it on his left arm, which was folded across his body. There was a hint of a smile on his lips. "*You* love her, don't you?"

Jacob froze.

Mr. Lacy stood still a moment and then began to pace back and forth across the gravel. "That is why you were so concerned, why you had to know if I cared for Anneliese, and why you took such an interest in my affairs."

Lord Haversley strode closer to his friend and then stopped, extending his arm on his friend's shoulder while explaining. "Now hear me out. I am grateful for your friendship. Since coming to Elmbridge I knew you were a man of sense and someone I ought to have in my circles. I genuinely meant it. And Miss Grysham, I believe, *is* interested in you. Quite interested, if I am being truthful. And I did save your life well before I even realized any of this about Miss Spencer, so there is that bit of true friendship you must understand."

Mr. Lacy could not stop smiling. "Do you admit to loving her?"

Jacob dropped his arm and turned his back to Mr. Lacy for a moment. Then Jacob faced him and said quietly, "Completely. I cannot tell you of my devastation. She *has* been quite aloof and standoffish, but I was not deterred. I was going to ask for her hand yesterday afternoon. I have been in complete agony since I knew she was engaged. I have been beside myself."

"And what of Lady Florence?"

"I had considered marrying her, based on our connections, and only because Miss Spencer was engaged and so utterly unavailable to be my wife. But now . . ."

"Oh, never mind Lady Florence! She does not matter," said Mr. Lacy, interrupting him and throwing up his hands. "Miss Spencer is probably halfway to Berkeley by now. Do you not wish to speak with her?"

"More than ever."

"Then you had better be on your way."

Jacob spun on his heel toward the stable. "Oh, Lacy," he said stopping a moment. He turned around and raised one eyebrow almost off his forehead. "Miss Grysham will wonder where I have gone. Will you be so kind as to tell her for me?" He winked toward his friend.

"With pleasure." Mr. Lacy bowed. "And Godspeed!" he yelled.

Chapter 24

"An independent woman must have ways to secure her own travel," Suzanna said to Kate. "I think hiring a coach was the appropriate thing to do." They rumbled down the road in the darkness, although quite a bit of moonlight came through the carriage. "Thank you again for traveling to Elmbridge and for insisting on coming to Chalestry. You are too kind to me."

They were over two hours into their ride, and Suzanna kept convincing herself that all would be right as soon as they reached Berkeley.

"Of course, though you are lucky not all of the McCallisters' grooms were occupied tonight, miss. Bribing them at the last minute is hardly 'securing' your own travel. In the future, you may have to be judicious as to when you hire a carriage—and who you hire." Kate shuddered, and Suzanna was unsure if she was cold or nervous to be traveling at night.

"Let us hope the railway comes to us soon," said Suzanna with a smile. She was glad Kate had proved such a loyal lady's maid. She loved Kate. She needed her. For propriety's sake and for her own sanity.

"Are you sure we are safe? A carriage in the middle of the night . . ." Kate's emerald eyes widened toward her. Suzanna was sure the night seemed even darker with Kate's reduced visibility. "I am just imagining what happened to Mr. Lacy, although I do know the blond groom. I have met him a few times. I am sure he knows what to do if someone were to confront us."

"It is not quite yet the *middle* of the night. Do not worry, Kate. I am sure the coachmen are very skilled. The McCallisters have enough money to hire only the very best, most capable servants."

Kate nodded but Suzanna noticed her nervously rub her hands together. What if something were to happen? It *was* an unusual time to travel. Going to Berkeley could take a few hours. They still had a ways to go, and the night was not young.

The woods became thick, and the moonlight felt almost imperceptible. A cold twinge raced down Suzanna's spine. She had time to prepare only one small trunk. Surely a highwayman would not try to steal it. Yet other people had done much more to Mr. Lacy with only his leather satchel.

Suddenly she heard the two grooms talking. Someone was approaching. Suzanna stole a glance at Kate, whose brows furrowed. The carriage rumbled on rather quickly, and it suddenly felt like a reckless pace for so dark a night. Then, behind her, the sound of galloping hooves became louder and louder. The carriage kept its pace—surely her driver was not scared. What could she do against an ambush? If she were to be an independent woman, this was a horrible beginning.

The horseman now came beside her window, close enough that Suzanna could hear the labored exhale of the creature's breath. She peeked out the window and could see a strong, sable horse through the glimmer of moonlight.

"Stop your coach!" the rider yelled. "I demand it, this instant."

Suzanna looked across at Kate's white face. Why had she dragged her into this? She was barely healthy enough to travel, and now Suzanna had put not only herself in danger but her maid as well. Suzanna took her by the hands. Luckily it felt like the carriage was slowing.

She turned to Kate, trying to keep an even tone. "We must run for it." She gathered courage with an inhale. "When I count to three, I will kick open the door, and you must jump. I will be right behind you. Run into the woods and hide, and I will come find you once they have passed."

There was no time to waste, and Suzanna could hear the horseman yelling again at the driver. She prayed Kate would be healthy enough to escape. On three she kicked open the door and Kate jumped.

Suzanna watched her stagger into a standing position, gather her skirts, and attempt a stitled run toward the trees. Suzanna braced herself against the doorframe. Pushing the swinging door away once again, she jumped and rolled two times before stopping in a clump on the ground. The rocks stung under her palms. She prepared to stand and dart off when she heard, "Stop, please!"

The *please* caught her attention. A thief would not yell "please." He would have some type of weapon, and the tall figure calling to her had nothing in his hands. Whoever he was swung down from his horse.

The coach was still moving down the road, the driver trying to slow the spooked horses as he looked over his shoulder toward the swinging door. Suzanna knew that attempting to get away now would be futile, as the man was already off his horse and could outrun her in an instant. She stood still and waited as the man walked closer to her.

Her stinging, trembling hands clutched the sides of her dress as her knees quivered.

"Miss Spencer," said the man, his voice much calmer and suddenly more familiar.

He continued to to come closer until Suzanna could not believe her eyes. The man before her was none other than Lord Haversley. She felt her mouth fall open, and then she clamped it shut, wondering just how much of her sheer bewilderment he could register on her face in the silver moonlight.

"I do not know where to begin," he started, his voice a bit breathless. "But considering the situation, an apology for making you jump from a racing carriage might be in order."

Suzanna noticed a large rip in her traveling dress as she dusted herself off. She felt her hair next, which tumbled down one shoulder in a twisted, knotted cascade. She finally looked up, still shaking, trying to gather her composure, and swallowed hard.

"Lord Haversley," she said with a tight smile and a small curtsy, "to what do I owe the honor?"

"I thought . . ." He rubbed his hand on his chin. "I thought quite a few things, actually."

It was a strange moment. They stood alone on the side of the road, both catching their breath and standing a safe distance apart from one another.

What was he doing here? He was supposed to be at the ball, dancing with several lucky women, and no doubt choosing one of them to marry. Suzanna felt a tinge of jealousy toward Lady Florence, who must be his choice, and yet here he stood in front of her.

After a pause, he began again. "You see, I did not find you at the ball, and so I began to worry. Anneliese mentioned you had left, and Mr. Lacy said so as well."

He asked Mr. Lacy about her? Probably because he knew of their engagement. *Broken engagement,* she reminded herself. Lord Haversley seemed uncomfortable, for Suzanna could not remember him ever shuffling his feet as he did at that moment.

"He said he received a note."

What was she to say? She knew he wished her to speak, but she still quivered, and her heart gave a flutter. She did not trust herself with words. Not yet.

She fortified herself, taking a few deep breaths. Finally she tried to speak. "I told the servant to not deliver it until the ball started because I did not want anyone to leave, if they noticed, on my account."

Lord Haversley's eyes met hers. "I noticed, and I worried. Which is why I am here now, acting as though I would besiege your carriage. Although I promise that was not my intent."

He had noticed she was gone? Noticed so much so that he chased after her?

She shuddered. "A woman does occasionally jump to the wrong conclusion." Suzanna gestured to the open road. "And in this case, that was quite literally the situation."

Lord Haversley chuckled and stepped closer. Suzanna watched him with wonder. It was the first time she had been free of the engagement and alone in his presence. She hugged her arms around herself, noting the chill of the air on her sleeves, but she was not cold. Their conversation flowed freely, just as it had in his London home and her drawing room and even Mr. Lacy's kitchen. Something in their banter felt right.

He cleared his throat and lowered his tone. "When I knew you were gone, I had to know why. It is so clear to me now why you seemed to push me away. At first I liked the challenge. Most other young women fall at my feet on account of my title. You did not. Then I realized how genuinely I enjoyed your company. There was—there *is*—something in the way you speak, the way you interact with others. You are intelligent, aware, passionate, and unwavering. I admire that."

He tugged on the knot of his cravat, his eyes penetrating hers. "It was that early morning in London when I found you in the kitchen at Lysetter Hall that really won me over. Ever since then I have been trying to get to know you, to no avail. And then, in Mr. Lacy's kitchen . . . "

He reached out silently, unwrapped her folded arms, and held each of her hands in his. He turned them over, staring at them.

She winced a little, remembering how she had closed the door by inches in his face. Suzanna had suspected his feelings for her then. She had tried to avoid him. She had to. It was only right—until yesterday.

He looked at her hands and brought one of them to his heart. "Then Mr. Lacy told me on the fox hunt that there was an understanding between you two. I could not believe it. How it wounded my soul. You see, despite your curt behavior at his house, I had resolved that I would tell you everything. Nothing would allow me to forget you. Yesterday I was going to declare myself and try one last time to have you as mine. But with such finality as an engagement . . ."

His eyes were large and vulnerable, a look she had never witnessed before.

He dropped her hand lower and began to softly pull off her torn gloves. She watched him in amazement but did not pull away. Again he turned over her palms, caressing the scars with his fingers.

"I heard every word of your conversation, Lord Haversley," said Suzanna, gathering courage. "I was in those woods just after the hunt, walking toward my father's grave. I am sorry. I did not wish to cause you any pain." She pressed her lips together and closed her eyes for a moment, until she looked down and said, "And I am sorry to be keeping you from a perfectly wonderful ball." Suzanna swallowed. "I said in my note I left because I did not wish to cause pain for Mr. Lacy. But truthfully I also couldn't bear the thought of you announcing an engagement."

"There was nothing perfectly wonderful about that ball because it did not have you, Suzanna."

Her name from his lips fell upon her like a spell. She went slightly limp, and it took a moment to right herself. What was this feeling? This was something she had never experienced before. Not even when Mr. Lacy had said her name and flattered her.

Perhaps . . . perhaps this was love.

Slowly, a confirming warmth spread throughout her body, starting at the crown of her head, reaching her limbs, filling her boots. She must have drooped slightly because she felt a strong, warm hand let go of her palm and press on the small of her back. Lord Haversley stepped closer and put his other arm around her waist. She looked up at him in that moment, a smile drawing up her cheeks.

"Suzanna?" he said looking down at her. Until that moment she had never realized just how much taller and broader he truly was compared to her.

"You really must stop," she said. Lord Haversley pulled back slightly, his eyebrows knitting together with concern.

"Stop what?"

"Saying my name. It has an incredible power, unlike anything I have felt before."

Lord Haversley smiled. "Then I shall continue, Suzanna." He stepped closer again, a roguish twinkle in his eye. "Are you admitting that perhaps you do actually enjoy my presence, although you have tried so very hard to keep your distance?"

"My resolve"—she could not stop her smile—"has significantly lessened in the last twenty-four hours." Suzanna knew she was blushing but hoped the moonlight hid some of her color from Lord Haversley.

"And what would happen to your resolve if I told you I loved you?"

Suzanna looked into his dark eyes more fervidly than she ever had before. Her opinion of him had improved every time she was with him. And now, suddenly free of obligation, she realized that she did care about this man. Quite a bit more than she could quantify.

Every time they spoke, every time they were together, her interest toward him had grown. Something felt right. It felt like home.

She inhaled slowly. "I think I can say that for the first time in my life, I feel loved. And in love. And ready." She pressed her lips together and clasped her hands, taking a deep breath. "Ready to love you."

He pulled her toward him, and she rested her forehead on his chest.

"How I have longed to hold you close, to feel you in my arms," he said with a sigh.

She turned her head and looked at him. "I must warn you, though, until now I thought maybe I was incapable of really loving another person. But I will try with everything I have."

"Don't you see?" Lord Haversley answered, lifting her chin to meet his gaze. "You have already been doing it. I have already felt it."

He reached down and gently kissed her forehead. It was a feeling unlike any she had ever felt. Something like liquid happiness coursed through her as his lips touched her skin. She smiled at him, and he bowed a little further, his lips touching hers. They held each other for a long while, warm together in the cool night. Everything around them seemed to dissolve, and for a moment the dark road, the forest, the stress of the past months disappeared. Suzanna knew nothing except the two of them.

"Jacob," she said when their kiss finally came to an end.

"Yes?" Lord Haversley looked at her with a smile. She paused and then grabbed his lapels. He willingly came closer, closing his eyes as though to kiss her again. She ran her hands down the lapels, skipping over his arms, and stopped above his wrists.

He suddenly opened his eyes. She smiled, turning over his sleeves and taking his hands in hers. "Your cuffs are severely devoid of trim. Did you not just come from a ball?"

Lord Haversley shook his head and laughed, taking her hand and raising it to his lips.

"Someone, whose opinion I hold very highly, mentioned I might try a simpler style."

"I see," said Suzanna, again pulling on his lapels. She looked him up and down and then clicked her tongue. "Well, it suits you."

This time he clasped his hands behind her back and drew her in. Their kiss lasted even longer, became more familiar, until she noticed the carriage driver had turned around and was talking with Kate, while the other man inspected the wheel a good distance down the road. Had they all witnessed their scene?

Lord Haversley followed her gaze and began adjusting his waistcoat into its proper position. He looked at her, displacing one eyebrow, a mischievous grin pulling at his mouth.

"What shall we do now?" said Suzanna, looking about nervously.

"I suppose we ought to return to Chalestry."

"But I . . . I am not prepared for the ball. And what about Kate?"

"Perhaps this once the groomsmen can take her home in the carriage."

Suzanna looked again down the road at Kate and the groom, who seemed to be smiling.

"They look to be getting along swimmingly," said Lord Haversley as one side of his mouth drew up in a smile. "I always did like that young groom the McCallisters employed. Perhaps you ought to ride back with me. We could make it in less than an hour, and I am sure Kate will be safe."

Suzanna eyed him skeptically, but Lord Haversley bounded over to the carriage and explained everything, giving strict commands that they should go straight to Chalestry Manor and that Kate was to be watched over with the utmost care. He then leaned in toward Kate and whispered something and helped her into the carriage. He returned to Suzanna as the carriage rumbled past.

"So I am stranded here, alone, with no one to protect me, just as I feared." She offered a coy smile. Lord Haversley took her by the hand and led her toward Sylvester. Her mind reeled. How had it come to this? And how did she feel so comfortable?

"I would not say, mademoiselle, that you are stranded, nor are you alone. I shall have you back to the McCallisters' ball shortly."

"Oh, I do not plan on entering the ballroom. For starters, I do not have on the proper outfit."

"Hush, Suzanna. For a moment, just enjoy our ride."

She stopped and exhaled, telling her rambling mouth to stop moving.

Something told her it would not be hard to obey his instructions. She felt his hands around her waist as he lifted her onto the horse. He carefully mounted in front, gingerly placing his feet in the stirrups to not move her. They sat so close together she could smell his scent, again of horses and a hint of wildflowers. He reached down and turned her hands, placing them around his waist.

"I advise you to hold on," he said and took off abruptly, causing her to hug his waist more tightly. "We shall be back in no time," he said with a smile.

Chapter 25

Lord Haversley kept his word, riding exceedingly fast and making it back within the hour. As they approached the front entrance, he dismounted, grabbed her once again, and lowered her to the ground.

"You see, that ride was not all that bad."

Suzanna blushed a deep red. She looked around her, wondering if anyone had seen them riding together. She did not say to him just how much she loved every moment. She feared if she spoke about it, it would somehow wake her from the dream.

She came from her reverie when she saw Lord Haversley pulling her toward a servant. "Right this way, miss," said the maid.

Suzanna turned back to look at Lord Haversley, but he was nowhere to be seen. Where had he gone?

Suddenly the maid took hold of Suzanna's hand as she whisked her past a groom and into the house, nearly dragging her, full speed into her dressing chamber.

"Mighty good fortune you did not have time to pack all your trunks. Lord Haversley gave me all the instructions from your maid."

"Excuse me," said Suzanna, looking over her shoulder and trying to figure out what exactly was going on. With a furrowed brow, she looked back toward the maid. "But if you think you are going to help me dress for the ball, you are mistaken."

The maid looked to the side and shook her head. "Oh, Miss Spencer." She had already opened Suzanna's trunk and was airing her best dress, the dress she had planned to wear to the ball that evening. It was a bright satin blue with quite a bit of shine. The lace on the collar was intricate but not overdone, and pearl buttons studded the front.

"I have no intentions of going. It is nearly over, and I cannot show up now!"

"I am merely doing as Lord Haversley suggested, which was help you dress for a ball."

Suzanna rolled her eyes. "I cannot!"

The maid started to loosen Suzanna's outer traveling gown and slipped it to the floor. Within ten minutes Suzanna stood in a beautiful new gown with her hair reassembled in a full bun. The maid even managed to add earrings and Suzanna's mother's crystal necklace.

As Suzanna looked at herself in the mirror, she decided she *could* possibly enter the ballroom. She felt beautiful. Her mother's necklace gave her courage as she walked toward the main hall. She then spied Lord Haversley just outside the ballroom door, his brows drawn together and his hand over his mouth in what seemed a very serious conversation with another man. The man's back boasted a tight-fitting jacket and tall hat, and they appeared to be studying a document together.

The maid, who followed behind her, said, "Let us take a moment and fix your hair a little more, miss. Lord Haversley seems engaged at present."

Suzanna nodded, and the maid added a few more twists and braids, taming a few more unruly wisps. The maid placed the last pin and disappeared just before Lord Haversley finally pulled away from his friend.

He left his friend with the document and turned to the main stairway. He walked deliberately toward Suzanna, and she noted he moved with confidence, not with his old bravado or his hesitation on the road to Berkeley but with something more genuine and content.

"You look perfect. And perfectly ready to dance."

Suzanna glanced over her shoulder to thank the maid, but she was nowhere to be seen.

Lord Haversley took her hand. "There is still time to go inside. They have only finished dinner."

Suzanna felt her stomach rumble, but she thought perhaps it was filled more with nerves than actual hunger.

"I am afraid I cannot go inside. There are so many people there who I do not wish to hurt. What if Mr. Lacy feels slighted? And I do not want to begin to imagine the scathing look I will receive from Lady Florence."

The man who had been talking to Lord Haversley turned and folded the paper in his hands. He walked toward them and said, "You would deny Lord Haversley a dance on his day of triumph?"

"Colonel Unsworth?" Suzanna's eyes squinted in the dim foyer.

"The very same." He bowed, lacey cuffs drooping from his wrists as he did, his elaborate watch chain dripping down his vest. "I just arrived this evening from London. I would have been here earlier, had not my carriage driver been so daft! I could not help myself. I had to see my friend's face when he read the news."

Lord Haversley went to him and rested a hand on his shoulder.

"Not to mention you were drawn here by a secret missive from a certain young lady inviting you."

Colonel Unsworth pursed his lips. "Well, there was that, yes."

Suzanna's eyes went wide.

What were they referring to?

Lord Haversley seemed to notice the thoughts processing in Suzanna's head.

"Which is rather fortunate for us both, for *you* Colonel Unsworth, have solved not one but two problems for me this night."

Suzanna looked up at Lord Haversley, biting her lip. "What exactly are your two problems?"

Lord Haversley motioned his hand forward, giving Colonel Unsworth the floor.

"I have here," Colonel Unsworth continued, brandishing the papers, "the official signed document that says Parliament will pass the Vaccination Bill."

Suzanna withdrew her arm from Lord Haversley's and turned to face him. "Is it true? Is it everything you wanted?"

"Everything we could have hoped for," said Lord Haversley.

"You have done it!"

Suzanna threw her arms around Lord Haversley. "Just think of what this means for everyone! No more variolation. More help for everyone! All of your hard work has paid off!" She wished to say more but stopped exclaiming when she heard Colonel Unsworth clear his throat loudly.

Suzanna drew away from him and smoothed her skirts. She attempted to mask her excitement, trying to maintain an air of nonchalance. "And the second way he has saved you?" she asked Lord Haversley as evenly as she could muster.

"A few missives." The Colonel swallowed hard. He picked at his cuffs and looked sheepishly toward Lord Haversley. "I am sorry."

"No offense taken, my friend. As a military man, you ought to know that all is fair in love and war."

"Right. Yes. Well, there you have it." He slapped his hands together. "So if you will please excuse me, I am afraid Lady Florence will be missing me." He bowed and began walking backward toward the glimmering light of the ballroom.

Suzanna looked up. "Lady Florence?"

Lord Haversley smiled and took Suzanna's hand in both of his. "Apparently they had exchanged a few letters, and she invited him tonight. That might have been his real reason for coming. Lady Florence disappeared into the garden shortly after I danced with her this evening. Apparently he had just arrived, and Mr. Lacy had the good sense to secure the supper dance for the colonel with Lady Florence and inform me of your whereabouts. So our thanks must go to Mr. Lacy."

Suzanna shot her head back. "Indeed. It is that easy?"

"I do not know for sure, but the colonel seems to think she will accept his hand. He made sure to mention his holdings over dinner to Lord Chalestry."

Suzanna gave a nod. "Securing an engagement is not *always* so easily done," she added with a smile.

"So you will dance with me?"

"Do you think Mr. Lacy will be offended if I come in and do not dance with him first?"

"I can assure you he has already danced with my niece."

"Thank goodness for Anneliese. And Mr. Lacy. And Colonel Unsworth!" she said as he led her through to the ballroom.

The music began to swirl around them, deep sounds coming from the strings. Lord Haversley pulled Suzanna into the close embrace of the waltz. The room seemed to spin, and she felt almost faint with happiness. How could this be?

As they danced she could not help but think that the people who come into one's life come for a reason. She was never meant to marry Mr. Lacy, but through him she learned her own heart, and her journey had led her to Lord Haversley. And she felt if she asked Mr. Lacy, he would say the same thing for Anneliese.

"You know," she said as she looked into Lord Haversley's dark eyes, "all this time I had felt so alone, so empty. But somehow, when Mr. Phipps taught me how to help with smallpox, I felt better. A little closer to my parents, a little less alone."

"And it brought me to you," he said.

"It's like it healed me and taught me I could love you."

Finally Suzanna felt whole again.

They held each other, even after the dance ended.

Lord Haversley escorted her out through the garden at the end of the night. She noticed the carriage had returned but did not see Kate. She wondered if Kate might be talking again with the groom whom she had hired that evening. Suzanna would have to ask her about him, but that could wait.

They walked a bit farther toward the stables, and she found herself alone once again with Lord Haversley.

"Might we take one more ride on Sylvester?" Lord Haversley laced his fingers through hers.

"Alone, at night?" said Suzanna, placing her other hand on her hip.

"It has been done before," said Lord Haversley, his wide smile complementing his dancing eyes. She shook her head, and before Suzanna knew it, they had reached his horse and he had scooped her up and placed her on his faithful steed.

He jumped up behind her this time, holding her around the waist with his arms while he took the reins in his hands and led them down the hill.

"I need to ask someone a question," he said as they trotted.

Who could he wish to speak to at such a moment? Especially this late at night? Suzanna thought him wild, a bit crazy, and never more handsome. She settled completely into his arms as they rode.

Soon they came to a stop, the dark moonlit night surrounding them. He lifted her gracefully off the horse and onto the ground, and Suzanna recognized several grey headstones before her. Lord Haversley took her hand and led her a little deeper into the cemetery.

Before another minute passed, they stood in front of her father's grave. She wanted to turn Lord Haversley around, look him in the eye, and ask him how he remembered where her father's plot lay. How long had he cared for her? But instead, she walked to the other side of his grave and listened as he spoke.

"Mr. Spencer." He gazed down, employing a reverent tone. "I am a few months late, but I wish to ask for your daughter's hand. I know you trusted Mr. Lacy to do so, and your dutiful daughter promised she would comply." His eyes raised and met Suzanna's. "But I promise I will care for her just as much." He swallowed and took a step toward Suzanna, caressing the scars on her arms. "For there is not another man on this earth who loves her as I do."

Suzanna held Lord Haversley's firm grasp over her father's grave for what felt like a long time. He finally led her a few paces above the headstone and circled his arms around her shoulders, resting his chin on her head. Their breath caught in unison, more than comfortable in each other's arms.

"Do you think he approves?" he whispered, tipping her chin toward his.

"Most definitely, Jacob," she said, her crystal blue eyes memorizing his every feature.

His hand reached for her face, and he tucked a wayward lock of hair behind her ear, cradling her head in his hand as he bent toward her. Their lips met, his arms enveloped her, and Suzanna experienced every confidence she ever sought. In that moment, she felt more love than she knew possible. Unfettered, pure, magnificent love.

Suzanna acknowledged she had broken her promise to her father. But in doing so, she followed her own heart, freed Mr. Lacy's, and found Lord Haversley's. Together, with her perfect Jacob, they would make a difference in the world. Perhaps it was not so much her promise to her father that mattered but the promise her future now held that made all the difference.

Afterword

"*The annihilation of smallpox, the most dreadful scourge of the human species, must be the final result of this practice.*"[1]

—Edward Jenner, MD

The plot of this book and all of the characters are of my own invention, with the following exceptions:

Edward Jenner (1749–1823) was a local physician/scientist in Berkeley, England. He was awarded the title of doctor later in his practice, due to his great accomplishments and not a medical degree. He did indeed wish to eradicate smallpox and tested his hypothesis on eight-year-old James Phipps in 1796, using pus from a milkmaid named Sarah Nelmes, who had sores from cowpox. The cow's name was Blossom, and its horns are kept today in a museum in Berkeley, England, that teaches about Dr. Jenner's legacy.

Dr. Jenner's treatise on smallpox was published in 1798, and he coined the term *vaccination*. Jenner himself was variolated (given smallpox from another person on purpose), and this was such a terrible experience it affected his whole life.

Dr. Jenner left a house to James Phipps, which you can visit today in Berkeley, England.

---

1. As quoted in "History of Smallpox," Center for Disease Control and Prevention, cdc.gov/smallpox/history/history.html.

The milkmaid's poem referenced is an actual poem from the time period, as is the pseudonym for smallpox of the speckled monster.

Dr. Jenner had a small structure he called the Temple of Vaccina, and once a week he would vaccinate people there free of charge.

Smallpox has existed for thousands of years. Evidence of its plague has even been found on mummies. Queen Elizabeth the First wore so much makeup and had such a unique hairline because she had suffered smallpox. The Native Americans were exposed to the dreaded sickness when they were given blankets that carried smallpox. It killed much of their population.

The Vaccination Act of 1840 was the first act in England regarding smallpox passed in Parliament and was followed by more stringent regulation to vaccinate all of England.

While others did much for the eradication of smallpox, it was Dr. Jenner's vaccine that created a safer way to protect people against the dreaded disease without making others contagious. Napoleon Bonaparte, who hated doctors, said of Jenner, "Ah, Jenner, we can't refuse that man anything!"[2] and even returned some British prisoners at his request.

Today, smallpox is one of few diseases that have been completely eradicated from the earth. Samples of the dreaded speckled monster are frozen and held by the United States and Russia. The few last cases of the sickness were documented in Africa in the 1970s, and the disease has been declared extinct since.

---

2. Lawrence Andrews, "Smallpox," *Deadliest Diseases of All Time*, 1st ed. (New York: Cavendish, 2015), 35.

Acknowledgments

As always, a huge thank you to my incredible mother for being my best and most diligent editor—who also wins the award for reading the most iterations of this book along its journey. I also am ever grateful to my writing group—their fabulous insights and camaraderie help more than I can say. I also must thank Caitlin and Ashley, the "Arave sisters" as I think of them—for their ruthless, helpful, and historically accurate editing skills and suggestions. They have incredible talent and should start their own editing firm. Thanks to my brother Dave, for his ability to answer all medical detail questions via text when I need to know what happens to broken bones, coagulated blood, etc. Thanks to the real "Miss Spencer," whose deep and abiding care for her fellow man is truly unparalleled. The only thing better than her inimitable cooking is her huge heart.

And, of course, I thank my Daniel, who supports me, cheers me on, and loves me through everything. Thank you, Love, for always seeing the big picture. And thank you to my darling, amazing children, for sleeping well, encouraging me, and reading a bit over my shoulder and telling me you'll read it all when you are older. Last, I thank my Heavenly Father for giving me the ability to create and the desire to add a little bit of fun and goodness back into the world through words.

About the Author

S arah L. McConkie started her writing career in the second grade with a thirteen-page magnum opus about dinosaurs. Although the plot line and penmanship lacked polish, Sarah learned she loved retiring to bed thinking of what to write the next day. On a good night, she still does the same thing.

Sarah took up the pen several years later after tucking her own little dreamer into bed and now combines modern life experiences, a robust knowledge of Regency and Victorian details, and a passion for all things old fashioned and proper to craft her historical romances. She costars with her own Mr. Right in the real-life romantic comedy she calls life.

She has a bachelor's degree in music education and taught junior high choir for several years before becoming a stay-at-home mother to three darling children. Her first novel, *Love and Secrets at Cassfield Manor,* was published in August 2018. Sarah believes creating thought-provoking and moral stories promotes literacy in a world that needs more readers.

Scan to visit

sarahlmcconkie.com